THE AMERICAN PRESS HAILS BERNICE RUBENS . . .

"For Bernice Rubens, humor and pathos are constant companions. Just as you are about to exude a tear, she is there with the other side of sadness, laughter . . ."
—*Houston Chronicle*

"A SARDONIC CHRONICLER . . . A DEVILISHLY SEDUCTIVE STORYTELLER."
—*Kirkus Reviews*

"Bernice Rubens gives her characters hearts and brains—moods and wiles . . ."
—*The New Yorker*

"It is no surprise that [Bernice Rubens] was awarded the Booker, England's top fiction prize. The author knows all about her craft . . ."
—*Los Angeles Times*

"A WICKED WIT AND WISDOM . . ."
—*Newsweek*

Books by Bernice Rubens

Birds of Passage
The Elected Member
Favours
Go Tell the Lemming
Sunday Best

Published by WASHINGTON SQUARE PRESS

Most Washington Square Press Books are available at special quantity discounts for bulk purchases for sales promotions, premiums or fund raising. Special books or book excerpts can also be created to fit specific needs.

For details write the office of the Vice President of Special Markets, Pocket Books, 1230 Avenue of the Americas, New York, New York 10020.

GO TELL THE LEMMING

Bernice Rubens

WASHINGTON SQUARE PRESS
PUBLISHED BY POCKET BOOKS NEW YORK

A Washington Square Press Publication of
POCKET BOOKS, a division of Simon & Schuster, Inc.
1230 Avenue of the Americas. New York, N.Y. 10020

ISBN: 0-671-50328-6

First Washington Square Press printing October, 1984

Originally published in Great Britain by Jonathan Cape Ltd.

10 9 8 7 6 5 4 3 2 1

WASHINGTON SQUARE PRESS, WSP and colophon are
registered trademarks of Simon & Schuster, Inc.

Printed in the U.S.A.

FOR ROBIN AND BILL

GO TELL
THE
LEMMING

Chapter One

When Angela Morrow was unhappy, she would sit alone in her flat and play patience. When she was really depressed, she would cheat. And she was cheating now.

She needed a space to place her king, that red king that sneered on the pile at the end of the line, shielding, she knew, at least two aces and a black jack, without which further play was impossible. Cheating did not come easily to Angela Morrow, and though she was alone, with no prospect of being less alone, she looked furtively around her. Then she lifted the king and quickly spread the aces underneath. But no jack. With both hands she gripped her forehead, a device that she had recently discovered would hold back her tears, as one applies a tourniquet above a gushing wound. But the tears had nothing to do with the jack that wasn't there, or with the knowledge that crime didn't pay (strange how nowadays, and how often, some fatuous platitude would interrupt her pleading conversations with herself); no, the tears that she was holding back had been pricked at the sight of the mantelpiece, as she looked up momentarily from her patience. That was enough. Just to catch sight of the mantelpiece.

Sometimes an incident of the smallest significance can trigger off an event of dire consequence. The noise with which a husband slurps his soup can sky-rocket a time-worn wife into the office of a divorce lawyer. One baby-scream too many can occasion infanticide. There are several ways of breaking a camel's back. For Angela Morrow, sitting there, alone, playing patience, and cheating withal, it took only a thin layer of dust on the mantelpiece to drive her to the gas-oven.

She scooped the cards into a neat pack and hid them, as she always did, behind the record player. You never knew. Someone might discover them, and with them her shameful loneliness. She walked calmly to the window, and leaned, as she always did, on the sill, her thighs cleaving to the hot radiators—one of the reasons she stood at the window at all. Not that she looked, or even saw. What was outside the window was simply there, as her face insisted in the mirror when she could not avoid it. Just there. So she stood at the window as the landscape outside met her eye without surprise, and she wondered what to do with her life. Then she turned, with no pur-pose, and walked away from the window with nowhere to go, and on her way past the phone that didn't ring she saw the mantelpiece again, which only an hour ago she had dusted, nay, spring-cleaned, clearing away all the little possessions that made divorce so difficult; she had dusted it down, polished it, replaced everything, his and hers, nothing belonging exclusively to either, but each part of a history that would not free her. And now the dust covered it again, and in her inner ear a sickening drumroll pro-claimed that cleanliness was next to godliness, and the cymbals timed her screamings. So she went into the kitchen, closed the window, opened the oven door, and turned the gas full on.

Regulo five. That's how it stood. *Filet-en-croûte* heat. The standard dish for dinner-parties. *His* way. The rolls on the bottom oven-shelf for the last five minutes, then on to the dinner-table that had taken her a day to lay because everything had been dirty, not in her terms but in his. The table would look elegant enough, and the guests would gasp, 'I don't know how you do it,' and for some reason she found the remark faintly insulting. David would carve. Over- or underdone, she feared. Either way, it was never never right. So hard to tell with *croûte*. Sometimes the pastry was so misleadingly brown, sunburnt and shining, whilst inside it was as if the poor cow had skipped past a forest fire. And the dark-red blood would ooze through the pastry layer, and then she would be glad because it was a wash-out dish and she didn't like the guests anyway. Film producers, most of them, like David. A little more blood wouldn't harm them. God knows, they were vampires enough already. Whose blood didn't they drink? A pint of blood a day was basic fare. Dinner at the Morrows was a bonus. She was tempted to give them straws.

A crust of old mustard on David's fork. Why did it have to be *his* fork? 'This house is filthy,' he would hiss as she passed the vegetables. Not just the fork, but the house, the whole bloody house. And David would pour the wine, which was good dependable vintage. Neither over- nor underdone. *His* department. Reliable, those *filet-en-croûte* dinners. Good cannibal fare. *His* way.

She turned the Regulo up to twelve. *Her* way. Shove the chicken in, still frozen, with plastic giblets inside. Roast quickly. Stuff yourself with bread meanwhile. Diet tomorrow. You're not even surprised any more by the hammering in your head morse-coding that manners maketh man. So spite it. Eat, tool-less, like an animal. You know it's regression, clever you. And for dessert, if you're a good girl, you can suck your thumb. Read the papers. Every single morning paper. Stand up all the time. Alone, always alone. If the doorbell rings, or the phone, ignore it. You're eating, reading and standing up. Private pursuits. Eat without ceremony off the oven dish. Discard plastic bag when you come to it. Hurry. Not for any reason. There's no living to be late for, and dying can wait. But presto-eating anyway. Andante's for the dinner-table, set with husband, silver and guests, and side-plates and those bloody silly finger-bowls. *His* way. But now, alone, presto and standing, stuff yourself full. *Her* way. Now what?

She twiddled the knob, then back to his way at five. But she knew, and twenty years of marriage had taught her, that at five was no way of living, neither at twelve. So she turned the Regulo up to seven. Somewhere in between, between his way and hers, there lay a way of dying.

She knelt down in front of the oven and put her head inside. Filthy, but clean enough for what she had in mind. Then in a split lucid second, she remembered that she hadn't left a note, if to no one else but to her daily woman to clean the oven out after her. Was heaven clean, or hell as it might turn out to be, or that corner of limbo mutely reserved for suicides? Was there dust on the surfaces there, or crumbs, were cushions unplumped? The corners were the worst. Even when she was working in her cutting-room during the day, she wondered about the corners, and whether in her absence they gathered dust to spite her. Would she ever in a life- or deathtime overcome this grinding obsession that had sprouted and swollen inside her since David had left? Or would she take with her, through the oven fumes, her hand-luggage of vacuum, duster and polish?

The gas was beginning to giddy her, and call her back to what she was doing. She remembered the note again.

They were a note-leaving family. 'Gone to the piktures,' her son would misspell on her mirror with her lipstick. Or 'Gone to dinner with a client,' was David's euphemism, beautifully calligraphed on the back of one of his calling-cards. Over their twenty-year marriage, he had client-stuffed himself, never bothering to vary the lie because he knew that she knew, and that both knew that whatever he wrote on the back of the card was simply vocabulary. She had to leave words. So she switched off the gas, and tottered back into the living-room.

A pencil. She'd seen one somewhere. Not on the mantelpiece. Nothing functional there. In the bedroom? The study? In one or other of the various habitations of her day? No pencil. Only flowers. She would buy flowers before food, and on her desk, on her dressing-table and by her reading-chair, bouquets, as markers to her separate well-dug tenanted graves. But no pencil. The screaming in her inner ear again, and she had to let it out, bellowing into the room, 'I can't die because I can't find a bloody pencil.' Excuses, excuses.

The telephone pad with the biro attached. She would write it there on the small lavatory roll of paper that gave her, within its frame, three square inches to explain her drop-out. But three were too many, and a thousand not enough.

'Dear Mum and Dad, I am writing to you because I

want you to know why I'm going to do what I'm going to do.' Hopeless. She couldn't even write it down.

'Dear Jonathan, This is not the most suitable letter for a mother to write to her son, but . . .'

'Dear David, You're not going to forgive me for this, but you have driven me to it.'

Nonsense, she had to admit. Nobody is driven anywhere without some piloting on their part. Indeed, she reflected, there was no one she could write to, because the act of writing a suicide note at all was an act of accusation, an act of judgment. And she was entitled to accuse only herself. Moreover, she could not write to anyone she loved, because she could not bear their pain, and even if she did not live to witness it, she could not die with that responsibility. It was only her own pain that she could bear, because she liked herself so little, and only her own self that she could accuse. So she wrote:

Dear Angela, I can't stand it any more, so I'm going to put my head in the gas-oven. I've been alone now for two years, and I don't seem to mend. I would feel better, I suppose, if I took a knife and went over to Fulham and killed her, but I should have done that ten years ago when it all started. Jesus, is it that long? I should be mending, shouldn't I. Time should be healing me. But I don't seem to be able to give time time. Yes, I work, I cut films, good ones, bad, about fifteen documentaries since he left. I go to parties, dinners, theatres: Monday becomes Tuesday, days to weeks to months to years, and I am stubbornly blind to their passing because I *am*—two years ago—stunted and arrested by the moment he left. How boring it all is. What am I hanging on to?

It's dead, Angela, and I'm not sticking around to be strangled by the history of it. 'Cos that's all it is. History. D'you remember all those summers when I took Jonathan away to those expensive South of France beaches? Where's Daddy? He's on location. Client-stuffing. I counted it up once. Sixty-seven sandcastles in one season, not easy on a French beach, I can tell you. They're mean with their sand, the French. So I tried digging holes. One hundred and forty-seven desperate holes. Will we get to Daddy if we dig deep enough? Then into the sea to cry. Year after year, all that suffering. It's obscene. Give me time, David always said, and that's what I gave him. Come to think of it, that's what I'm giving him still, because, after all, women like us, Angela, we don't give ultimatums, do we? That's fishwife stuff. Not for us. Oh no. We went to the best schools, we've got degrees. We understand. We cripple them with our understanding, you and me. Listen, what's bugging me, Angela? Is it hate? Is it bitterness? Is it—you should pardon the expression— love? Maybe. But I think, most of all, it's history, and even time, given time, won't heal that. So I'm putting an end to it. It's no good telling me to change my mind. Here I am on the brink of the gas-oven, so you may as well go tell the lemming to pull himself together. I've tried, Angela. There've been escape routes. And the first thing I've done is run along and stick up a roadblock. God help me if I ever voluntarily gave up my suffering. There've been other men. Remember Simon? Nothing wrong with Simon, was there? No. But suddenly we decide we don't like red hair. Not only do we not like it, we loathe it, and how dare that red-headed son-of-a-bitch think for one moment that we might be attracted to him. And Charles? Nothing wrong with Charles. It took us six days to find a reason to loathe him. Something *had* to be wrong with poor Charles. After a week we found it. He was so obviously working-class. Jesus, Angela, we've become bigoted. If you're desperate enough, you can build barricades out of anything. We cannot go on like this. I'm sick of it all. I'm sick of analysing. In truth I am bored by my stiff upper lip, and my talent for endurance offends me. Come to think of it, Angela, the whole weary tale is a great bore. Man meets woman. They fall in love. They marry. They have a son. They stick it out for twenty years. Man then falls in love with another woman. He leaves his wife. Sounds like the script of one of David's 'B' pictures. Such a bore, Angela. Not really worth wasting a good death on it.

She put down the biro and saw how the streamer of used paper had curled itself like lichen around her legs. She smiled. Shit-paper, that's all it was, and fitting enough to declare such a rotten exit. Unworthy of her. How ridiculous it all was. For every cloud, after all, has a silver lining. Laugh and the world laughs with you; weep and you weep alone. But you're never alone with schizophrenia.

Dear Angela, We're sticking around, you and me, and one of us has got to stay sane. One of us must always find it ridiculous . . . Between us we might just hold the balance. I'm going on, Angela, and you're staying around to make me laugh. Your obedient servant.

P.S. I loathe Women's Lib.

She ripped the note off the frame and took it trailing into the kitchen. Then she set fire to it with the pilot flame. She opened the window and scooped the ashes on to the sill. Then she opened the oven door, turned the gas on and put her head inside. She counted up to ten; mindful of the danger, she counted fast. Then she turned the gas off and closed the oven door. No one would ever know that she had made a pretence at dying. The gesture was part of her survival-kit, and had been for herself alone.

She went to the window again, avoiding the mantelpiece, and leaned over the sill, snuffling like a horse on the fresh air. She looked at the birch trees lining the street, and she acknowledged that they were growing in the street where she, Angela Morrow, lived. She dared even to turn her head and stare at the mantelpiece and to decide to let it be. She trembled. Angela, who in her crisis had lately been so close, now gently but confidently receded into cable distance.

"Angela Morrow London Determined To Survive Stop Even If It Kills Me."

Chapter Two

Film producers grow on trees that grow in Mayfair, and each one believes himself to be unique. Yet a more unexceptional group of tradesmen would be hard to encounter. In order to become, or more truthfully to *be,* a producer (for there is little growth in the process), you have to be beset by a desperate need to tell people that you're in the movie business. Because for people who know nothing about the movie business, and they are after all in the majority, a film producer spells power, glamour and money. Power he most certainly has, and glamour too, if the eye of the beholder is sufficiently jaundiced, but money, never. At least, none that he can call his own. David Morrow, like most of his fraternity, conducted his life in a style that would have become a *nouveau riche* millionaire. He was never short of the thousands: it was the pence that gave him headaches. He bought himself a new limousine equipped with television and telephone, but he couldn't afford to mend the wipers on his mistress's Mini. He was always readier to sign for a thousand pounds than pay out a penny in cash. He had offices in Mayfair, which was right and proper for one of his calling. He had a separated wife in Chelsea who refused his money, and a mistress in Fulham with whom he lived and with whom he was growing increasingly bored. Ten years ago she had sat at the desk opposite him, where now Ruth sat, that great misshapen monument to clipped efficiency, the sort of girl he should have employed in the first place. Ruth was a treasure. Having little of a life of her own she entered his with plans, notebooks and files, and an unfailing memory. He was able to be a liar because it was Ruth who kept score. He could swindle in his ever-so-gentlemanly way because Ruth was always at hand keeping the books. He rarely read scripts because Ruth was his amanuensis. She had consciously made herself indispensable. She told lies for him, fobbed off his mistress, kept his wife in indecision, kept his creditors at bay on the one phone while booking a first-class return to South America on the other. Ten years ago Carol had sat at that desk, prettily and uselessly, and with much telephone elocution. Most of the time she used to stare at him, with a vacant look of worship, a look that to this day she had never discarded. Yet, whereas in the old days this bewildered puppy-gaze of adoration became her, now the look had turned hang-dog. Her jowls had slipped, and in unsuspecting sleep she even snored a little. She was ten years younger than Angela—but, by God, he thought, Angela had worn a lot better. He had a sudden longing to see Angela, to be with her again, to try—yes, really try this time. He would take her to dinner. Of course she would be free. He could safely tell Carol he wouldn't be in for supper. 'Get her, Ruth,' he said, and irritation already grated in his voice. 'Get her for me, please.'

'Her' could only have referred to Carol. Ruth knew of

his aversion to naming her. Even on the phone he avoided any reference to her name. In the early days it had been 'darling,' then a diluted 'dear'. Nowadays it was practically 'you'. He picked up his connection, and with no preamble, 'I shall be late tonight.'

'Again? You haven't been home for dinner the whole week.'

He hated her use of 'home'. How dare she assume even after the two years he'd lived there that it was his. Home was where Angela was, though he could not bring himself to reenter it. It was where his son had been born, where Angela had made those dreadful curtains that slouched across the window with threads hanging. Suddenly he longed for those curtains, and all the hurried living that had gone into their making. The restless staccato-fighting evenings, her dirty fingernails, her hair that fell into that terrible soup that she had spent a whole day preparing. And he had screamed for peace. Now, with Carol, he had it. A bellyful of it. She was devoted to him still, with the passionate idolatry of a neuter nun. It was what Angela could never give him, that blind devotion, that unquestioning faith in his sincerely felt infallibility. Now he had that too—and, by God, how it sometimes bored him. Bored him to poker sessions as many nights of the week that Angela could or would not see him. He never took Carol out, except sometimes to the pictures, where it was dark and he could rush her out before the end-titles for fear of meeting those who knew Angela, who would look balefully at Carol and wonder. 'I know I've been out a lot this week. But I've got four productions going. Don't wait up for me.'

He put the phone down quickly, pressing his hand to his forehead, trying not to acknowledge that a decision had to be taken. Often in the past two years he had owned that a choice must be made, a total commitment one way or the other, and he had talked himself into thinking that the simple acknowledgment of its necessity was enough. With Angela, apart from everything else, and of that there was plenty, there was his son and history. But Carol, even as she faded, gathered history too, ten years of it; but hers, unlike Angela's, was a history of a foreign land, and it was natural to take it less seriously. It was exotic, but not quite the way we did things at home: it was faintly uncivilized, faintly unprincipled. It was tempting, but even if you immersed yourself in it totally, as he, in his folly, had tried to do, you remained for ever an alien. Besides, there was another reason for staying with Carol, and it had nothing to do with love or even convenience. It was his stubborn refusal to acknowledge that somewhere along the line he might have made a mistake, and he was a man who would dwell miserably in his errors rather than confess to a fault in his judgment. It was a limbo life, negative and hurtful, and no one was more aware of it than David. Each morning when he awoke in Carol's bed, he thought of Angela. In the car, as he was driven to his office, he saw himself central but unproud to the sad balance of both women, and his power did not please him. He went through each day, his heart screaming.

He wondered where he would take Angela for dinner and what he would talk about in order not to talk about the only subject that mattered. He would tell her on the phone that he had some news, in case she might refuse to see him. During the day something of import might happen or Ruth would invent something for him. Ruth had a fund of inventions which, over the years, she had catalogued. Each story had a number and a file, and a simple cross-check ascertained on what date the lie had been used, on whom and for what purpose. Ruth was not only efficient. She had a quaint sense of morality. She did not believe in double-crossing.

For a moment, David entertained the possibility that Angela would not see him . . . But only for a moment. For he knew that she would need little persuasion. Somehow he wished that she would deny him totally, yet he dreaded that she might divorce him, for he knew he would return to her rather than face that finality. He knew too that Angela would never use divorce as a lever, that when the papers came, if they were ever to come, it would be a sign that Angela, in her heart, had dismissed him. Sometimes he dreaded opening the post and he would keep the letters marked 'Personal' till last. Then, when it failed to be among them, he would feel the need to celebrate. Leave the office perhaps, for an afternoon poker session at the club, where he would stay till the early morning, limboed and secure. It could not go on like this, he knew, and simply by acknowledging it, he intended it to go on for ever.

'What appointments do I have this morning?' he asked.

'Tom Welland is coming at eleven. He's bringing his agent.'

If there are dirty words in a film producer's language, agent is one of them. In a business in which it was imperative to get away with as much profit as possible, this portable side of honesty, an agent was a prime stumbling-block. From an agent's viewpoint, a film producer was *ipso facto* his writer-client's enemy, and you took it from there. Whenever a film contract for a novel was mooted, the agent would tutor his client in the required vernacular. Slowly he would introduce him into a phraseology that might, but did not necessarily, mean what it said, schooling him in producer's language. And so when meeting-time came, the producer was faced with a writer, an erstwhile gentle creature who hitherto had concerned himself only with the finer points of metaphor and idiom and who now spouted airily about producer's profits, percentage of gross, below-the-line costs and, to cap everything, union minimums. Tom Welland's agent in particular was a fine language coach. Colin Waterhouse had himself once been a writer, and though he had failed, he still harboured a narcissistic admiration for the man who sat alone and did the work without which no film producer, star or profit-seeker could make an appearance. And when Colin Waterhouse walked into a producer's office, he arrived hostile.

David motioned them to sit down, and in the same gesture dismissed Ruth. He had not met Tom Welland before. A moderately successful writer who had ten novels to his credit, and this, his latest, the first to be considered as a film. Preliminary negotiations had already been handled between Colin and himself, and this meeting was to discuss the film adaptation. David noticed that the writer sat aloof, with an assumed shyness and modesty, but he wasn't fooled by that one. He knew from his experience of writers that it was the modest unassuming types who, by the end of the picture, were telling you your business, accusing you as a castrator of their work, a philistine, a parvenu. Money-bags was their final spit-out, and of course, as David knew, they were right. That's all he was, a money-bags, and not even that, but a great nose for where money was to be found, and a great sniffer-out of what the public wanted. He had that talent—that was acknowledged even amongst his rivals, who added that though David had never made a good picture, every one of his pictures had made money. He had never read a book or a script. That too was a widely known fact. Ruth was his reader. She would synopsize each story, and on the basis of her résumé he would discuss the book with an author with such cunning and intelligence that often the writer himself might be fooled. Ruth's synopsis on Welland's work had run to four pages, twice as long as her usual offering, since Welland's book was thick with complicated plot, to say nothing of a mass of psychological detail. The synopsis lay now on his desk, in his eyeline but out of Welland's vision.

'I like your book,' David said, with as much confidence as if he had read it. 'Very much. But I think from a film point of view, we need to open it up a bit.'

Try that bit of phraseology for size. 'Open it up' was a phrase all producers used to all writers, whatever the work. Most of them would have used it for *War and Peace*.

'Open it up?' Tom Welland asked innocently. Was it not already open? Were its contents not patently visible?

'I mean, we must enlarge the canvas. Take the wife, for instance. She has no friends. We know she works in a bookshop, but we don't meet any of her colleagues.'

Tom Welland sighed. 'She's a very isolated figure. Her withdrawal is voluntary. The whole point of her story is her disaffiliation. It drives her to suicide.'

'Well, I was coming to that,' David said, and the writer shifted in his chair. Along with 'agent', 'suicide' was another dirty word in a producer's office, especially if it was successful. 'I don't want her to commit suicide,' he said, and it sounded like a personal plea. 'I'm not talking about box-office sensitivity either. I just don't feel

24

convinced that she would have done it. She would have gone on—doggedly and miserably, it's true. But she was too much of a survivor to die by her own hand.'

The agent smiled. He knew the source of David's objection, and he had expected it. He had sent him the book in the first place because the story was uncommonly like the story of David's own marriage. It had appealed to David largely for that reason. It placed his shabby behaviour between hard covers at two pounds a throw, and that made it respectable. It gave his double dealings the dignity of literature. And what with the current heart-throb of the screen playing the role of husband, why, his behaviour might even be celebrated. But he couldn't have the wife going off and doing herself in. That would complicate matters and cause much inconvenience to everybody.

There was silence. The agent looked at the writer, who swallowed. Then Tom Welland gave a shrug, a non-violent gesture, which registered, he hoped, his disapproval, yet at the same time did not preclude the possibility that he might give the matter some thought.

'A film is very different from a novel,' David pressed on, taking advantage of the writer's obvious availability. 'Your novel is very interior, very cerebral. This style does not easily translate into pictures. With good direction it can be conveyed, but you cannot hang a whole picture on it. Her suicide, as I see it, is the end-result of an essentially interior monologue, and we cannot, in a film, just produce the effect without having been able to underline the cause, since the cause in this case is a literal one.'

Vocabulary, the agent thought. Well-sounding but meaningless. He knew that, in the end, David Morrow would have his way. He just wished he'd be a little more honest with his reasons.

'Look,' David went on, 'I know it's a big decision, but I think in the end you'll see it my way. I suggest you go ahead with the first draft-script, and in the process of opening it up you will find that not only is there an alternative ending, but the present one will no longer be logical. Take it along this first stage, as you wish,' he said. 'Then you can start working closely with the director. D'you think that's a good idea, Colin?'

'What does Tom think?' Colin said.

'I'd sooner not commit myself to a new ending at this stage,' he said. 'I'll do as you suggest. I'll work on the first draft.'

'Fine,' David said. 'How soon can we have it?' He knew from experience that a writer wanted for ever. He was prepared in this instance to allow ten weeks.

'Six weeks?' the writer said timidly.

He really is an innocent, David thought. 'That's O.K.,' he said. 'And don't forget. You can be in touch with me at any time.'

When they had gone, David poured himself a drink. He was pleased with the way the interview had gone. From a business point of view, it was a good beginning. He knew that his objection to the ending was not only personal: that ending was not a commercial proposition. That was the essential nature of the business he had become embroiled in, and sometimes it disgusted him. His argument about literary devices that would not transfer to film was contemptible. Unlike many of his fraternity, he was still sensitive enough to recognize his own dishonesty, and to be appalled by it. He suddenly wanted to drop out of everything, to go away somewhere, alone. Or maybe with Angela, to meet as strangers and to start all over again. He drank to that, although he knew it was fantasy. He offered to pour one for Ruth, knowing that she would refuse. Why couldn't the girl enjoy herself a little? It worried him, sometimes, what Ruth thought of him. The lies she told on his behalf; how she played Carol off Angela and vice versa. She liked Angela. They'd been friends for many years. He wondered whether Angela was using her too.

'I'm taking Angela to dinner tonight,' he said. He felt suddenly very happy at the prospect of seeing her again, and he needed to tell someone, to proclaim it with joy, to be proud that he was taking his wife to dine. His wife? Yes, he thundered to himself, and it didn't matter how he was living or what anyone else thought. His indecision was his own agony. It would deal with itself, given time. Time that would serve *him,* and nobody else. So he could not acknowledge that across London another day had started for Angela, which made it the seven hundred and forty-first day of their separation. And that time has no preferential creditors. It was serving her, too, to her first day of survival.

Chapter Three

When one makes a resolution one is doubtful of fulfilling, one postpones it till the morning. Which was what Angela Morrow did, and recalled it as the alarm woke her from her half and fitful sleep. She remembered her decision and approved the theory of it, but in her exhausted awakening her enthusiasm had drained. She dragged herself out of bed, and marvelled at the uncrumpled sheets and the still neat folds of the blankets. How was it possible that the torment inside her had not in some violent way expressed itself, while she, drugged with resolutions, was not looking? It bothered her too that she still kept rigidly to her side of the bed, leaving David's untouched, hallowed almost, as a dead man's room is sometimes left unchanged, unopened, since the day he died.

On her way to the bathroom, she intoned her daily litany. 'It's half past seven,' she said aloud. 'I'm going to run my bath and then I'll make some coffee.' No earth-shattering conversation this, but enough to confirm that she had woken, that she had seen another day arrive, and that somehow or other it must be consumed. At least the sun wasn't shining, and with luck it might rain all day. She had no appetite to invest in anything to wear for hot days. Inside, she was winter, always, and, as such, she dressed, clothing herself in her own logic.

In her bath, she counted her blessings. It was something she usually refrained from doing, for she saw it as an act of abdication, but since today marked the beginning of her survival, it was permissible as ammunition. A son, enough money, a pleasant flat, and a job that she liked and was good at. All that and history too. She spoke them aloud, omitting the last. The nagging recall of history was no way to survive. She showered the soap away in cold water. They said that was good for you. It made you pull yourself together. Before dressing, she dared to look closely at her body, an act of considerable courage, and for the first time in many months she saw it as the possible object of someone's concern. Yes, for forty, she was wearing well, a little overweight perhaps, but that she could deal with. Her skin needed attention too. She would buy some lotions on the way home from work. Yes, it was all dealable with, except the history. There was no cream for that, or diet. It would have to wait. She would have to put it aside until she could deal with it, but she knew she could no more put it aside than her hair.

She dressed with care, mindful of her resolution. For a moment she thought of skipping breakfast, but on her first day she had to give herself every chance. She knew that people did survive on empty stomachs, but it was sheer indulgence to inflict further pain on oneself when there was hardship enough without hunger. So she decided to have an extra good breakfast, and moreover to set the table meticulously. Even to a linen serviette. David would have been proud of her. She propped the morning paper against the flower-vase and started on her grapefruit. As she moved the sugarbowl, the paper fell down. 'I'm sorry,' she said, looking across the table. She began to tremble.

"Dear Angela, Why can I do nothing decent, just for me, *me*, ME. Now I think I know the ingredient, the yeast of the primal scream. It's not a scream at all. That's only what it sounds like. It's the pure emission of that two-letter obscenity. Me. It comes from the navel, where it first found its simple and innocent expression, slowly unwinding itself with creeping crescendo, as a snake hisses to its full height. Yes, it's hissing all right, Angela, but when it's fully stretched, what then? Does the 'me' evaporate into the diminuendo of death, or is there another scream to come, and another? Is this survival? Over to you, my strong and captive listener."

She finished her breakfast standing up. Much more comfortable, and the tempo of her eating increased. She pulled on her coat as she finished her toast, and as she left her flat, running down the stairs, she heard her phone ring.

Every phone call, either at home or at work, was David-expected, so that anyone else received her disappointed short shrift. She didn't like the telephone. She had enough conversation talking to herself. But the non-conversation that she had with David, negative and painful as it always was, had become as essential a part of her day as her work itself, and her survival was yet too young and too green to forgo it.

'Hullo?'

'You sound out of breath. I'll ring back if I've disturbed you. It's Stuart.' He wanted a favour from her. It

30

was obvious, and he didn't want to catch her in a bad mood. 'I'll ring you later.'

'No, it's all right. I was just on my way to work.'

'Then I won't keep you. I'll ring you at the office.'

'For Christ's sake, Stuart, what d'you want? I'm here. I'm listening.'

'I, er, I thought, if you were free, er, you would have dinner with me tonight. See my new flat at the same time.'

'That would be lovely,' she said quickly. She could always phone him during the day and say that something of vital importance had turned up. She didn't have time or courage to say it now. It would involve too much explanation.

'I'll pick you up at eight,' he said.

She managed to get a seat in the tube, darting for it in competition with a very fat lady whose girth was against her. The fat woman stepped on Angela's foot in revenge, accidentally of course, and likewise Angela stabbed her bottom with her umbrella. Two-one, she scored, but when the train stopped abruptly, the fat lady fell on to her lap. Level-pegging.

"Dear Angela, Look at me and my London Transport Encounter Therapy. A fat anonymous lady is happily sitting on my lap and I'm surviving. This is my station, Angela. Stand by."

As she walked out of the station, the sun broke through the clouds and, for some reason or other, did not disturb her. She was early. There was time to walk slowly through Soho Square, past the meths drinkers, drunkenly guiding cars into parking spaces, their function at that early hour as superfluous as a traffic warden in a desert. She watched a large white car reverse into an unlimited space that the self-appointed guide circumscribed with his drunken embrace. 'Want it cleaned, Mister?'

You'd bloody well better have it cleaned, Mister, or your tyres will be down before I go off duty.

And Mister, knowing the form, says, yes, helplessly, staring at his elongated face in the gleaming bonnet of his car that his son had polished only yesterday. The meths drinker winked at Angela, screwing up his already screwed-up face, and reminded her suddenly of Stuart. Now the sun began to irritate her, and all the good resolutions that she'd slept with, and in diluted form had awakened with, now dissolved completely.

"Dear Angela, I'm trying, but it's hard. I can't see Stuart tonight. I know he's kind, and he's decent and he loves me, and because of all these things he's contemptible. So let's say, just for now, that I don't want to see him because he's David's best friend. My God, some barricade. Hacked together from strips of loyalty. Well, I've used just about everything else for my defences. The design, the purpose, is exactly the same. Let me just experiment with a new material. It's odd, but when David and I were together, I had so many affairs, and never once did I consider myself unfaithful. Now, for the first time, I allow for the notion of adultery. And that includes loyalty too. But I'd sooner go home, Angela, and spend the night alone, and dust the mantelpiece and stare out of the window. And you can stand inside me and laugh and call me a bloody fool. But for the moment, soul-sister, stop bugging me."

She trudged along St Anne's Court, her daily short-cut to the office, a sleazy alley that by rights should have been covered with lino. Along one side, three permanently out-of-order telephone booths/urinals. Along the other, strip-clip joints, and morning-suited barkers, who even at this hour hoarsely insisted that no greater enjoyment could be found in all London. The passers-by, mostly can-carrying film assistants, doubted it, but knew the patter by heart, and joined in the chorus. Even the man in the fingered mackintosh was not fooled, though he'd come back for more, as he did every morning. Alone, like Angela, but unlike Angela, having to be alone with others alone. Even dusting a mantelpiece must be better. She smiled at Chico, the front-man at 'Tearaway', the posh joint, the Folies Bergères of the alley, where the tits were bigger, and the teasing longer, and there was no casual trade. So Chico didn't bark. He simply smiled, and waited for his punctual customers. If you were queer, you took care to avoid the alley, or you would have been hooted off the line. All good clean fun in St Anne's Court. None of your perverted filth. Open now, doors and raincoats. First show of the day. And at nine o'clock in the morning the men dribbled in, saddest of all in the morning, with sleep still in the eye, and the mouth dry and panting for the fix that would see them through the day. Till the next morning.

"Jesus, Angela, is there *anywhere* beautiful?"

She hurried out of the alley. She knew most of those who passed her by. Film-makers, from any one of the dozens of little studios that peppered this side of Soho, scratching a living from bewildered sponsors who thought in their hearts that film promotion was a waste of time and money, but who had to participate because of their competitors, who, in their turn, thought likewise. They were a kind of fraternity, the film-makers, especially those who worked in documentary, a close-knit unit, who, for the most part, still retained a genuine inter-

33

est in cinema. When you graduated to features, you tended to walk in the road in Wardour Street, daring the one-way cars with your kinship, while the short-film-makers still minded their manners, and kept to the pavements, hugging their cans and their unfinished commentaries.

She crossed the street into the market, hurrying through because there was such patent life there, and raucous shouting that interfered with her conversations with herself. She was glad to reach her small cutting-room, where she could be alone for a while, and try not to think, try to soft-pedal into a whisper the screaming inside her head. She had to ring Stuart. But not now. Later perhaps when she could think of a good excuse. She picked up a pencil from the bench, and added to the jumbled graffiti on the wall. 'Ring Stuart.' Above it, someone had written 'Madame Tussaud has gone to seed/To seed has gone To saud.' It seemed a fitting commentary.

She laced up the cutting-copy on the moviola. Chris would be in early. As the film approached its fine cut, he came in earlier and earlier, his panic mounting. Over the shooting-period, he had had a whole crew to blame or hold responsible. The sound was muffled, the lighting flat, anything at all but his lousy direction and inadequate script. Now that same crew were off on some other picture, screwing it up for some other director, while he was left alone in the cutting-room. Alone with his wretched rushes, with an inadequacy of cutaways, master shots and linking material that would make up an ensemble. So he took it out on Angela, who had gradually convinced him that the cutting-room was too late for miracles. So he came in earlier and earlier, and faced a jumble of material that even he had to admit to himself was a crashing bore.

And his commentary got wordier and wordier, vocabulary covering pictures that simply were not there, until the fine cut was a mere series of lantern slides, with his illiterate commentary on the side. He had already twice postponed a viewing for the sponsors, and now they were pressing. He knew that the film in its present state didn't fulfil their minimum requirements. Yesterday he had asked Angela to find him some music that might blur the poverty of his film material. That's how desperate he was. He came in just as Angela was finishing the looping.

'Let's look at it on the projector this morning,' he said. Somehow he felt that on a larger screen and without the whir of the moviola, the picture would look better.

'I'd sooner you see it like this,' Angela said. 'I can mark up the changes as we go along. There are bound to be some,' she said, from her tired experience of him, 'and quite frankly, Chris, I don't want to look at this picture one single more time than is absolutely necessary.'

'You're charming this morning,' he said. 'Full of compliments. Go and have some coffee. I'll go through it myself and make notes.'

She regretted her rudeness, but she had had him on her back for the last six weeks, and there was Stuart to ring and her own unhappiness, and her weakening resolve to survive. She started to unlace the machine. 'I'll take it along to projection,' she said. 'What's more, I'll even stay with you and watch it. Sorry. Just a bad morning.'

He smiled at her, unlacing the sound track.

In the viewing-room, he grumbled about the sound quality, blaming the speakers. He complained of others' inefficiency throughout the viewing. Very occasionally, after an intelligible sequence, he would enjoy a moment

35

of supreme optimism. 'It's great,' he muttered, 'it's going to be great.'

"Dear Angela, Great. D'you hear that? What word does he use for Tolstoy?"

The film ground to its dismal end. She looked at him, waiting for his words. But he looked at her with similar intent. Then they both wordlessly left the room.

'I'm going out for some coffee,' he said at last. 'Lace it up again. I've got to rethink the whole thing. Rethink it entirely.'

She'd heard that one before too.

'It's going to work,' he said as he reached the door. 'It's going to be bloody marvellous.'

She went back to the cutting-room, and when she'd laced it up, there was nothing to do but wait for him. Ring Stuart. She'd feel better once that had been dealt with. Look Stuart, she rehearsed, sorry but I won't be able to make it tonight. I've got to work late. Yes, very late. Much too late, always and for ever too late to see you, you runt-faced stupid crud with your dreary decency and your loving of me so get off my back you simpering runt you. She hissed it into the receiver, dialling his number while the anger was still upon her. She let it ring. Three times was enough for Stuart. He deserved no more. After three rings he deserved to be stood up. She hesitated before putting down the phone, distancing the earpiece. She let it ring six more times, and then with confidence, knowing that he must be out, she left the receiver on the cutting-room bench while she went into the adjoining office to make coffee. When she returned, Stuart's phone was still ringing. He was most likely at the butcher's, she decided, supervising a sophisticated french cut. Probably saddle of lamb, which was Stuart's invariable offering whenever he performed in N.W.I. He had probably already set the table, candled in anticipation. No doubt, and with the same hope, he had changed his sheets as well. She shuddered, and replaced the receiver. She had tried, and the attempt convinced her that she had honourably cancelled the appointment.

She started to drink her coffee and read Chris's morning paper. A global picture of murder, sanctified in different areas by the names of war, independence, patriotism. On the back page was a real live murder, excused by no euphemism, but simply and straightforwardly wanton, and somehow that one single strangulation was the cleanest deed in the news.

Her extension rang, and she hesitated before picking it up. Probably Stuart, on the point of rosemarying his lamb, confirming the evening, pinning her down, forcing her to repeat her yes, because no was possible only to herself, or into a dead telephone line. Yes, she would go with him, and while they ate dinner she would wonder how to stave him off afterwards, knowing that she wouldn't, that she wouldn't even try, because a no would hurt him terribly.

''Dear Angela, Why do I diminish myself so? How can anyone be that guilty?''

She picked up the phone.

'Angela?'

'Who's that?' Though she knew very well who it was, trying to pretend that his voice after twenty years had sieved effortlessly through her mind, that it did not reverberate through the back of her head through the whir of the moviola during her days, and the screaming silences of her nights.

'It's me.'

37

"The arrogance, Angela. It's me. Who else would phone you? He wants me to go to dinner with him. Tonight. Not even a day's notice. 'Cos I've got to be free. And if by any chance I weren't, it would be automatic to change my plans. But I'll say yes, like I always say, 'cos this is how he wants it. Candlelight without commitment. No. This time it's no. Positively no. Yours absolutely decidedly.''

'Have dinner with me tonight?'

'If you like.'

'I'll pick you up at the flat at eight.'

She pictured the unhappy collision with Stuart. 'No. Pick me up at the office,' she said. 'I'm working late.'

'Got news for you,' he said, hanging on to his end of the line.

'What is it?'

'I'll tell you when I see you.'

'All right. I'll see you at eight.'

She replaced the receiver and waited a second before dialling his number. She had changed her mind. She would not see him. His number was engaged. Of course. It had to be. Every decision, such as she could make, thwarted.

"Dear Angela, I tried. I can't bring myself to try again.''

He picked her up at eight o'clock. He had always been punctual. All the others had left the office, and Angela was glad of it. Her encounters with David could do without witnesses.

'Are you ready?' he said, seeing that she was far from it. 'I told you I'd be here at eight.'

She turned on him swiftly. 'Don't you bully me,' she

screamed. 'I don't have to put up with your shit any more. I'm not your wife. Offload it on that slut of yours.'

"Jesus, Angela, no fishwife stuff. It gets us nowhere. But, by God, the relief of it. Oh the full-blown and fleeting consolation. Forget the aftertaste. You've been decent and noble and tight-lipped for so long, and look at you. Oh Angela, if only I could break without breaking."

'Shall we go?' he said, knowing that he held all the cards.

'I'll be five minutes.'

In the car he put his hand on her knee. She did not respond, but neither did she remove it. She thought about it, its motivation, its possible consequences. Then she took a deep breath and laid her hand on top of his. But David, fearing she was sealing a pact when a pact had not been offered, withdrew his hand.

'Where are we eating?' she said, trying to pretend that nothing had happened, and thinking how foolish her hand looked caressing her own knee.

'Italian, I thought,' he said. 'There's a new one in Knightsbridge. It's very good. I ate there a couple of weeks ago.'

She stifled the 'With whom?' and swallowed. "See how I'm trying, Angela."

'I went with Tony Childs. Remember? He used to work for me.'

'I thought he'd gone to Canada.'

'He came back. Didn't suit him. Wants to get back into films.'

'You taking him?'

'I may. Depends on what gets off the ground.'

It was her cue to ask him about his business. But she refrained, because she knew that that was what he wanted above all to talk about, not only because he loved talking about his wheelings and dealings but because it kept him safe from every other subject. They were silent, passing Harrods. Menopausal shoplifting for the better class of person. If you lifted a jar of strawberry conserve from Harrods, they called it a nervous breakdown, but further down the road in the supermarket, where the only proof of strawberries in the jam at all was the label on the jar, they hauled you in and called it shoplifting, and bound you over till your flushes ceased.

They pulled up at the lights. On their right, the air terminal.

'I'd love to go away,' she said, almost to herself.

'Then let's,' he said. 'I can take a couple of weeks at the end of the month. Shall we go to Paris?'

She heard Angela laughing and thanked her for that. 'In what capacity?' she asked. 'Wife? Mistress? Friend?'

'D'you *have* to play a role?' he said. 'Look,' he stopped the car. For once he was going to say what he meant. 'Can't we just have an evening together, a pleasant evening together without reference to the past or the possible future. Can't we just *be* together?'

'I'll try,' she said, and the rest of the drive was silent. If one cannot speak about the past or a possible future, only the present is left. And what is the present save a hangover from the past, and hope for the future.

'How's your new project going?' she said. The present. Safe.

'I think we'll be able to go ahead. Saw the writer today. May have some script problems.'

'What's the story about?'

Not safe. Not safe at all. All over the world and every minute of the day, men leave their wives and go to live with other women. And guilt and sometimes regret drives them back again, back and forth, until one of the doors is suddenly closed. No, he couldn't tell her the story. She would personalize it, as she did everything. 'It's nothing awfully exciting,' he said. 'It's just about a marriage.' That was as general as he could manage.

'You're always making films about marriage,' she said. 'Rather as if you were an expert.' ''Sorry, Angela, just couldn't resist it.''

'Is it going to be one of those evenings!' he almost shouted, the vein swelling in his forehead.

'There's nothing safe to talk about,' she said. 'Even the future is history.'

She was right. He understood that. He knew how over the years he had hurt her. He knew too that he was sorry. Terribly sorry. Much too sorry ever to tell her, because that too she would twist. Yet after all these years of pain, an apology was all she wanted, was all she would settle for; just a simple acknowledgment of what he had done to her, a simple attempt to compensate. But he had his own ways of saying he was sorry. 'Give me time' was one of them, and 'Don't close the door' was another. The fact that he laid his head on another's pillow was in his mind irrelevant; he had neither left Angela nor joined Carol. He was living in a limbo, and as long as there was limbo, there was hope. He wanted so much to enjoy the evening. He tried to recapture the excitement he'd felt from the very beginning. Because he wanted to live with her again, to love her again, but the fear that it might now be too late turned into an anger that he directed against her. 'Do you want me to take you home?' he said. 'Home' was a loaded word too. There was nothing on earth that you could say to her, without begging some historical question. Between them language had become too imprecise, too flexible. Silence was the only honesty that could lie between them, and even that silence depended on its duration. There was as much artistry in its timing as in a poem whose silence the poet interrupts with his impatient words, or in a painting whose space the painter punctuates with spasms of colour.

'Let's try,' he said, after a pause. Then he smiled and tweaked her nose. 'It doesn't get any shorter, does it?'

She started to cry. It was a gesture he'd always teased her with in their happier days. He put his arm round her as she snivelled, automatically giving her his handkerchief. 'How have you managed for hankies without me?'

There is nothing more insidiously blackmailing than nostalgia, and though Angela was totally aware of it, she let him comfort her. After all, what did it matter why one loved, for what tortuous reasons one felt part of another. If a victim loved her persecutor, was that less of a love? If all logic, if all sanity were against you, could you love still, or did you have to be the girl next door to qualify?

They pulled up at the restaurant and she took a little time to comb her hair. 'How do I look?' she said.

'You're always asking that,' he laughed. 'Now how do *I* look?' he mocked. 'Is my hair all right?' He primped the back of his head.

Always double-edged, the tease. If I met him now for the first time, she thought, I would fall deeply in love with him.

The patron of the restaurant greeted them effusively. 'Lovely to see you again, Mr Morrow,' he said. He smiled at Angela.

'This is my wife,' David said.

"A Word Is A Word Is A Word Stop Love Angela."

42

The manager handled her duffle coat as if it were a mink as he led them to a small table at the rear. He lit two red candles in silver sticks and placed a single rose between them. His set, and he was loath to have no part in the play. So he hovered for a while. 'A drink?' he suggested, sensing that some ice needed breaking.

'I'll have a whisky,' David said, 'and a Campari for my wife.'

"Dear Angela, He's been away from me for two years, for over seven hundred and thirty days. It *is* possible, just slightly possible that on one of those days, something, some quite trivial thing about me and my habits, might have changed, even ever so slightly. It *is* possible. Come to think of it, Angela, he's right. I still drink Campari. Nothing has changed. All that's happened to me in all those days is time. Leave me alone, Angela. Let me eat my meal in peace."

The manager left them to sort it out for themselves. Angela regretted his departure. In the presence of a third party they were safe, she and David. They could join together, even in hostility. Now, face to face, all that was between them was silence, a sick silence of which both were deeply aware, each delving into their minds for something to say, anything unloaded, straight, simple, without possible undermeanings.

'What news did you have to tell me?'

'What news?' he said, playing for time.

'On the telephone you said you had some news. Remember?'

'Oh, it's nothing really.' He clutched desperately in Ruth's remembered files. 'I just had an idea. Thought you'd like to work with me on my new picture.' My God, he thought, what have I said. It had come right off the top of his head, inspired as if by someone else to get him out of a jam. 'Only if you'd be out of work yourself, that is,' he said, trying to reverse it a little.

'I'm starting a new picture next week.'

'Really,' he said, infinitely relieved. 'Whose picture is it?' He was willing to talk about it for ever.

'It's Robert's, alas, but it's work. What kind of job were you thinking of for me? I might consider it if you made it worth my while.' She tried to make a joke of it.

'Not editing,' he said. Then, when she still showed interest, he added helplessly, 'I thought you might like to try the production side.'

'Like what?'

'Well, Mr Worcester might be able to use you. Location-hunting mainly. We'll have to shoot in Italy. It's a co-production.' He shrugged, feeling that it had already gone too far. 'Well, you said you wanted to get away.'

'D'you think it's a good idea for us to work together?'

'Strictly business,' he said, chucking her under the chin. Keep it light, the only way to deal with it, and slide off the whole business as quickly as possible. 'Just a thought,' he said, hoping that that would end it once and for all.

'I'll think about it,' she said. 'Don't really fancy working with Robert again. How much are you paying?'

'No salary. A percentage.'

'That puts me in the executive class,' she said. 'Alongside you. Would you like that?'

He wished to God he'd never mentioned it. It could, when he wasn't looking, become a reality, rather as his affair with Carol had finally broken his marriage. He had a complete inability to understand cause and effect, and the consequences were upon him while he still considered himself involved in preliminaries. This inadequacy did not point to selfishness or cruelty. All it spelt out was his irritating innocence.

'What will you have to start with?' He moved towards her in order to share the menu. 'Vichyssoise, I suppose.'

But though she wanted it, and it was her favourite and her usual, she declined. She had to show him that during their separation her taste, in food at least, had undergone some change. 'I'll have the pâté,' she said, 'if it's coarse.'

'Pâté?' he asked. 'You never liked pâté.' Or: How dare you threaten the order of my memories. Her sudden taste for pâté was a danger, and God knows what she would order next. Game perhaps. It was the season, a season to which she had always been sublimely indifferent. 'And afterwards?'

'The pheasant sounds good,' she said. 'I'll have that.'

He felt suddenly uncomfortable, un-at-home. If he were ever to go back to her, it had to be to precisely the same person as she had been two years ago. Going back to Angela was going home, and what point was there in that if home was unrecognizable. 'There's *coq-au-vin.*' He almost pleaded with her, knowing it to be her favourite dish.

'No. I prefer the pheasant.'

'Then I'll have *coq-au-vin,*' he said. Somebody had to keep the home fires burning.

She let him order the wine according to his taste, which she knew to be more reliable than hers, and over the *hors-d'œuvres* she felt suddenly comfortable with him, with a total willingness to forgive all the hurt he had done her. As for David, he began slowly to recapture his earlier anticipation, gathering a solid conviction that in time, his

45

time, everything would be well between them. It was with such silent thoughts and the occasional smile that the first course of the meal was easily enjoyed, but when the dishes were taken away, it was as if they faced each other, unprotected. He poured her more wine, even though her glass was still reasonably full. He scratched in his mind for something to say.

'Tell me more about this new film of yours,' she said, helping him. He was glad to be able to talk about his work. It was an area in which he felt safe and in complete control.

'Daphne Wells is playing the lead,' he said.

'In that case,' she interrupted him, laughing, 'I *will* take a percentage.'

'Well, between you and me, she doesn't have the box-office magic of the old days. They're still paying off on her last two pictures. Don't let it get around, though.'

'It's all a myth, isn't it,' she said. Angela tried to tell her to shut up, sniffing the beginnings of a destructive brew. But the inner voice angered her, and she went on relentlessly. 'Your whole business is a myth. It has absolutely nothing to do with anything that's real.'

Mercifully the second course arrived. David decided not to take her up on it. He knew it would lead to all kinds of recriminations, but Angela would not let it lie, and hardly had the waiter left their table than she was pursuing the old argument that for ever lay between them. 'It's a total reflection of your life,' she said, 'the kind of unreal job you opted for, the people you mix with. Performers, all of them. The actors, the producers, the money-bags, they all perform. I used to be like that when I lived with you. D'you remember our dinner-parties? Are you going to the Morrows on Wednesday night? They're performing. Or the Bankses on Sunday? Saturday was the Thomases' night. The ever-so-clever performers of s.w.3.'

He wondered if she realized that she was shouting. 'Stop it, Angela,' he said, as kindly as he was able. He knew that she was saying none of those things. It was all a sad translation of, 'I want you back, David. Please come home.' It was language used to by-pass rejection and to clothe the nakedness of her simple plea. He put his hand on her hair. She started to cry, turning her face to the wall. And as she tried, handkerchief-less, to dry her tears, she heard a violin, and she thought of Chris's dreadful picture that she had cut and recut over the past six weeks, and how only today he'd decided to lay a violin obligato over the whole rotten shambles. Was the picture she, at this moment, presented so utterly boring and meaningless that only the addition of music track could make it passable at all? She turned her head, and found herself serenaded by a North Kensington gypsy. He saw the tears on her face, and his bow hesitated. Wrong number this time, most certainly, but he could right it perhaps with his soothing strain, and he promptly reinforced his air with a desperate vibrato that almost mocked her tears. David looked at him and motioned him to leave, and as he started to move, Angela smiled at him apologetically, not wishing to hurt him. 'Let's get out of here,' she said, grabbing her duffle-coat from the stand behind. She looked at her pheasant and David's *coq-au-vin*, steaming on the table. His and hers, and interchangeable. ''Then why, dear Angela, when we're so close, have we collided, he and I, in a tangled encounter that scathes us both? I have destroyed so much in the last five minutes, and it's not what I wanted at all. Forgive me. Somebody forgive me. It's just that I keep thinking of how he will drop me off at the flat when the evening is over, and I feel like a whore. If someone were to tell me about me, I'd have her hide for masochism. Stand by, Angela. I haven't heard you laugh all evening. Is it patience for us at home, or the mantelpiece again? Am I still writing you my suicide note? Awaiting your reply. PS. That violinist had a very good staccato.''

She waited for David in the car, terrified. After a few minutes she saw him at the door of the restaurant, smiling sadly at the manager as if apologizing for his lunatic wife, and the patron returned an understanding nod of the head. David would have paid handsomely for any inconvenience caused, but it was unlikely that he would go there again. He got into the car, and without a word, without even looking at her, he started to drive away. They crossed through the park, and all the while he stared doggedly ahead of him.

"Dear Angela, Fancy even being aware of that violinist's technique. Does the fact that I can entertain thoughts outside my situation make my pain mediocre? Now, for instance, as we drive in this car, I think of a second-rate movie. The tight-lipped hero at the wheel, his feelings brutally hurt, his pride mutilated, his ego shattered, driving through London at night, the cause of his pain sitting mutely by his side. It is the end. Nothing can mend them now. A crash perhaps? And he, unscarred, looks down on her pale broken corpse beside him. And that'll make him bloody sorry. Oh Angela, stop me, stop me.''

'I'm sorry,' she said, 'I'm terribly sorry. Come home, David. Please come home.'

'To this? To all your bitterness? To all our history?' He put his hand on hers to soften the words, for whatever he

48

would say, he knew that she would take it hard. He kept his hand there until they reached the flat where once they both had lived. He stopped the car and looked at her. 'I left you because I needed the peace, Angela. I've got it now. I can't pretend it's what I want. But your pulse terrifies me. Tonight, for instance . . .'

'I'm only like this because I can't forget that at the end of the evening you'll drop me off, and go and lie elsewhere. It puts me on edge.'

He turned the ignition. He had to get away. 'I'm terrified of coming back to you,' he said.

She scrambled out of the car and walked helplessly up the front steps of the house. He watched her, her back desperately straight, clenched, as he knew her jaws were, fighting back the tears that she would hold until she was alone. He watched her disappear inside the house and he waited until her lights went on. He followed her into their bedroom and he saw her take the corner of the pillow into her mouth and scream into the feathers her deafening loneliness. Then he let in the clutch and drove away, because he could bear it no longer.

Inside, Angela walked up the stairs, and by the first landing the tears had broken. She made no effort to control them. She rarely cried—tonight was an exception—but now she decided that she must, that once and for all she must rinse out her pain, totally and with loud mourning. She was bereaved, and she must weep for seven days, and then, by the law of God, it had to be over.

"Dear Angela, I have completed my first day of survival. I am here to prove it, and I shall never, never, see David again. *Now* you laugh. Be my guest."

As she turned the corner of the landing to her own flat, she saw, through the gaps in the banisters, a pair of polished shoes and the beginnings of corduroys. Stuart. She had forgotten about him completely, and as she climbed the last flight of stairs, she fuelled her hatred of his servility. God knows how long he'd been waiting, patiently no doubt, with no anger, only with thoughts for her safety. When he saw her, he smiled, almost apologetically. She touched his arm. She had decided what she must do. 'Please don't ask me for an explanation,' she said.

She unlocked the door, and with one arm around him she guided him into the bedroom. In view of what he felt was about to happen, Stuart was more than willing to forgo an explanation and, to show his willingness, he desperately embarked on a subject that could have nothing to do with the evening's mismanagement. He spoke about himself, as he always did—his concern for, and interest in, other people being minimal. He embarked on the latest bulletin of his political progress. Stuart was an ambitious man; after years of decent, straight and honest spadework, he had managed to get himself nominated as the prospective candidate in a very safe Labour constituency. Tonight he had had the news of his nomination, in view of which he was willing to forgive Angela her neglect. Stuart always spoke as if from a platform. He did not speak as much as herald—his whispers would have filled the Colosseum—and he never used one word when a dozen would do. Angela dreaded his performance in bed. She would have to shut her eyes and play patience and she could cheat as much as she wanted to.

'As you know, I've been giving my services to a project of children's playgrounds in my area, and I think that it was this very pursuit of mine that finally won over the committee. I consider this work to be of prime importance in a community venture . . .' All this while he was unbuttoning the flies of his combinations. Angela hoped he would go on talking. His sloganized and pedantic delivery robbed him of all identity. He was the anonymous fulfilment of a whore's needs. She did not help him to undress, nor mercifully did he approach her. She merely opened the bed, unobtrusively so as not to interrupt his manifesto.

"Dear Angela, I've got to do it. It's not a lot to pay for that dreadful saddle of lamb that probably even now lies cold and congealed on his hopeful candle-lit table. How unattractive he is, Angela, and how skilfully I diminish myself. But being aware of that doesn't stop me. My ego doesn't exist. It has something better to do."

She got into bed and waited for him.

'I must say this is a surprise, that even I, in my wildest dreams of fantasy, never entertained.' He lay down beside her, his mouth drooling with non-stop self-advertisement, and as she moved over him, his speech quickened, and the terrible fear that he would not acquit himself with her plunged him into an oration worthy of a maiden speech, which indeed, in a way, it was. She helped him out, not from understanding or affection of any kind, but because it all helped to pay for his abortive lamb with rosemary astride the saddle. She looked at him while she performed, cheating outrageously at her patience, while he earnestly and frantically declaimed the fundamental rights of every human being, black or white or black or white or black . . .

"Dear Angela, How like a pig he looks. If I were to put a lemon in his mouth, he could be President of the United States. What do I want it for, I ask myself. What's the going price for a saddle of lamb on the sex market nowadays. I've paid, I reckon, and I'm tired. After all, what with surviving and mourning and paying my dues, it's been a very busy day. When we've managed to get rid of him, we'll sleep tonight, you and I, and perhaps in the morning, as token of our survival efforts, we will know that time has moved today, and that occasionally we were able to move along with it. Thanks for everything.''

Chapter Four

Chris's film was finally dubbed. In the last week of editing, Angela had cut and recut the film a dozen times. A day before the mix, Chris had soaked the whole lot in the second movement of the Brahms Violin Concerto. It gave it tone, he said. It was certainly the only tone it had. It's great, he added, which it was certainly, if you didn't look at the picture. The sponsors were satisfied enough to commission a follow-up from him. There were enough violin concertos to keep a man like Chris in business, but Angela swore she would never cut a film for him again.

Yet Robert was no picnic to work for either. Not as talentless as Chris, but slightly less honest. Years before, he had made his first film, which was about crippled children, and with the help of a superb cameraman, a miracle editor and a shooting-ratio of forty to one, he couldn't help but turn out a reasonable picture. In Robert's own insensitive phrase, it 'went down a bomb', and from that time onwards Robert had cornered the documentary market on handicap. Angela had worked for him twice before, and each time she had decided never to do it again. There was something unethical about Robert's film approach. If a situation made good viewing, it really didn't matter how you got your material or how much it would cost in human terms. In the finished film, this violation was hard to pinpoint, but if you were the editor and you saw his rushes as they came in, you were horrified at his monstrous manœuvrings to achieve the desired result. But he was charming, and it was difficult to dislike him, even though you knew that he charmed you and everybody else only in so far as he thought they could further his career. He was not exactly a nasty; he was a side-lines creeper, a slobbering puppy needing your approval. At this moment he was up North, shooting a film on the parents of drug-addicts. God knows, Angela dared to think, what heartbreak he would create up there in the name of his art and she was sitting in the projection room waiting to see the first of his rushes. Three and a half hours of them, and that was only the first batch. It represented two days' filming. She shuddered to recall that his shooting-schedule was three whole weeks. The first reel and a half showed Robert getting his bearings. Robert would get up, eat, think, prepare and rehearse on camera. He left nothing to chance, just in case, he would say, you never know, you might lose that one divine moment of truth. Well, it was not until the fourth reel that such a moment flashed by, and then it was unusable because Robert's ubiquitous gesticulating shadow lurked across every frame.

"Dear Angela, There's a budgeted eight weeks for editing this picture, but it'll probably take that long just to see his rushes. I don't know what got into me to work for him again. I could have taken that job that David . . .

Angela, it's six weeks now since we met, and next Wednesday it'll be seven. You know, we make and break records for ourselves. One week, two weeks, three. Then we say it's a month, lunar reckoning, and then maybe two. I suppose when the months become years the pain must cease. But there may also come a time when the pain is unable to go any further, when, having been measured in years, it tracks back on itself, it retranslates, and that which has lasted a year is reckoned as a duration of twelve months, fifty-two weeks, then the days and the hours and the minutes on a narrow spiral of never-ending descent. Perhaps, Angela, that's what's going to happen to my pain. Am I making a cult of it, or is this what you call surviving? Or are they both the same thing? Am I using Stuart, or others like him, for survival, or do they cultivate my pain? I feel I'm digging my trenches all right, but I'm burying the logic within. Perhaps the very road to survival is through self-destruction. So let it be.''

The sixth reel. Robert still rehearsing. The mother of the family answers the phone. It's the wrong number. Even that has to be recorded for Robert's posterity. Suddenly she missed Chris, and his terrible lack of confidence that made him scream to others that he was great. Robert never questioned his own talent. It was there, solid, irrefutable, and he was divinely entitled to use other people's feelings, time and money to nourish it. Patiently and conscientiously she sat through the whole batch. Out of the three and a half hours she reckoned there was five minutes' cuttable material. With that ratio, anybody on earth with even less to say than Robert could somehow or other produce a picture.

She went back to the cutting-room. Robert had already phoned, wanting a report on his rushes. She was instructed to ring him back when she was ready. Let him wait, she thought, but the phone rang, for Robert had waited long enough.

'How are they?' he said, full of confidence.

'I don't know what you're trying to do,' she said. 'There's very little continuity. Out of the whole batch there doesn't appear to be a complete sequence.'

He laughed. 'Then you'll have to look at it all again,' he said cockily. 'We've got some great stuff there. That kitchen stuff, for instance.'

'Yes, it's fine,' she said coldly, 'but totally unusable.'

'Why?' he demanded.

'Because your great hulking shadow is on every frame.'

Long pause. If that was so, it was truly unusable.

'It's not enough to keep out of the picture,' Angela went on ruthlessly; 'you really ought to take your shadow with you.'

'I'll set it up again,' he said. 'I need that sequence.'

'O.K.,' she said, 'but don't forget. Our editing schedule is only eight weeks.'

'Don't worry,' he laughed. 'I'll be with you every single moment of the day.'

'That's exactly why I'm worried,' she said, and put the phone down.

On the seventh it was one week, on the fourteenth, two. Then three, four five six. Almost seven weeks. She was back to record-breaking again, and somehow she knew she wouldn't make it seven. This was the longest time she had not seen him, longer than at any period during their separation, and she was aware, too, that he hadn't seen her. Did he sit at his desk, reckoning, gloating over his records, wondering, as she did, what was the point of it all? Did he, at such a moment, reach for the phone, as she did, as an addict for his fix, and then, with pious resolution, move away?

As she turned away from the phone, Gavin came in. Her assistant. Late as usual, his eyes still watering from his headwind motor-bike, his stitch-dropped woollen scarf wrapped round him from head to foot, yet still seemingly flying, though the air was still. Gavin was a continuation of the wind, which would, in Gavin's own time, calm itself. He was smiling, as always, his face so full of good intent that it was impossible to be angry with him.

'Sorry,' he said. 'Bike trouble.'

It was the same excuse every morning, and it was always true. Gavin had no cunning. If he had taken the morning off for his grandmother's funeral, you would know that the old lady had died undeniably, and that she was not likely, during the course of Gavin's working life, to die again.

'That's O.K.,' Angela said. 'All you missed was Robert's brilliant rushes. Three and a half hours of them, and half of it, I'm afraid, is unslated. You know Robert. It's going to be a hell of a job synching them up. You have all my sympathy.'

Gavin laughed, unwrapping himself. Nothing could ruffle him. He started to set up his table.

'Aren't you having lunch first?' Angela said.

'No. I'd better start on them right away.'

'Shall I get you a sandwich?'

He nodded. 'Get one for yourself too. Then you can make coffee and we'll eat together.' He loved this period of a film, the initial period of editing, when in logging and synching-up he was king of the cutting-room. Angela would ply him with coffee and sympathy, remembering her early days as an assistant and the dull menial chores of the job. Often, if she wasn't busy on something else, she would give him a hand with logging, writing down the edge numbers as he called them out from his bench. It was a neat reversal of roles during that time, and both of them enjoyed it.

When Angela came back with the sandwiches, and she had made coffee, he was well into the first reel. He refused to be irritated by Robert's incompetence, although it doubled the time he would have to spend on the work. He ascribed the mess to difficult shooting conditions, and Robert's fear of losing something that was vital. Gavin always took care to understand why people behaved the way they did, and as a consequence he found few people unpleasant or unworthy. His inability to dislike anybody might have marked him out as a bore, but he was not without passion. He would react violently against injustice, and do what he could in the proscribed area of his acquaintanceship. He would never join a protest march on behalf of a million people he did not know or couldn't understand. There was no glamour in his kind of protest, no exciting possibility of spending a night in gaol. He was too busy marching for the old lady who lived next door to him, or his young friends who lacked money, jobs and shelter. Gavin was a man who really cared, who really would lose sleep over a friend's misfortune, and when he looked at Robert's rushes, he knew that Robert didn't care, and he cared deeply for Robert who was not able to care himself.

Angela passed him his coffee. He went on working and she watched him, finding pleasure in his absorption, the nostrils that occasionally flared with interest as the pictures jerked by. He had been her assistant on their last three pictures, and she worried sometimes that he had so little ambition. They worked well together, and he would have been happy to remain an assistant all his life, especially to Angela who occasionally gave him the odd sequence to cut on his own. He had a considerable talent as an editor and he knew it, as he knew he had talent as a painter, a pursuit that happily occupied most of his spare time. But his talents did not bother him. He felt perfectly fulfilled, even without totally fulfilling them. He had no grievance against those who got ahead with less talent than himself. He simply knew that he had different priorities.

'Take a break,' Angela said. 'Your coffee's getting cold.'

He swivelled round in his chair, and faced her, smiling. 'They're not too bad,' he said. 'I'll work late tonight and get this batch finished. You can take the day off if you like.'

'Don't you want me to give you a hand?' She wanted to stay. There was something so peaceful about Gavin, it infected you when you were close to him, it smoothed the crinkled edges of your agitation. It held you close and, like a benevolent leech, drew out into itself your pain. Suddenly she wanted his arms around her, strong Mr World arms like they always were in the women's magazines—but, goddammit, she thought, no matter how s.w.3 you were, those strong arms were the only thing that mattered when the nitty-gritty came. Those tough, dependable and laughable he-man qualities that you mocked at in waiting-rooms or under hair-dryers—''But, dear Angela, we need them more than most. What's so extra special about us that we put ourselves beyond the moonlight loves and passions on those pages. So we don't go to Bermuda, and we don't use cream shampoo, and we don't drink Martinis, but even on a railway siding, with greasy hair, love is possible. I'm mending, Angela. Just a little, I think.''

'What's the matter?' Gavin said, gently putting his hand on hers. He knew what the matter was, not the details of it. He didn't need those, nor was he interested. He simply wanted to tell her that he knew, that he was there, and that he cared.

'Come here,' he said. He was much younger than Angela, but there was enough father in him, enough lover and brother, to hold her close without fear of motive or consequence. And he did just that, his innocence transfusing into her. That was all there was to it, with no preamble and no sequel, and as she unbent in his embrace, she knew that for the first time in many years she was happy.

''Dear Angela, It *is* possible. I know that it is possible. Remind me every morning, for God's sake, that it can, and that it must be.''

She went back to her chair. She was not free enough to look at him fully. She felt herself blushing. She knew he looked at her, because he could afford to, and gradually she turned her face towards him, knowing that he was possibly the only man she knew whom she did not want to destroy. 'I'm going for a walk,' she said. 'I need to understand it.'

'Don't question it,' he told her. 'It was everything, but it was nothing. Here,' he said, handing her a can, 'take this reel and start logging. You need to do a very boring and mechanical job. It's the best way of being on your own.'

For the rest of the day they worked in the same room, but separately. Occasionally she caught him looking at her, and she was reassured. They worked till early evening, when he started to wrap his scarf around him. 'See you tomorrow,' he said, his hand on the door. 'I'd offer you a lift, but the pillion's broken. Unless you'd like to stand.' He laughed.

'Thanks. I can do that in the tube. I'll stick around till the rush-hour's over.'

When he had gone, she was alone in the office. From the high window over Wardour Street, she could see the beginning of the Soho change-over. It was an area leased during the daytime to a totally different community from that which rented it for the night. At this time, the early evening, the last of the day renters were starting for home, and the night squatters were dribbling in. Dolly, the stripper from Tearaway, was rushing along to Milo's in Old Compton Street for her evening shift. Across the way, Tony, who made industrial documentaries to a very strict budget, and a two-to-one shooting-ratio, was locking up shop, and putting his almost empty dustbin outside, while a few doors down, Cedric, who specialized in *cinéma vérité*, was lugging two dustbins brimming with celluloid on to the kerbside outside his office. Then he hailed a taxi and was off. And from nowhere they came, out of the alleys and from hidden corners, the film-makers who had to do it on the cheap, converging like hungry tramps around the dustbins, pawing inside for the odd rolls of short-ends that Cedric would have deliberately overlooked because he knew that every evening they would come. A handful of her colleagues were moving into the corner pub, waiting, as she was, for the rush-hour to subside. The Japanese restaurant opened its walls, while Mrs Muffet of the daytime sandwiches put up her shutters. It was the twilight hour of comings and goings, of conveyance before settlement. She sat down at Gavin's bench and saw how neatly he had catalogued the first of the rushes. She was content to think of him, and she held him in her mind, pinning him there as an anchor.

It was almost seven o'clock, the beginning of her daily safe period. David would have left the office and she did not know his other number. So she was not tempted to linger around the phone. Yet she did not relish this safety. His telephone availability during the day tempted her always, and to resist it gave her something to do. All she could do after seven o'clock was to tick off another day of separation in her mind, and know that that tick was reliable. She was safe until morning. So idly she picked up the phone and dialled his number.

When he answered almost immediately, she was startled, having no idea what to say to him. 'What are you still doing at the office?' she said, angry that he had broken one of the rules. He was not supposed to be there. After seven o'clock, his number was a toy that she could play with. He had had it all day. Now it was her turn.

'I've got a meeting,' he said. 'Look, Angela,' he sounded anxious to hold her, 'I'll ring you back on another line. We've got a call coming through on this one. You at the office?'

'Yes,' she said tonelessly, and put the phone down. Then quickly she gathered up her things and rushed out of the door. When she reached the second landing, she heard her phone ring. She pinned herself against the wall, listening and counting. Twelve times. He really wanted to speak to her. Fifteen, sixteen. Now he was angry that she wasn't there. Twenty, twenty-one. Now perhaps he was worried that something had happened to her. It stopped at twenty-six. Now he didn't care any more.

She walked slowly down the stairs, holding Gavin in her mind's eye, clinging to the positive proof he had given her, that love, even for her, was possible. They were shutting up on the first floor, another documentary company where she had often worked. She needed to be with people she knew and liked, people who with their work-talk could take her mind off her mind. She opened the main door and went straight to James's room. He was still at it, working overtime on a sponsored nut-and-bolt film that was due a week ago. James was never on schedule. It wasn't that he was slow; he was a perfectionist, and he applied his high standards to everything he cut. 'Shan't be a minute,' he said. 'Shall we go for a drink?'

'I was just going home.'

'Too early,' he said. 'You won't get a seat on the tube. I've got my car in town. Let's have a drink and I'll run you home.'

She went over to look in his machine. The sequence showed a lathe in operation. James was laying the sound-track and cutting picture to sound. He was basically a musician, and it is possible that he went into the editing business with his eye exclusively on the sound-track. Sound was almost sacred to him. He would never have worked with a man like Chris who tossed symphonies around to save his lousy pictures. When he'd heard the Brahms Concerto filtering down through the floors, he knew that Chris was in production.

'It's a manual on machine tools,' he said, explaining the context of the sequence. 'Not really as bad as it sounds. I've found this marvellous electronic music. It really looks as if the machines are talking, doesn't it, and, what's more, talking in synch.'

'I envy your enthusiasm,' she said. 'You're never bored, are you?'

'Depends who I'm working with. I hear you're with Robert again. And you swore you never would after his last picture.' He stopped his machine. 'Angela,' he said kindly, 'why d'you do it? You've got a choice. There's no shortage of good work. Why d'you have to make yourself so unhappy?'

'Stop it, James,' she said, 'I don't want to talk about it. Let's go and have a drink.'

He ran on till the end of the sequence, then he switched off the machine. 'You've sentenced yourself to eight weeks' miserable labour,' he insisted, 'and you've done it with your eyes wide open. You make things tough for yourself.'

"Dear Angela, I've known James for many years and now, for the first time, I dislike him a little. By the end of the evening I shall dislike him so much that you know as well as I what we'll do. All in the name of survival. Is there no other way of keeping one's head out of the oven? Or shall I die from a malignant arrogance? 'Cos that's how I'm heading. I shall take James, as I took Stuart and countless others, though no doubt you've got your reckoner ready, and I shall fabricate a charge. I put them on a cursory trial, and then sentence them to coital destruction. I appoint myself executioner. And you'll be there, my little voyeuse, and if you can find it in your heart to laugh, it'll help keep the Assizes open. Am I your disobedient servant, Angela?"

The pub was full of film-makers. The talk around the bar was of film. There was a Union meeting later on to which all of them were positively not going, but then and there they held their own, mocking each other with the title of Brother, and Sister-ing Angela with Union slogans that hadn't been changed in a quarter of a century. Stuart would have been horrified. She hadn't seen Stuart since his saddle-of-lamb evening, but they had talked politely on the phone. He couldn't understand why their connection had to cease, but how many times does one need to lie with a man in order to destroy him. Once was enough if you were, like Angela, diligent enough. It wasn't as if she wanted to make a habit of it; it was momentary, a gesture for that evening, and having made her point, a relationship of sorts might still be possible.

She sat with James in a corner, as audience to the bar-clingers' speechifying. 'Look, there's Harry,' one of them shouted turning to a newcomer. 'Brother Stoneham, thought you were on location.' Harry approached the bar.

'I was,' he said. 'Chucked it in.' His eye caught Angela's and he went over to her.

'What happened?' she said. She sensed that something had gone very wrong. Harry was Robert's sound engineer. He'd worked on all of Robert's pictures, and each time, like Angela, had sworn never to work with him again. This time was obviously his last.

'I got the first train I could,' he said. 'I just can't work with that bastard.'

'What you drinking?' James said, getting up.

'I'll have a whisky if you don't mind. God, Angela,' he said, sitting down. 'It was terrible.'

'What happened?' A number of them had moved across to the table to hear Harry's story. He gulped his drink.

'It was a nightmare,' he said. 'You know what Robert's like.'

The others nodded their approval. Even those who didn't know Robert knew his reputation.

'Well, we were shooting in a family—marvellous people—they were terribly co-operative. Would do anything we asked. You know how people are sometimes when you film them. Well, they've got a son, a heroin-addict, and it's pretty terrible. He fixes himself in his bedroom, and his mother's breaking her bloody heart. You probably saw her in the rushes, Angela. She's so sweet, she just doesn't know what's hit her. Well, Robert has the great idea to get this boy to give himself a fix in front of his mother. I thought he was joking, but he was absolutely serious. Said it would make great television. So he suggested it, and the mother, being timid—you know how some people can be with any kind of authority, and there's no father, she's completely on her own—she sort of said it was O.K. if it helped the film. And Robert said it was dramatically imperative, or some such crap. You know how he twists people. So he set the whole thing up, and I was getting sicker and sicker, and in the end I couldn't do it. Benny wasn't too happy shooting it either, and if I know Benny, he'll be on the next train. But I couldn't do it. I just had to get out of there.'

'Did he go ahead and do it?'

'Oh yes. They were shooting when I left. It's the sort of thing you can shoot mute. Robert'll find a scream loop from somewhere. He's a monster.' Harry finished his drink. There was silence. Angela felt James's eyes on her.

'In that case,' she said at last, 'he'll have to find another editor. He'll be phoning me in the morning. I'll tell him.'

'Oh, the shit,' somebody said. 'Still, there's plenty of sound-men out of work, and editors and cameramen for that matter. He'll finish the film and it'll probably be a resounding success. Only a handful of people will ever know what it cost. And before we know where we are, our little Saint Robert will be running a symposium at the I.C.A. on the ethics of film-making.'

They ordered more drinks. Nobody, least of all Harry, wanted to talk about it any more. Although the story sickened her, Angela was relieved that she was shot of Robert's film once and for all.

'Let's go,' she said, turning to James.

'Let's have supper in town,' he said. 'Or would you like to go to the pictures?'

''Dear Angela, What's the share index on the sex market for pictures as opposed to suppers. Not that it makes any difference. What one offers in return is a fixed service of a consistently mediocre quality, whatever has been paid for it. So we might as well make it pictures. Less conversation.''

On the way to James's garage they cut through an alley, and she knew from the spasmodic throttle-rattles that somewhere along the lane Gavin was still trying to start his bike. At the turn of the alley they found him, sitting with supreme confidence in the saddle.

'We're going to the pictures,' Angela said. 'Come?'

'No. I must get it started. Got to take it to a garage.'

'Harry's back,' she said casually.

'I know. Saw him before he went to the pub. It's sad.'

'I'm not cutting it,' she said.

He put an oily hand on her shoulder, and smiled. 'Good, and I'm not cutting it with you. Job-hunting tomorrow. But I'll be in early. Clear it all up first. See you.' He went back to his examination of the numerous pipes. 'Don't worry,' he called after them, 'I'll win the Grand Prix yet.'

At the box-office, James insisted on paying, and Angela felt immediately in his debt. Inside, he fumbled for her hand. Might as well start paying now, and she gave it to him. First instalment. But there would be no second or third. In connection, there is only the first and final payment, and sometimes not even the first. Hand-holding was a bonus.

It was a Czech film and the high-hatted lady in front of her obscured the subtitles. James leaned forward and asked her quietly to remove her hat, which she did, only to reveal a cone-shaped head and a beehive hair-do that sprang up with a sigh of relief. Hand in hand, they moved to another row.

The film was an indifferent message-piece, but she was content to sit down, tucked in the half-dark, holding a hand that could have been anybody's. James was playing with her fingers, interlocking them with his other hand. He played with her wedding-ring, pushing it up and down. For a moment she wondered whether it was symbolic, but she couldn't be bothered with undercurrents. If James got some kind of kick out of easing her ring, demonstrating how loose and unreliable it was, he was welcome. Many people left during the film—its message was transmitted early on; the rest was mere elaboration. At the end of the picture there was only a handful of people in the cinema. All seemed to dawdle, savouring the aftertaste of escape, adjusting the eye to the green velvet curtain that a few moments ago had been Prague. They dawdled as if to avoid the rain outside, or, like Angela, to delay the first payment.

'Let's have some coffee,' she said.

'Why don't I take you home, and you can make coffee there.'

''Dear Angela, How dare he. *I* am organizing this production. It's up to me to put him in the dock, with or without a cup of coffee. It's not easy to hang a man who whistles his way to the gallows. Even destruction has its moral code. Did we make the bed this morning, Angela, and is the mantelpiece clean? Don't want people to think I'm letting myself go. A clean house makes a good impression. Are all tyrants so provincial?''

In the flat she made him coffee. He followed her into the kitchen, touching her hands and body with as many accidents as he could manoeuvre. But Angela wanted no part in wooing. No small money. She was prepared to pay with a large single-note unit and keep the change. He could save his courtship for one who could eventually love him. It saddened her that she could not qualify.

She led him into the bedroom, and cursed Angela for not having made the bed. James undressed without her help, and with terrifying shyness, suddenly unacquainted with his buttons and zips, and his once so familiar tie. She did not look at him. She lay in bed and waited, her purse open.

She had dealt out her patience when the phone rang. James crumbled guiltily. Angela leaned across him, and felt his frightened heart-beat under her elbow. 'Hullo?'

'What happened to you? I rang you back almost immediately. You weren't there.'

'I had to see someone downstairs.'

'What were you phoning for?'

She groped for something to say. Then, knowing she would regret it, 'I'm out of work. Walked off Robert's picture. You still serious about that job?'

'Can we talk about it tomorrow,' he hedged. 'Have dinner?'

Well, she was prepared to give her whole body just for a kind word and the pictures. It would be petty to deny him her presence only in return for a job. Misguided economics. 'Ring me in the morning,' she said. 'I'm nearly half asleep.'

James could not help his sudden fit of undeniably male coughing. It half expressed his need to be known, not only by her husband but by Angela herself, and half was due to the pressure of Angela's arm on his chest.

'You're not alone,' David said with offended certainty.

'Oh yes I am.' With James lying by her side, she might just as well have been alone. 'I'll ring you in the morning.' She was anxious to put the phone down. She knew he didn't believe her.

'If you like,' he said, 'if you can manage to get out of bed.' He dared not specify further. He could not face the suspected truth, and it was he who had to put the phone down on her.

As she turned back to James, she heard Angela laughing.

''Dear Angela, We'll deal with that one tomorrow, but meanwhile, if you can stop laughing for just a moment, what am I going to do with this one? I don't know why you laugh while I lie here hating myself and wondering if this is the price of survival. And all the time, all I want is to be able to love him, him, Stuart, anybody, as proof that I value myself slightly higher than the price of a supper, a kind word or a seat in the pictures. When you laugh like that, Angela, I really hate you. Jesus, Angela, he's tickling me. I do believe he's a virgin. I'm tired now—and, my God, so disgusted. Angela, you bastard you, I pay, you keep the score. I reckon the most we can say about this one is that he's a collector's item. Chalk him up.''

'Dear God. Now that Angela isn't listening, help me. Please.'

Chapter Five

David was reading the last page of Tom Welland's script. Tom sat in the armchair and waited.

192   EXT. WIGGLESDOWN RAILWAY
          STATION.   NIGHT.
There is a thin drizzle of rain. The station platform is deserted, except for CAROLINE, who stands, wrapped in furs, at the edge of the platform. (O.S. FX roaring train.)
CAROLINE's POV train gathering speed into the platform.
CAROLINE takes a step forward.
Train speeds through the station past camera.
(Camera on empty platform. Hold.)
       FADE.

David threw the script on the table. 'They already made *Anna Karenina,*' he said. 'Fourteen versions.'

Tom Welland smiled. 'I thought gas was a bit messy. I know you don't go for the suicide ending, but I felt, maybe, what you really took exception to was the method.'

'I don't care if she takes a hundred sleeping-pills off screen, and goes out like a fairy light over a bed of roses, I don't want her to die. In the context of her story, her suicide would be psychologically inept.'

'I wish I could see it your way,' Tom said.

'Look,' David went on patiently, 'it's a beautiful script. You've opened it out very skilfully. I like that party, for instance, that she gives just for women. That party pinpoints her isolation. But throughout the script she's a survivor. Her clutch after life pierces every page.' And he had sincerely felt it. He knew at that moment that in all honesty she could not die. He thought suddenly of Angela, and clenched his fist as he remembered that distinctly male fit of coughing. 'She can't die,' he said aloud.

Tom sensed that he was no longer referring to his script, and that it was more than his novel that David Morrow was bargaining for.

'I'll tell you what we'll do,' David said. 'We'll get Hal Butler to look at it. If he can be free, he's going to direct it, so you'd eventually be working with him anyway. He'll say the same as me about the ending. I'm sure of that.'

'I'll try it,' Tom said. 'I'll try it your way.'

When Tom had gone, David noticed that he was sweating. There was something ominous about this day, a feeling of impending judgment. And all he could feel was innocent. He had done nothing, he convinced himself. All that had happened to him had happened without his interference. Ten years ago, love had come to him. Over the years it had gathered habit and history. These were

natural developments that he could not hinder. Boredom
had come to him, irritation and terrible guilt, all of which
responses had been activated by others. Twenty years
ago, love had assaulted him from another direction. He
was still trying to cope with that too, with that sitting ten-
ant whose rights he knew. And no matter how difficult he
made it for her to remain in his heart, she had sat doggedly on. Then why should he panic when it looked as if
she might be moving out. He wiped his forehead. He
knew why he was sweating. He sweated with the memory
of that coughing in her night; he sweated with the terror
that he might lose her. His eye caught the watering-can
on the end of the window-sill and he rushed to the cloak-
room to fill it. He would water his plants and his sweating
would cool. He started at the beginning of the row with
the cyclamen, and he saw its earth moist, the saucer underneath almost overflowing. He moved to the fuschia,
and that too was watered, as all of them were along the
line. Was there nothing that Ruth forgot to do? She knew
he liked to tend his plants. It was true that occasionally he
overlooked them, but she had exploited his negligence by
taking over the job completely. He would have bawled
her out there and then, had she been there, but she had
gone to the bank with all her terrifying efficiency to jug-
gle with the manager on his behalf. So he sweated still.
He had to phone Angela. He had to know the source of
that coughing. Or he could go to their flat—he had the
key still. She had never taken it from him. He would go
straight to the bathroom, the most tell-tale room, and
check if there were more than one toothbrush in the rack.
If she hadn't made their bed, yes, his and hers, his and
Angela's, and it was more than likely that she hadn't, he
could count above one, the dimples on the pillow. And

suppose there were two, and two toothbrushes, and maybe suits in the wardrobe, and additional books and records of another's taste, obscene signs of another's life and work that added up to his irrevocable displacement. The sweat was now pouring from him, and he reached for the phone.

She answered herself, and he was surprised at the terrible gentleness in his voice as he asked her how she was, and did she want to talk about working for him. She too was startled by his tone, having expected a brutal cross-examination, and she answered him with equal kindness, grateful for his concern, and suggested that they might meet, lunch perhaps, and talk about it.

When he replaced the receiver, his hands and forehead were dry. He was a little proud of himself that he had refrained from questioning her, and he determined to say nothing during lunch that would betray his jealousy and fear. On the whole, he realized, he didn't really want to know. He knew he could not cope with what she might reveal. It was easier to pretend that nothing had happened, that nothing had changed, that in time, his time, all would be well between them. Now he could get to work on his pre-production plans. Tom Welland would change that ending without any difficulty, especially once Hal Butler got to work on him. Butler was an experienced director, professional and totally commercial. There had never in the course of his long career been any great expectations of Butler. He had never shown extreme promise. He just turned in the goods on schedule and within the budget, and nobody was ever disappointed. David made a note to arrange the first meeting with Welland.

There was a knock on the door, and without waiting for

a reply Mr Worcester came inside. 'Got a minute?' he said, sitting down, whether David had a minute or not. Mr Worcester had been David's Associate Producer on all his pictures. They had known each other for over fifteen years, yet David, like everyone else in the firm, still called him Mr Worcester. He had been loath to offer his christian name, and when it was discovered that it was Hayzel, one could understand why. The fact that it was spelt with a 'y' didn't make it less feminine, so it was right that he insisted on Mr Worcester, which was how he was universally addressed.

'Just had a call from Tina's husband,' he said, lighting a cigar. 'She's got hepatitis, poor devil. She'll be out of action for a couple of months. I'll need a new assistant. Any ideas?'

'It's a rotten thing to get,' David said. 'Takes ages to get over.' He hadn't wished hepatitis on Tina, or any disabling condition on anybody. He could have created a job for Angela even though it might have looked engineered. This way it appeared more natural to include Angela in his work, and he offered the suggestion to Mr Worcester.

'Marvellous idea,' Mr Worcester said. 'Why haven't you used her before? But would she want to? She's sort of stuck on documentaries, isn't she?'

'Well, she's just walked off a new one. Told me yesterday. I could suggest it to her if you're in agreement.'

'Why not?' Mr Worcester said with all his good nature. 'Won't do her any harm to see the feature world from the inside. They're a bit snooty, the documentary lot, aren't they? No offence to Angela, of course. I think she's a darling. I'd love her as an assistant. Haven't seen her for so long. Put it to her, will you.'

'I'm taking her to lunch,' David said proudly. 'I'll let you know this afternoon.'

Mr Worcester roused himself out of his seat and went towards the door. Then, with his hand safely on the handle, he turned and said, 'Isn't it time you two got together again?' In the goodness of Mr Worcester's heart he wished David back with his wife. But that was a totally private matter. He felt perhaps he might have gone too far, so he added, 'It's all so confusing. You know how I like order in things. I'm silly, I suppose, and unimaginative, but irregularity of any kind unnerves me.' He was offering a purely pedestrian plea to excuse his interference. 'I hope she agrees,' he said fervently. He had high hopes that working together might bring them together.

David smiled. 'Well, she always had a soft spot for you, you know. I'm sure I can persuade her.'

She was waiting for him when he arrived at the sandwich bar. She had insisted on a lunch place in her area, claiming that she could only afford an hour's break. But, in truth, she had wanted to be with her people, in her natural surroundings, in a non-posh place, where David, for a change, would be the outsider. She needed to feel safe because she dreaded that David would question her about her night companion.

"Dear Angela, What was his name?"

She shivered. This morning James had come to her cutting-room, ostensibly to borrow some spacing. He had dawdled at her bench for some word from her, any word that would acknowledge that they had lain together. But she had remained silent. Their coupling had gone from her mind, leaving only traces of his name. It had landed her in trouble with David to whom she would have to lie to save from pain. For in spite of all the hurt that David had caused her, she knew that inside his uncommittable heart he loved her. She hoped to God he wouldn't question her, though she had her lies at the ready. It was a play on television, she would say. She had gone to the trouble of checking on the programmes at that time, and mercifully there was a play on, a play in fact on the subject of adultery, a situation in which any character at any time might conceivably have coughed for recognition. It was a thin excuse, so she needed support of some kind, in the sandwich bar where she was known, and where Alice the counter-hand knew her tastes, and where she could rely on friends whom she could join if the going got tough.

She saw him come in through the door, and he looked uneasy. Suited and tied, he was obviously no regular, and it was clear to him from the casual bonhomie of the clients that Mrs Muffet's sandwich bar was as much of a club as his exclusive 'Members Only' in Mayfair. He looked around, not seeing her, and she, moved by his outsider-ness, shouted his name. But hardly had it left her mouth than she realized that her cry had drawn all eyes on to him. He reddened, hating her, but had no option than to join her. It was not a happy beginning.

'Must we sit here?' he said, seeing a quieter table in the corner. Angela had deliberately chosen a table in the middle of the room, where sniping was more difficult. But she got up dutifully and followed him into the corner. She had already exposed him enough. There was no need to keep him on stage. When Molly came to take their order, she let David choose for both of them, and gradually he became more at ease.

'What happened with Robert's film?' he said. He wanted conversation right away and all the time. He wanted to avoid any silence in which he might be tempted to discover what he needed to be told, but what he desperately needed not to know. And Angela, sensing his fear, wanted suddenly to tell him the truth, that in spite of the coughing, there was no usurper in the flat, no claimant on his rights and, God help her, no claimant on her future. But instead, she told him the story of Robert's film, spinning it out, avoiding any pause.

'You're absolutely right,' he said. 'What are you going to do now?' His hand lay on the table, and she wondered whether he'd put it there for her to hold. But she was frightened to touch it because such a gesture could be construed either way: that there was only one, or that there was more than one, toothbrush in the flat. She looked at him and smiled. 'Well,' she said, 'you did say something about a job. Have you changed your mind?'

'No,' he said, leaving his hand there. 'In fact, one came up this morning. Tina's ill. Hepatitis, poor devil. She'll be off for a few months. Mr Worcester needs a new assistant.'

'Did you mention me to him?'

'Yes. He thought it was a marvellous idea.'

'And what do you think?'

'It's up to you.' He didn't really know what he thought. He looked at his hand and realized why he had put it there. It was to take hold of hers to squeeze it with his love and his determination to get the truth out of her. He grabbed by the wrist the hand that was holding her fork, which dropped with a loud clatter on her plate. People looked in their direction, then quickly looked away, eyeing them from time to time to gauge the progress of their strange encounter.

'Who was with you in the flat last night?' That wasn't

the question he had meant to ask. He was not interested in *who* it was. The quality of the competition did not concern him. He wanted to know whether there was competition at all. 'Was there somebody there?'

'No. I was alone. Like I'm always alone,' she said, trying to free her hand.

He gripped her wrist viciously. 'Then who was coughing?'

'What coughing?'

'Someone was coughing,' he said limply, regretting that he had asked the question at all.

'The television was on,' she said coldly. 'I was watching a play.'

'You said you were half asleep.'

'My God,' and every syllable was against her better judgment, 'supposing I did have someone there, coughing his bloody lungs out. Supposing I did.'

He let go her hand. She had told him nothing. Now the silence between them didn't matter. He took his hand from the table.

'If you're so worried, David,' she said, as gently as she could, 'why don't you come home and see for yourself?'

He started eating again, without answering. Then, after a pause: 'Dreadful food in this place. Do you always eat here?'

'Most days. And the food's not too bad. Neither are the prices.'

'What shall I tell Mr Worcester?' he said.

'Tell him I'd be delighted to work for him.' She watched for his reaction, but his face registered nothing.

'He'll want you to start right away. I think he wants to go to Italy in about a week. Can you start tomorrow?'

'It'll take me a couple of days to hand Robert's film over. I can start on Monday.'

He insisted on paying the bill, though it had been given to Angela.

'I'll see you on Monday,' she said, when they got outside.

He hung about, not wanting to leave her. 'What are you doing over the weekend?' he said.

'Oh, I've got lots to do,' not wanting to hurt him with anything specific, but at the same time unwilling to divulge that she had nothing to do except dust the mantelpiece, stare out of the window, play patience and dust the mantelpiece again. 'What are *you* doing?'

'Carol's parents are coming for the weekend. I shall be tied up.'

'Why did you ask me then?' she shouted at him. 'Did you have to tell me that? Is that why you asked, to trap me into asking you?'

He knew why he had done it. It was to punish her for what she hadn't told him, and he turned away when he saw the tears fill her eyes. She felt them too, and wondered why they didn't drop. Were they welling there, defying gravity, cooling themselves a little before they fell? And when they did, scalding her cheeks, she bit her lip hard, outraged by her endless capacity for pain. He put his hand on her shoulder and she seized it as she might have seized her pillow in her desolate night, and she bit it, screaming silently into its flesh. Then she felt his fingers squeezing her nostrils, and she let go, silently too, and turned away from him. He made a move to follow her, then shrugged with the hopelessness of it all, and went his own way. Passers-by, who had stopped to watch them, now skirted the place where they had stood, as if it vibrated still with their wordless and desperate passion.

"Dear Angela, What have I done? How far have I removed him from me this time? I want him back, Angela, and the waiting is destroying me. Yet I cannot not wait, I cannot free myself from him. I know he doesn't help with his constant phoning and inquiries, but that's his problem, and I must let him solve it and see to mine. Yet they are inseparable. From a distance of twenty years, even parallel lines meet, and I see it still from twenty years ago, and I cannot bear to look at us now and face our patent separation. It's history again. Save me from it, Angela, for God's sake. Don't tell me to pull myself together. I've heard that one before. I've said it to you often enough. Don't tell me to look at myself either, as sometimes, like now, I can't bear to look at you. What's more, I haven't heard you laugh for ages, and, if you remember, that's the only reason I'm keeping you around. I must have hurt his hand terribly. I've got to phone him to find out how he is. I've got to. Dammit, I would make inquiries after a stranger. O.K., O.K. So I made you laugh at last. Angela, you and I are back in business. We have one or two phone calls to make."

Back in the office, Gavin was stacking the rushes. A new batch had arrived that morning, delivered by the cameraman himself, who had stuck it out till the end of the day and had taken the night train home. A new cameraman and sound engineer were collecting instructions from the producer in the next office, and Benny saw them through the open door and was sorry for them. Robert's assistant had stayed up with him, and they were probably wondering together what all the fuss was about. Angela had phoned Robert early that morning, and told him that, after Harry's story, she could not cut for him any more. Robert had said that she was mad like the rest of them, and that good editors were two a penny. And their assistants.

So are heroin-addicts, she had said. And their mothers, no doubt.

Now all the phones were busy. Harry and Benny were job-inquiring and Gavin would need the phone as soon as one was free. She didn't need a job like the others. All she needed to say was that she was sorry, but she couldn't wait for that, for a delay would give the impression that she was none too sure of her repentance. So the moment Harry put one of the phones down, she grabbed it, and dialled his number. He answered himself, and with no preamble she said, watched by Harry and the others, 'I'm sorry, I'm terribly sorry. Are you all right?'

'I'll survive.'

She said she was sorry again, to fill the pause, and he said, safely out of her touch, 'It was my fault. But I didn't mean to hurt you. I was trying to tell you that I wanted to see you this weekend, but that it was impossible.' Long pause. 'You are coming in on Monday?'

'If you want me to.'

'I told Mr Worcester. He's delighted. Shall we have dinner in the evening?'

''Angela, Will you please shut up. I'm not employing you to give me advice. Except when I ask for it. Your sole *raison d'être* is as a laughter-machine and you can start winding yourself up right now, 'cos I'm just about to give you plenty to laugh about.''

'Yes, that will be lovely,' she said and for some reason it sounded very formal. 'I'm sorry about your hand,' she said again. She could barely hear herself speaking through Angela's laughter. She had wound herself up good and proper this time, to a pitch of mirth spiced with loud malice.

"Enough, Angela, enough. It's not that funny."

She replaced the receiver. 'It's all yours,' she said to Harry, who had a list of phone numbers to get through. She wanted to be alone somewhere, but the office was so crowded, and she needed to be alone with Angela. So she went outside on the terrace.

Directly in front of her, on the fourth floor of the opposite building she could see Elliot Wall Jr, working at his moviola. Elliot had been at that same bench, editing the same picture, for four long years, and over that period, from the terrace, she had from time to time looked through his window and watched him age. His beard, that had sprouted as a ginger chin-fluff, now almost covered his face, red, unruly and terribly angry. Before he had set up his quarters in the cutting-room opposite, he had spent a whole year shooting a film on the buskers of London. Every day and evening he was to be seen in Leicester Square, recording over and over again, with the apprehensiveness of a beginner, the monotonous routine of the tap-dancers and singers of the kerb. Then, as his remittance dwindled, and even the laboratories which had grown fat on Elliot Wall Sr's indulgence of his son complained at last that they had seen enough, so Junior moved his two hundred and five hours of film into the cutting-room opposite to begin his marathon job of editing. He worked obsessively and without an assistant. It took him six months to view and to log his rushes. And then he began. Progress reports on Wall Jr's cut filtered through the cutting-room floors beneath and into the sandwich bars and pubs of Wardour Street. After the first year, he'd cut it to four hours, begrudging the loss of every frame. During the summer months the reports on Wall Jr's dwindling footage vied with the test-match score, but in winter he had a clear field. At the end of the second year, he was down to an hour and a half, and it was rumoured that even now he could be seen in the Square of an evening doing a little extra shooting. As he pared his material down, his beard raged around his neck, each newly grown hair a protest against yet another lost frame. At the end of the third year, rumour had it that he'd reached a commercial twenty minutes, but that he was now too addicted to stop. Any day now it was inevitable that he would reduce his two hundred and five hours' marathon to a single frame, which he would, no doubt, contemplate for a while, until he understood the necessity of cancelling out that one too. That day, perhaps, he might have reached his moment of truth, and he would stand up and walk over to the window, and notice for the first time that there was a terrace opposite, and that Angela sat there, as she had sat occasionally over the years, watching him and wishing him well. She was reminded of a painting exhibition she'd been to years ago with David. Starting on the ground floor, the pictures were dense with colour and movement, reeling drunkenly from one unreliable signpost to another. On the first floor, the paintings had sobered a little, less dense, their movements sparse and controlled. Gradually the canvases grew larger, some with but a single line or circle, until, on the top floor, the final canvas covered one wall and was totally blank. After a painful climb of mumblings and stammerings and loud stutterings of colour and shape, the painter had reached articulation in the orgasm of silence. When Elliot Wall Jr would cast off his last frame, he too would have arrived at that eloquence, like a writer who, after paring down his thousands of words, is left with one, and that too—in the process of undergrowth, growth and clearing—must be, in all honesty, discarded.

She pulled a chair over to the railings, and folded her hands on her lap.

"Dear Angela, You and I must have a little talk. Let's get a few things clear. I'm the one who makes the decisions around here. Your role, unless otherwise stated, is to sit around and say nothing. Just now, for instance, when I was talking to David on the telephone, I was so happy. He hadn't meant to hurt me. He was trying to save me from hurt. And his concern made me suddenly happy and proud. I know you think it's pathetic, but nevertheless it strengthened me. I was like the tiger, and then I heard you laughing at me, I looked at you as if through a series of diminishing mirrors, and, in the very last, I saw myself reduced to a simpering kitten. You are not good for me, Angela. I won't have you diminish me. Do not ever again interfere with my happiness. It's only in my despair that you must bother me. Can we be friends now?"

Chapter Six

For Angela, Monday arrived immediately after Friday. Over the weekend she had contracted time into a continual step-march. Monday had gone well. She had been a little nervous at first, unused to any aspect of the production side of film-making, but Mr Worcester had assured her that only intelligence was necessary. He had guided her throughout the morning with his instructions, and by the afternoon he was asking her advice. There was a lot of telephoning to be done, and for the first time in her life Angela was happy to hear it ring. No one knew where she was working. There was no fear that it might be Stuart on the phone, or James, or any one of half a dozen plaintiffs bewildered by his broken connection. She was happier to speak to anonymity, imagining a face on a voice, acquainting herself with the unfamiliar phraseology of feature-film language, the style of which seemed to be based infirmly on hyperbole. Mr Worcester had decided to leave the arrangements for the Italian investigations to her. It was a big responsibility and she was glad of it. She was grateful for the trust he placed in her, for his confidence in her intelligence, for his small and constant kindnesses, for his . . . "Dear Angela, No. I need not take Mr Worcester to bed."

In the evening she had had dinner with David and they had talked mostly about the film. He had told her the story in detail, which was uncommonly like their own, but this did not disturb her. She was able now, for her own sake, to see it purely as a business venture. They were calm together, without effort. Observers in the restaurant might have envied their natural gaiety, and no eavesdropper would have heard Angela talking to Angela, for they were together this evening and using the same language.

After dinner, David wanted to prolong their mood, and he suggested an hour or so of roulette at his gambling club. In the earlier years of their marriage, they had occasionally spent an evening at a casino. Neither of them had been seduced by the sport, and they had gone rather in contempt for those who had. But Angela, too, wanted to savour the ease that was between them, so she agreed.

In the car he said very little, but it was not a silence of evasion.

"Dear Angela, I'm not going to spoil it. I promise. But it's going to break, I know. And it's not going to be my fault. You just stand by and listen, and stop my mouth if necessary. Why is it that sometimes, like now, it can be so good, and then when I think about it, I'm afraid that it will not last. I must not think of being dropped off alone at the end of the evening, because that is the thought that will kill it. That is the thought that will open my mouth in quarrel. Don't let me think of it, Angela. You bear it in mind the while, but keep it from me, please, until we get home."

When they entered the club, Angela was surprised and a little disturbed by their reception. David was obviously well known and liked there, a regular, who commanded that kind of obsequious attention and respect given to one who loses like a gentleman. To some who acknowledged him, he introduced Angela as his wife. She smiled, and when later on in the gaming-room they ran into Jack Walters, an old friend of hers who worked in animation, she introduced David as her husband. "Dear Angela, Look what a good girl I am."

Jack tagged on to them. He'd had a run of bad luck and was about to change his table. 'Let's go to the one at the far end,' he suggested. There were fewer people at that table and the minimum stake was higher. But what players there were, were all sitting down, serious betters, with a determination to go on losing till closing time. There were three vacant seats at the far end, and they took them. None of the other players looked at them as they sat down. Their chances did not depend on who or how many laid their bets. It was an alone game, a game of patience extended into company and with no possible cheating. Jack Walters was sitting between them. It had happened that way, and when he found himself in the middle, he offered to change his seat. It was Angela who took up his offer, and as she sat down next to David, he placed his hand on hers.

"Dear Angela, It pays, it pays. Maybe you can go home now and wait for me there. I feel strong tonight, a tiger again, and I can't risk your diminishing mirrors. You understand, don't you, Angela. Go home and wait for me, and don't bother about the mantelpiece any more."

David gave her a pile of chips. He took four from the

top and handed them to the croupier. 'Douze, quatorze, seize, dix-neuf,' he said. He turned to Angela. 'That's right, isn't it?'

Yes. Her numbers hadn't changed any more than her taste for Campari or *coq-au-vin*. He was right to assume that she waited for him, unchanged, changeable only through his presence and on his ratification. She counted out nine chips from the pile and passed them to the croupier. 'Huit partout,' she said. David pressed her hand. The mutual understanding of each other's gambling habits was a tenuous enough thread on which to hang a relationship, but between them it was more than that. It was a recognition of a past that they had spent together, a past that neither of them was prepared to let go or see change.

Jack was playing safe. He put one chip on Rouge and another on Pair. The betting was heavy and crowded on the higher numbers, and David's covering of eight winked like a lonely star. The wheel spun, but none of the players seemed interested in watching it. Most were intent on sorting out their systems on their cards. They expected to lose, all of them, and they seemed to be waiting for the wretched wheel to stop, so that they could bet again and gather yet another statistic for their cards which would take them nearer to the winning formula.

'Douze,' the croupier called.

Angela's was the only bet on twelve, but David with his carré had benefited too. So had Jack. It was a good round for all of them. David passed Angela her winnings, and replaced their bets, doubling the twelve. Now suddenly the twelve was fully covered by many of the players, as if some of the luck might still linger on the square. And when the wheel stopped spinning, it was twelve again, and a losing round for the casino.

'You bring me luck,' she said to David.

'My poor little carré's working for me too,' he said.

Suddenly she felt guilty, and called for Angela, and Angela, knowing her place, had remained, because the mantelpiece, as both of them knew, could wait. "It's because I'm winning more than he is, Angela, and I don't want to put him in a subordinate position. What is this dreadful sickness with me, that I must always be a victim, and that only in the most degrading circumstances, with people like Stuart, James and the rest, do I need to be a conqueror. It's a monotonous pattern, like an endless stencilling of masochism. And somehow it's all so middle-class. So s.w.3. Let me lose the next round, Angela. There is less fear for me in a loss, and let's go home soon, you and I, before the mood breaks. Let him leave us outside the flat, and for once we can say, We did no damage today. Today, we mended it and us a little."

The wheel stopped spinning and the ball obligingly slipped into eight. David, having doubled his bet, had a killing.

'Let's go now,' she said, ashamed of all the money they had won, anxious to leave that circular sea of faces who should have been staring at them with disgust. But they were at their cards again, and their new bets, working out the formula. Somebody had to win and lose every time. Their faces were irrelevant.

David was loath to leave. Only sensible people left on the crest of a wave. Most stayed to splutter and submerge, until closing time mercifully washed them ashore. Besides, the mood would break in hot tears, anger and simpering, and he didn't want to risk breaking it, and the only way of avoiding that was to call it a day for the time being. Jack Walters was going home anyway, and he lived close to Angela. He could take her home. It was that part especially that David dreaded, dropping her off at the flat, where, sitting in the car, the mood would break in hot tears, anger and simpering, and none of these could he bear. 'I think I'll stay on a bit,' he said.

'I'll take Angela home,' Jack said, collecting his chips.

Angela watched them as they programmed for her.

"Dear Angela, What happened all of a sudden? What happened when I wasn't looking? Who and what turned me into a mere passenger? He's afraid to face the drive home, the arrival at the flat, to face me waiting, boringly waiting for one word, one gesture that would signify that things were going to change. And Jack lives so conveniently close. Not out of his way at all. Shall I stay, Angela, and make it difficult for him, or shall I go with dignity, with my silly chin held high, with that sickening so-called self-respect when this is the very last thing on earth you've ever encouraged me to have."

'Shall I drop you off?' Jack said.

'Drop me off?' She looked at David. 'That'll make it twice in one evening. Quite a record.'

'Oh, Christ,' David said, replacing his bet.

"Stop me, Angela. Stick out my chin, hold my head high and propel me on Jack's arm through the betting-hall with all your sickening, home-made unpalatable dignity." 'Good luck,' she said, because she had to say something, and she took Jack's proffered arm.

'He's on a winning streak,' Jack said as they drove out of the car park. 'If I had his luck, I'd have stayed too.'

It did not please her that Jack found excuses for David, apologized for him as it were. She didn't want anybody else to think that David had behaved badly. 'So would I,' she said, laughing it off. 'Anyway, I'm tired. I've got a heavy day tomorrow.'

After that Jack was silent. Over the years that she had known him, they had spoken very little together. He was not in any case a gregarious man and few people knew him intimately. She didn't even know whether he was married and now was certainly no time to ask him. She'd seen most of his films, and thought them all skilfully lunatic. With his minimum-line martian drawings, impossible happenings, all clothed in a strict Knightsbridge dialogue, he gave to insanity his own irrefutable logic. It was to be expected that he would be a silent, private person, and Angela wondered in what language and accent he spoke to himself.

"Dear Angela, Well, it wasn't my fault this evening. You did not urge me to one syllable that might have broken the mood. So where did we go wrong? It's hope that misleads us, Angela, that's what it is. And if you ever smell it again between David and me, I want you to take it by its deceiving neck and throttle it. Yes, strangle it, whatever I may say and however badly I may treat you, help me to free us both. You know, Angela, I'm going to do a crazy thing. I don't know what's driving me to it. It may be revenge, it may be the need for self-assertion, or more probably self-annihilation. It may just be a coda to this suicide symphony that on and off I score in your direction, or simply the acknowledgment that whatever one does carries within it its own hope and its own hopelessness. Everything succeeds and everything fails. Very simply, we're going to take Jack to bed. We're going to charge him, put him on trial and sentence him, when he is completely innocent of any decent gesture towards us. That's progress, isn't it? Or is it the logical act of a tyrant? After all, in many countries in the world, one is plucked from one's bed in the night, plucked in one's innocence, charged with nothing, tried with nothing and shot into nothingness. So maybe it is progress into that trivial despot that I really am. Yes, Angela, I'm going to take this man who has done nothing, to whom I owe nothing, who has given me no hot dinner, no seat in the pictures, nor even one desperately kind word. He is as totally innocent of compliment as I am totally out of his debt. So stand by for this one, Angela. We are not likely to sink any lower than this.''

'Would you like to come up for coffee?' she said as he pulled up the car outside the flat.

''Is coffee an emotive word, Angela, or 'come up for' a leading phrase? Then why is there a gleam in his eye? He's not going to make it difficult for us.''

'That's a lovely idea,' he said, opening the door for her.

In the kitchen, she went through the formalities.

'D'you live all on your own?' he said, shouting from the living-room, his hand on the mantelpiece.

Angela looked at him. He was pretty well hanging himself. 'Yes, all alone.'

'Don't you get lonely?'

'Sometimes.' She brought the coffee in. 'Would you do me a favour?'

'If I can.'

'It sounds crazy, but I need a coughing loop. I'm cutting a film on smoking for the Ministry of Health. I need all kinds of coughs, the long and hacking kind, the itching cough, the splutter that tries to hide itself.'

He laughed. 'I'll have a go.'

She got out her recording machine and placed the mike

on the table beside him. Then, after a preliminary testing, he got to work. He coughed in every conceivable coughing manner, and then, having exhausted the human cough, moved happily into the animal kingdom. He gave her the wheeze of a sickly rhino who, on his own admission, had smoked three packs a day for a hundred and twenty years; the death rattle of a feverish elephant who swore on his mother's tusks that he had never smoked in his life, and the polite puff of a flagging sparrow who pleaded that she had always used a filter.

"Dear Angela, I'm beginning to like him. Save me from that."

'Would you like some more coffee?' she said.

'No, thanks. It'll keep me awake. After all that coughing I'm a bit tired.' He smiled at her. 'Aren't you?'

'A bit,' she said. Then coldly taking the plunge, as she might have named her price, 'Shall we be tired together?' She turned and went into the bedroom to undress, knowing that he would follow her.

Which he did, shortly afterwards, and possibly only to say good night. But when he saw her lying there, the gleam came into his eye again, and, without taking his eyes off her, he slipped out of his shoes. Then he undressed completely, looking at her all the time. 'Just a moment,' he said, as he took off his vest, and he went out of the door and she heard him foraging around in the kitchen. He was back very quickly carrying a bowl in his hand.

"Dear Angela, What have we got here? What freak of nature have we invited into our bed? What's he going to do with my Special Offer mixing-bowl? Two tops of a pre-mix cake packet, send fourpence in stamps, and in your opinion tick off in order of importance the qualities of a good cook. A trip for two to the Bahamas if you win, which we didn't, 'cos who could we take with us, and a consoling mixing-bowl for each entrant. Those great pre-mix deceptions, when all your guests think you're such a fantastic cook until some enthusiastic home-loving tit amongst them asks for the recipe, and then you're stuck. What, Angela, does he intend to do with my bowl and will I ever be able to use it again for chocolate gateau, coffee fudge and sunny madeira? Now he's putting it on the floor beside the bed. I'm not frightened, Angela. I'm just curious. Strange how the less sex has to do with love, the more curious one is about its technique and its paraphernalia. He gets into bed quite normally, Angela. He holds me like a whole man. He seems to have forgotten about the bowl altogether. But who am I lying with, Angela? A voice in a recording machine, not even a voice, a cough, a wheeze, a snort that could belong to anybody. I lie with the anonymous man who bets evens. An unidentifying creature as terrified possibly of his own self as we are in our self-imposed tyranny. I can't tell you what kind of lover he is, Angela. What is a good lover or a bad, anyway? All that matters is that you want him, and then it is good. We shall have no good lovers, Angela. This one just functions. He thinks of me as tangentially as I think of him. We are but machines for each other. Are you watching us, Angela? Can you see that he functions, that he now reaches for that mixing-bowl, which I shall never again be able to use for fudge, and how, at the time of his climax—watch Angela, and tell me about it afterwards, because I cannot bear to look—he vomits his guilt into the bowl? *We* have problems, Angela?''

Jack got out of bed, taking his clothes and the bowl with him. She heard the tap run in the kitchen, and then silence. She presumed he was dressing. Then she heard him go into the living-room. He stayed there for a while, and then the front door mercifully closed. She lay there, and thought about him, of Jack Walters, animator, that quaint misnomer, who probably now sat weeping in his car, cursing the shame that he had no need to feel, because for her there was nothing shameful in what he had done. She got up and went to the living-room, meaning to look out of the window to see if his car was still there. But on the way to the window she saw a drawing he had left on the table. She picked it up. On it, in pencil, he had drawn an angry man, looking uncommonly like David, holding a frightened bird by the scruff of its neck. At his feet, the meticulously decorated mixing-bowl was full to the brim. Underneath he had written in a childlike hand, 'The sad story of the cuckoo who coughed.' She rushed to the window, but his car had gone.

"Dear Angela, I could love him now. But it is too late for that. He is like us, Angela. His love-making, like ours, is a declaration of self-hate, and he need express it, with one woman, only once. Maybe tonight, Angela, we got our come-uppance. Us and Special Offer. Can't use that bowl again. I wonder how many other Special Offer bowls have gone the same way. Beware of the pre-mix. You never know where it's been. How sad it all is. Let's go to bed now, and for a change we'll take someone else's sadness with us."

On the way to her bedroom the phone rang, and she knew it was David. Before answering, she went over to the recording machine, wound back a little, and then switched it to playback. Then she picked up the phone. 'Hullo?'

'It's me. Did you get home all right?'

'Yes,' she said, with assumed weariness. 'I'm in bed. I'm half asleep.' She held the receiver into the room to catch the playback. He would know it was too late for television. 'I'll see you in the morning,' she said, and put the phone down. She had done it partly for revenge, but mainly to keep a little of Jack Walters by her, even if it was only in the guise of a spluttering and puffing sparrow.

Chapter Seven

"Dear Angela, Nowadays I look out of the window a lot. I put the mantelpiece behind me to make things easier. You see, I do try. I count my blessings often. I like working with Mr Worcester. I have Italy to look forward to. And I know that however lonely I am, I wake up every morning and know that I am not living a lie. I wake up clean. So what's so good about clean? I lead a life of total sterility and kid myself that it's mature. But I'm coping. And what d'you know? After weeks of total inactivity, my busy Lizzie has suddenly got busy. I took it off the mantelpiece, you see—I think that mantelpiece has got greenfly—and now it's on the windowsill, sprouting its heart out. Such a simple obvious move. Yet it was the difference between living and dying. Is there a like simple move for me, Angela? Where lies the greenfly that withers me inside, and is there a lighted site where I could flower? When I read this over, Angela, it makes me slightly sick. If I were ever to meet someone like me, she would turn me off completely. I would hate her self-pity, her unwillingness to allow the past to be past, her inability to, yes, let's say it, pull herself together. I would say to her, for God's sake, have you heard of Vietnam, or, if that word is too out of earshot, have you heard it whispered around that there are people without jobs, without food, without shelter? And all you are without, is love. But I know all that, Angela. I am not hungry, I have a job and a fully tiled roof over my head, yet I am without love, and that seems to me to be a supreme deprivation. It must be about three months or so—I don't have to keep records with you around—but it's about that time since you persuaded me that I ought to survive. Well, how have we been doing? Dare we have a recap? What battles have we won or lost, or have we only fortified our trenches and buried ourselves within? Well, we took away some roadblocks. We made ourselves available. There was Stuart, James and Jack. There was a Frenchman called Pierre, whom I never told you about. He was much the same as the others, Angela, and, like the others, I lay with him only once. Why, even a whore could, by accident or design, lie twice or more with the same partner. But when my shame is reflected in a man's bewilderment, I can face it only once, and then move on to other mirrors, for though the reflection is the same, the framing is different and that somehow makes it less shameful. Why do I diminish myself so? It's paradoxical, for in the mind of me I feel so superior, yet in my gut I feel so absolutely a nothing, and so I must find outlets like poor Stuart, James, Jack and Pierre that cater obscenely for both. Somebody, somewhere along the line, must have diminished me—my mother, my father, David. But those are words for the couch and all that is a middle-class waste of time. Besides, it is fruitless now to seek out someone to blame. Who needs whipping-boys?

It's only when you cease to accuse that you can start to grow. But stick around, Angela. I need you for all kinds of reasons, whipping included. I need you too to stay my hand.''

She had arranged with David they should both visit Jonathan at school before leaving for Italy, and now she stood at the window waiting for him. He would turn into the street and start blowing his horn to give her ample warning of his coming. Since he had left, he had never been up to the flat. She had insisted on that, the only right perhaps that she had clung to. At first he had been stupefied, unable to understand that he no longer had right of entry. He had refused to give her back his key, and in a moment of sanity and self-respect, she had changed the lock, regretting it later. He had settled for blowing his horn to announce his presence to the whole street. Only once had she weakened. It was about a year ago, when she had, on her own, laid a carpet in the bathroom. Apart from a new bedside lamp, it had been the only change she had made in the flat since he'd left, and she wanted desperately to show it to him to prove that decisions could be made without him and changes wrought. He had ignored the bedside lamp, and found the carpet poorly laid and its colour tasteless. She had managed to laugh it off, because his irritation was clear; for good measure she announced that she was buying a four-poster because their marriage-bed was worm-eaten. But the bed was still there, and his side untouched. Some of his clothes still hung in the wardrobe, and the desk was still stuffed with his papers. She didn't know why she left them there, whether it was her lethargy, her stubbornness, or the simple fertilizing of her pain. Whatever it was, it disgusted her, and as she waited at the window, she made the decision to get rid of his clothes.

She ran to the cupboard for a suitcase and threw all his clothes inside. It was an action she might have performed two years ago, logically and at leisure, but now she worked with the frenzy of one whose decisions are taken in violence and anger, and later, with the same violence, regretted.

"Dear Angela, I should have done this ages ago, but why should I be doing it at all? It's *his* rotten stuff, and he has left it here like a down-payment. And there's nothing here that he himself would wear. Just clothes he can't bear to part with. His school blazer, sizes now too small, with his conker still in the pocket. His dead father's evening-suit and overcoat. My God, Angela, he's left me his nostalgia, his bloody rotten sentimentality. Hope feeds on such poison. His school scarf and his tie, and his father's walking-stick. He has bequeathed me his childhood and his dotage, but he took away the 'now' of him. But I cannot be a repository for his memories. They are *his* dreams, and he must lodge them."

As she clamped the case down, she heard his insistent horn. She ran to the window, fearful of his anger should he be kept waiting. But halfway across the room, she decided to take her time. Let him wait while she packed his history. She did not go to the window. She locked the flat leisurely and went downstairs with the case. She wished he'd stop blowing his horn. Outside she signalled to him, and he got out of the car and took the case. 'What's this?' he said. 'Are you going away?'

'Your clothes,' she said coldly. 'I'm not a storage depot.'

'Jesus.' He put the case in the back of the car. 'Is it going to be that kind of day?'

'No,' she said airily, 'but since you've got the car, and you're here, I thought you might as well take them, as you should have taken them when you left. The desk is still full of your papers. I'd like you to take those too.'

'Are they getting in your way?' he said. 'Are they obstructing your way of life?'

'Yes,' she shouted at him, 'and why can't you understand that?'

'I do,' he said wearily, 'but what I don't understand is that you've managed to live with them for so long and then suddenly, and in terrible rage, you discard them. Get in the car.'

"Dear Angela, He's right, of course. My inconsistency is crippling. Why am I calm when I am calm? Why am I occasionally content? How can such anger and such peace dwell on the same site? Are they both one and the same, like the sides of a coin that I cannot keep spinning on an equilibrium? Am I *really* hurt? Am I *really* sad? Do people feel like me just for the fun of it? I made a mistake with the suitcase, Angela. Not the decision itself but the frenzied haste of it. I must take decisions in my calm days, and not allow them to irritate my peace. Tonight when I get home, I shall sort his papers, slowly and calmly. I shall not vent my spleen on them. I shall do it as a job that has to be done."

He switched on the engine, and the car-radio blared, and he, sensing her mood and the need for silence, switched it off. They drove through the suburbs without speaking, but once on the open road, he said, 'What shall we do with Jonathan today?'

She was glad that he hadn't referred to the suitcase

again. 'Let's see first what he wants. He said something on the phone about there being a fair in the village. He'll probably want to go to that.'

'I hope so,' David said. 'Maybe they'll have an up-and-down roundabout for you.' He knew her passion for round-abouts, how she would stand open-mouthed on the perimeter, waiting for the slow-down and then following her favourite horse around until it stopped just in front of her, so that she could secure it for her turn. Always the outside horse of the three, where the swing was higher but still gentle enough to allow her to move with the steam-organ music, clasping the gleaming silver bar in front of her, riding back into the sandy bucket-and-spade summers. He put his hand on her knee. 'Let's have a good day,' he said. 'Want some music?'

She nodded and he switched the radio on. He hoped for Mozart, whose music he knew would carry her beyond their history. He twiddled into a recitative. 'Yes,' she cried, and waited for Elvira to cry out her rejected heart in 'Mi tradi'.

"Dear Angela, What a great bore Elvira is, never accepting the Don's rejection. Yet her weeping is beautiful, and her pain cries out with a heartbreaking joy."

The opera lasted till they reached the school, and they sat and listened to the final quartet outside the gates, and though she had listened to it hundreds of times, she never ceased to be surprised at its sudden and undramatic ending fretting with the impatience to start something new.

She was singing as they got out of the car. Zerlina's duet with the Don. And David played his part. He had a good voice, and often in the old days they would sing together, usually Mozart, leap-frogging from one stave to another in a quartet. He put his arm round her as they walked up the steps to the school, and it was thus that Jonathan found them as he rushed down the corridor, chasing nothing but the prospect of a free day. He stopped when he saw them, and frowned. He was as unnerved by their togetherness as he was by their strained separation. Not the one or the other, but the total unreliability of both. He could never depend on either. He didn't much care which one they chose as long as they held to it consistently. Since their separation, there was nothing reliable about them any more. He had dreaded their coming as much as he had longed for it. They rarely came together, and whether it was his mother or his father, each was at pains not to mention the other. He felt that they should have been using him, as all separated parents used their children. Most of his friends at school could boast a disunited home, and they loved to profit by their roles of confidants. Jonathan wanted this power too to play his parents off, one against the other, as his friends did—with infinite and conscious strategy. But his parents insisted on his making his own choice, his own judgment, without their interference. So he didn't know where he stood. It would have been easier for him sometimes to hate one or the other, to be on somebody's side. But they enforced his neutrality, and he felt isolated in the dormitory at night when tactics were discussed, and the validity or otherwise of every new and twisted move. Now they were coming towards him for all the world as if they lived and loved together, and he knew his father was living with another woman. Why didn't his mother kill her, or why didn't his father leave his mother alone, not like now with his arm about her as if they were well and truly married. They got on his nerves really, and he wished again that he had been born orphaned, avoiding the responsibility of others' partnerships, or even worse, as in his case, neutrality. Still, they would go to the fair and have steak for dinner, a welcome change from the school vegetarian diet, and he would talk them into a new three-gear for his bike, and with luck a silver strap for his watch. His friends had little difficulty in milking their divorced sires. Their parents expected blackmail, and in their guilt they were glad to pay up. Why, Millbank even had his parents begging him to be allowed to replace his old bicycle, each of them vying with the other to provide a better make. But he was clever, was Millbank. He was saving up his blackmail for a sports car. He had two years to go before he could get a licence and it was enough time to stockpile his bribery. There was a faint chance that they might be reconciled during that period, in which case he was taking a mighty risk in not settling there and then for a new bike, but Millbank was a gambler by nature, and his hunches, with dogs and horses anyway, usually paid off.

He slowed down as they approached him, feeling his smile fix. They stood there waiting to be received, for the act of receiving him could not be done simultaneously and would have seemed like competition. They left it to him to greet them, either one first, or, as they expected of him, both together, which he did, in a large embrace, without target, and without affection. 'How are you both?' he said, strictly impartial.

'As you see us,' Angela dared to say. 'And you?'

'Ditto. I've got another boil. That's four since I saw you last.'

Jonathan was a boil-prone boy, and he totted up his gatherings and carefully followed their progress from their first simmering through their pickable stage to their seared falling-off, as other children studied their mice.

'Have you seen Matron?' Angela asked.

'Yes. She gives me the usual stuff. I've had a record crop this term, more than Bill Winters, and last year he beat me by six.'

'What's Bill breaking records in this year?' David asked.

'His moustache. He counts the hairs every morning. He's always late for breakfast. Twenty-two this morning, and I don't have a single one.'

Angela looked at the fair down on her son's upper lip. Like David, he would reach his twenties before he had need of a razor. She tried not to see David in him. Their striking resemblance often pained her. She looked for images of herself in him, but apart from the shape of the fingers, there was nothing.

'Shall we go to your room?' David said, 'and we'll talk about what we're going to do. You need to put some shoes on anyway.'

Jonathan looked at his stockinged feet, surprised, and turning round, slid along the parquet floor. They followed him to his room and, on entering, refrained from asking him to open a window. He apparently did not notice the thickness of the air; he had lived so long with boy's smells that fresh air seemed to him polluted. A mixed odour of sock, lead pencil and hamster hung almost palpably in the air. Angela sat on the bed nearest the open door, whilst she watched him stuff his feet into his shoes, not bothering to lift up the backs, but letting his heels sit on them as if they were sandals. She would leave it to David to correct him, but he, watching too, was leav-

ing it to her. So Jonathan walked down the corridor between them, bouncing on his neutrality.

'Let's go to the fair,' he said, 'and then we can have
lunch and go back to the fair and have tea.' A very simple
programme that he planned for them, knowing how relieved they were to leave it to him. 'We don't need the
car,' he said, as they reached the school gates. 'We can
walk over the fields.' Then, 'Oh, Mother,' with dismay,
looking at her shoes.

'I'll manage,' she said.

He scrambled over the fence, while David and Angela
took the turnstile, and he ran before them over the fields.
He was glad to be alone, and glad too that they were behind him with money in their pockets for shove-
halfpenny, dodgems, the figure of eight, and steak and
candy-floss and lemonade. And for their love too, which
he desperately needed, but he wished he could touch
them, each one, without prejudice, and they would hold
him close, without rivalry. But he settled for the knowledge alone of love, and left it to his dreams to cater for its
physical display.

When he reached the outskirts of the fair, he turned and
waited for them. He looked at them, and tried to see them
as strangers. But it was easier to see strangers as one's
parents. It was a game he often played while walking to
and from his music lesson in the village. He would pass
by an unknown couple and wonder what kind of boy he
would have been had they sired him. He would make an
amalgam of their looks and bodies and try to print it on
his own frame. Then he would begin to walk like them,
and sometimes the illusion became so real that as they
passed him, he waited, expecting their embrace. Now
two people came towards him—in his knowledge and in

107

theirs, his parents—yet he could see no resemblance between himself and them, a fact that they themselves had always stressed, saying that he looked like no one else except himself. But he was floundering in the knowledge of who himself was, and he would have given anything to be anchored to one or both of them. He scuffed his shoes as they approached, and parted to be on each side of him.

'What d'you want to go on first?' David said.

'Let's go on the mat, all of us.'

They threaded their way singly through the crowd. The mat seemed popular only with little children, and he felt suddenly embarrassed to be in the queue. Yet he loved the mat, especially when no one else was on it and he had the whole downward spiral to himself.

They climbed up the interior stairway. It was dark inside, and the stairs were steep, and when they reached the top, they were all breathless.

'I'll go first,' David said, 'and you follow me, Angela. Then give us a couple of minutes, Jonathan, and then you go.'

He settled himself on his mat between the uprights. He pushed himself off and was gone. From the top, they could see his head skirting the bends, and it was time for Angela to take off. Suddenly she was frightened. The height and speed of it worried her, and she could see David landing and gathering himself up together, as it were, from the ground. It looked the end of a rough ride.

'Go on,' she heard Jonathan say.

She steeled herself to go. 'Give me time,' she said to him, trembling on her mat. 'I'm going down slowly.'

'If you can,' he laughed. He gave her a slight push, and speed gathered before she knew of it. And when she understood that she was travelling, and far faster than was comfortable, she gripped the sides in panic and came to a sudden stop. She didn't care what happened. She was not going to move from that spot. She had stopped on the far-side bend of the tower, invisible to both David and Jonathan. When she didn't arrive at the bottom, David would assume that she had lost her nerve and was returning the same way as she had come. Jonathan presumed she had landed, and, settling on his mat, he gave himself a great push and was off. He was happy with the speed he gathered and looked forward to an accelerating slide. But round the second bend, Angela put up a solid block. He opened his knees to clamp her, and then, with his arms on her shoulders securing her, she caught his speed, and within seconds they landed. He still held her, knowing her to be afraid, and then he picked her up solicitously. She turned, and without any thought of proprieties she hugged him, sobbing a little for the love and protection he had shown her. And he was glad of it too. She had done something that the strangers on the way to the music lesson had had no right to do, whatever his expectations. And for a moment in her arms, he wished that his father was not there.

'Where now?' David was calling, slightly irritated by their public display of affection.

'The roundabout,' Jonathan said, knowing that it was his mother's favourite. He held on to her arm, not taking it—he was too unsure for that—neither holding her hand, because for that he was too old; so he hung on to her sleeve to show that he belonged.

The roundabout was in full swing when they reached it, and Angela and he walked round in contrary motion to pick their mounts. The outside horses were of the same mould, and the choice lay in the colour of their manes and saddling. Angela picked out one with a purple stuccoed mould of hair with green nostrils flaring. Jonathan picked the one behind, to be close to her. They ran after their choice, and then stopped, waiting for the horses to come to them. As the roundabout slowed down, David joined them and took Jonathan's other arm. 'Have you chosen?' he said. They pointed them out, and then followed them till they stopped. Then up on to the platform, Jonathan reserving the horse behind for his father. Within seconds, they were all mounted. The music continued to play while the attendant collected the fares, and then they were off, slowly at first, until, with the music's crescendo, they reached top speed.

"Dear Angela, D'you remember how Mum and Dad used to stand watching us, holding the buckets and spades. How, at top speed, you counted up to ten, and on the eleventh you would pass them by and start from one again? And then it took twelve to see them, and then fifteen, and when they didn't reappear till twenty, you knew that the ride was nearly over. You probably don't remember, Angela. I don't think you were around in those days. Come to think of it, were you ever around when I was happy? When did you first come to bother me? Was it David who introduced us to each other? What good are you to me if you cannot recollect my happiness?"

She saw a couple standing near the platform waving to someone on the roundabout. She started to count. Twenty before they met again, and the music was already slowing down. They dismounted.

The figure of eight was next, and then the haunted house. Within an hour they had exhausted all that the fair could offer them. Jonathan had won a teddy-bear that he was too embarrassed to carry, and Angela, a goldfish, astonished in a plastic bag, which didn't look well enough to last the journey back to the school.

'Let's get back quickly,' Jonathan said. 'I'll put it in the big tank in the hall.'

He ran on ahead, steadying the bag with his two hands. He went gently through the turnstile, and they glimpsed him on the school steps and then he disappeared.

The tank was at the far end of the hall, alongside the platform. When he sang in the school choir, he used to watch the fish, and sometimes he was so intent on their movements, in and out of the rocks and flora, that he missed the rhythm of the song, and his neighbour would have to nudge him back into harmony. He ran to the tank, and carefully balanced the bag over the top. Most of the fish in the tank were tropical. There were only a few goldfish, and Jonathan hoped that his would pick out his own kind. So he balanced the bag over an area where three goldfish were clustered, and he opened it to let his fish enter. The stirring on the surface disturbed the group and they scattered behind a rock. Jonathan's goldfish dived, looked around, startled by the unaccustomed warmth and luxury, sank to the bottom and promptly expired. It was a fair-ground fish that thrived on cold, polluted fish-bowl, which, placed in luxury, could only die. He watched the other fish move towards it, hover and turn away.

He screwed up the bag in his hand and went out to meet his parents. 'It died,' he shouted from the school steps as they approached him, and he wondered why it had upset him. He walked slowly towards them, settling himself in the middle. 'Sorry, Mom,' he said, finding it easier to make it her loss, 'but it died as soon as it got into the tank.'

'Probably too warm for it,' David said.

'I left it there,' Jonathan was saying. He hoped someone would come and take it away. Jones of the Sixth looked after the fish, and knew each one by fin, and would furiously investigate the presence of an immigrant corpse. He would announce it at assembly and ask the culprit to make himself known. Jonathan had thoughts of admitting it, and condemning once and for all, and in front of the whole school, Jones's rotten old fish-tank that was only good enough for posh fish. He hoped his poor little corpse would pollute the whole tank and the whole rotten crop of them expire. That'll teach Jones to tropical name-drop. He scuffed his shoes as he walked, not understanding his anger. 'Can we have lunch by the river?' he said, wishing to break the silence that only he was conscious of.

'Is it warm enough?' Angela said.

'Let's go and see. We can eat inside if it's too cold.'

'We'd better take the car,' David said. 'Want to drive, Jonathan?'

He was suddenly cheered and ran ahead of them to the car.

'Let me reverse it first,' David shouted after him.

He drove the car into the country road and let Jonathan take over. They rabbit-hopped at first, and Angela, in the back, laughed to cover her anxiety. Then, by top gear, he was running smoothly and calculating the months to a legitimate licence. At the end of the country lane David took over again and drove to the river restaurant.

They ate outside on the terrace. Jonathan indulged in his monthly steak, lacing it with ketchup and chips, forbidden foods at school. He was glad that his parents hadn't ordered fish, though it was a speciality of Le Bon

Pecheur. They ate chicken, which he liked too, but which
did not represent sufficient a rebellion against his school
diet. His monthly lunches with his parents were a ven-
geance, and not only on the level of food. He looked at
them eating, and they were strangers again. Tonight in
the dormitory he would have to listen to Millbank reciting
the bribes he had refused. He would admit to having
driven his father's car, because he didn't see that as
blackmail. His mother had voiced no objection. He
would not mention the fish. Its story had become as private as his diary. He would talk about his father's film,
and how both of them were going to Italy. He would con-
centrate on the work aspect of it and skirt around the domestic discords.

'What d'you want from Italy?' they both said together.

Put that way it was acceptable, and he asked for a set of
boules. He remembered going to France with his mother
when he was still in the junior school. In the evenings she
would shower the sand off him, and he would marvel
each day how the brown line above his hip grew browner
and browner. Then she would put on his white shirt and
his body would feel full of sun, and they would walk
down to the port to have dinner. All evening he would
check on his brown line, laying his white shirt against it.
After dinner they would walk to the village green and sit
on a bench and watch the old man play boules. On the
other benches old couples sat, and he remembered looking at his mother who had a brown line too, and thinking
that she was very old, and he wondered why she was always alone. Now he knew, though he had never been
told, but he had gathered it painfully from all their non-
truths and non-information. He moved closer to his
mother. He wanted to oust his father. His father had not

113

seen fit to share his childhood, to build his castles in the air or on the sand, to dig his holes, and now he must be expelled from their reminiscences. 'D'you remember how we used to watch them in France?' he said. 'We used to sit on a bench every night after supper.'

'Yes,' Angela laughed, not caring that David was not included. 'You were always looking at your brown line, and comparing it to mine.'

He touched her hand. Yes, he had things to remember, concrete things—he could catalogue a list of recollected trivia, of nurtured snails, tadpoles, stitches in his knee, shrimping, stealing from his mother's purse. And brown lines. And the sum total he could call his childhood. And none of them, since they were all holiday items, had anything to do with his father. He looked at him, his silent out-of-place self, and was sorry for what he had missed. But he would torture him a little, nevertheless.

'D'you remember,' he said to his mother, 'that hospital where they put stitches in my knee, and you bought me some underwater goggles to stop me crying? What happened to them?'

'You left them on the rocks, and then you remembered in the plane going home. Don't you remember jumping up and shouting, "My goggles," and hitting your head on the roof?'

They both laughed. Now Angela was sorry for David, and she noticed how he was fiddling with his food.

'Eat your lunch,' he said to Jonathan, sieving his anger, 'it's getting cold.' He was trying to think of a comeback, and he tried very hard, but there was nothing that was exclusively his and his son's. He wondered if many fathers were in the same position, but that thought didn't make it easier to accommodate. He wished he could have it all over again. He wished he could meet Angela for the first time and de-Carol his life henceforward. He hated these moments when he was forced to contemplate what he had done, the decisions he had half-heartedly taken, and the poor harvest he had reaped. For though he had colonized two women, he missed out on double gratitude. For, after all, what had they to be grateful for, either of them. To the one, he denied his presence, and to the other, whose presence he graced, he denied all else. He knew in truth that what he wanted most was to live alone, but his character was not tuned to inconvenience and solitude. He listened to the two of them as they recapped on those holidays they'd spent without him. And he had to admit to himself that he was envious. Yet he would not interrupt them. He could feign pleasure in their stories, as long as he related them to someone else. In rare moments he wondered whether there was something lacking in him, whether sometimes he was in the wrong, and those moments made him tremble because he had nurtured his power, both in his business and his private life, on the unquestionable assumption that he was in the right. And it had paid off, hadn't it. In his business at least. And his private life was not so miserable that he had to change it all, but what worried him was that these moments were getting more frequent, and occurred even when he was alone, with no spark of Angela or Jonathan or Carol to ignite them. Yes, there would come a time when he would have to make a positive choice, and having reached this stage in self-argument, he again felt absolved from decision.

'What d'you want for dessert?' he said. He seemed the whole morning to have been organizer, having contributed nothing except his laying of plans and his ungiving presence. He put his hand on Jonathan's, and Jonathan took it as a simple plea for forgiveness. He moved towards him and scratched in his mind for a subject that could include him. But he had the same difficulty as his father. So he gave him his order, a *crème brûlée*, because he knew that was his father's favourite.

After lunch, Jonathan suggested a row on the lake, and Angela, wanting him to be equally shared, said she would prefer to sit on the bank and watch them. She sat on a bench alongside the jetty, and watched David manoeuvre the boat from its moorings. Jonathan had already settled in the rower's seat. He wanted his father as passenger. He waited for him to settle, and David saluted an O.K. Jonathan gave him a response smile, and Angela knew they were entering a silent conspiracy and she felt no resentment.

"Dear Angela, All could be so well, and now I regret packing his clothes. Why do I vacillate so, and between such extremes? Is my inconsistency a signal to my own tortured hopes, and would it not be better for the sake of constancy to abandon them altogether? We are back where we started, Angela, at two years ago, when we froze ourselves into time, and there we have remained despite our survivals. So no more decisions, Angela. We cannot trust ourselves to uphold them."

After half an hour, she saw the boat turn into the port. David was rowing now and she was surprised at his strength. Jonathan was lying across the opposite seat, obviously exhausted. From where she sat, he looked like a child, and their boating away together was an incident that they would both recall as vividly as the game of boules.

They tied up to the bank and David helped Jonathan

out. They would have to get straight back to the school because Jonathan had a prep at four. 'That was marvellous,' he was saying, stretching his legs. And to Angela, 'He rows pretty well. He went right over to the other side.' His cheeks were flushed, and she remembered how he had looked when she had taught him to ride his bicycle and he had managed to go several yards without falling off. But she kept the memory to herself.

They walked back to the school. 'When will you be back?' Jonathan said.

'In a couple of months. We'll miss the next Parent's Day.'

'I might go up to London and stay with Danny. Is that all right?' Danny was a close friend who'd left school the year before.

'If it's all right with Danny,' they seemed to say together.

He said goodbye to them on the school steps, as a host sees his guests off the premises. 'Have a marvellous time,' he said. 'I hope the film goes well.' It was such a formal send-off that no one would have been surprised had they shaken hands all round. Then suddenly he came forward, and looking quickly around to ascertain that there were no witnesses, he clasped them both together, without touching them himself, holding them close as if to will them to join again. He stood back and they looked at each other, embarrassed. It was the closest they had come physically since David had left, and it was not of their doing, but both knew that it was a plea that could not be ignored. Angela wanted to hold Jonathan close to thank him for trying, and David giggled, covering the embarrassment for them all. Then they kissed him, each one separately, and waved goodbye as they went down

117

the steps. From the car as they reversed out into the lane, they could see him still standing there, waving and smiling as if he was satisfied with his work. And Angela winced at the hope on his face, that temporary hope that she had so often known, and she moved close to David, hoping that Jonathan could still see them, though she knew she was misleading him.

As they turned into the main road she shifted back into her seat and prepared for the silence that they both wished. They had reached the outskirts of London before either spoke.

'I think Jonathan enjoyed the day,' David said. For the whole length of the journey he had obviously been weighing the arguments for and against Jonathan's enjoyment, and, still undecided, he was proclaiming his wished-for result.

'Yes,' she said, not wishing to contradict him. 'I think he'll miss us on Parent's Day. It'll be the first one we've missed since he was there.'

'What are you doing tonight?' he said.

'I'll start packing, I suppose. And you?'

He looked at the case in the back of the car. 'I'll be unpacking,' he said.

"Leave it, Angela. Leave it."

'Did you notice how Jonathan tried to bring us together when we left?'

"Dear Angela, How ham-fisted I can be. And my insensitivity is deliberate. I am bringing his attention to something which has no doubt occupied his mind since we left the school. How can he answer me?"

And of course he didn't answer. He stared fixedly ahead of him, wincing at her lack of good taste.

When he drew up at the flat, he stopped the car and

turned to her. 'Don't you ever use Jonathan again,' he said.

"Dear Angela, For that I could kill him. He speaks as if using Jonathan is a habit of mine, and I have never, but never, included Jonathan in the rage between us. What a coward he is, Angela. What an eel, that can so slip out with such agility from every predicament. Let me hold on to this hate, Angela. Let it drive me upstairs to the flat, and to his erstwhile desk and study, and let me empty it of all his behaviour. And let me hold on to this hate till it boils over and dies, but let me never never never forget it. Let me hold on to the peace that must come, and another kind of hope that depends on me and me alone.''

She got out of the car, and without shutting the door, knowing that he was waiting for her to bang it, she ran up the stairs to the flat. Her keys were at the ready, and she lost no time in getting in and straight into his study. She sat down at the desk and calmed herself. Then she opened the top drawer. It was full of copies of contracts and business letters that he had failed to file. She took them all out, and laid them in an untidy pile on the desk. The second drawer was full of letters and photographs, and she hesitated before investigating. She recognized his father's handwriting, and as she turned the letters over, she noticed that almost all of them were from his father. Some were still in their envelopes and she saw that they were addressed to David's old school. She did not want to read them. They reminded her of the clothes that David had left in the wardrobe, David's past and his dotage. Underneath the letters were scattered photographs. David at school sports, David at prize-giving, David as a baby. She looked at each one in turn, and felt the tears welling.

She tidied the photographs and put them in a pile beside the letters. Then she refilled the top drawer and closed them both.

"Dear Angela, Where have I moved today but backwards and forwards from the same destructive spot, like a fern that curls close with fear and unfolds with hope, while firmly anchored to its poisoned root. Let me try again tomorrow, Angela. At my lowest ebb I have such faith in you, which makes ours such a sterile partnership. Will there ever come a time when you will leave me, so that I can be whole again?"

Chapter Eight

Hal Butler had freed himself to direct David's picture, and he had found his main location in a village some miles south of Rome. It was a small hamlet, straddling the coastline and built into the rock. It was a village which tourists had sadly to by-pass because there were no hotel facilities there and no available land on which to build. A few miles further south, the Italians claimed their annual tourist dues, mainly from the suede pockets of German lederhosen folded neatly on the beach while their owners obeyed the rules of the grim games organized along the shore. Mr Worcester's job, and Angela's, was to find convenient accommodation for the cast and the crew—no easy assignment, since it depended almost entirely on private billeting. So it was a case of winning over the natives.

Angela had flown down to Rome with Mr Worcester, and from there they had hired a car. Hal Butler, and Tom Welland, who, on Hal's instructions, was making daily alterations to the script—the suicide had been dropped at least four drafts ago—were drinking an aperitif on the piazza when Mr Worcester and Angela arrived. It was late afternoon, but the sun was still high, and Angela felt town-dressed and inappropriate. Mr Worcester loosened his tie, but refrained from taking off his jacket because he was shy of his braces. Hal and Tom were in shirt-sleeves, and, after their two-week stay, already bronzed and Sunday-magazine-worthy. Tom put his hand on Angela's pullover. 'Hope you've got some summer gear with you,' he said. 'During the day, it can get terribly hot. D'you swim? The sea's so calm and so beautiful, I just had to write it into the script.'

"Dear Angela, D'you mind letting God know that His third day's labour has not been entirely overlooked in literature? And that if He wasn't satisfied with Moby Dick and Lord Jim, He might be flattered by the acknowledgment of one Tom Welland, of His gathering together of the waters which He called the Seas. Look up your records, Angela. Have we got a novelist on our books? We tend to specialize in film people, don't we. We ought to spread ourselves a little. A writer is part of life's rich tapestry, you should pardon the expression. And after all, even whores don't specialize. Make a note of Tom Welland, Angela, for our next rainy day."

Hal had fixed them both up in the house of Sam Weiner, an American who had married a girl of the village. Sam had draft-dodged to Italy from his native Minnesota. In Rome, he was innocently involved in a gang shoot-up, and had lost his little finger in the fray. So he could have safely gone back home. But he chose to stay, because he had already met Giulietta, who was visiting her father, a patient in the same ward as Sam in the hospital in Rome. She came almost every day to visit them both, and with her father's permission invited Sam to their village to convalesce. In a few months they were married, and together they ran the café on the beach. Every morning Sam went fishing with Giulietta's father, while Giulietta made the day's pasta. Few villagers came down to the beach to eat, but there were enough day-trippers from Rome and other places near by to keep them in business. They lived in the family house with Giulietta's parents and her younger brothers. The house was built on to the outer cliff, and over the years Giulietta's father, with grandchildren in mind, had extended it in the form of a wooden annexe built on the beach itself. It was in this annexe that Mr Worcester and Angela were to be lodged during their stay.

Hal and Tom took them down to the beach to introduce them to their hosts. Sam Weiner greeted them effusively—rather excessively, Angela thought. He monopolized the four of them, without bothering to include his wife or her family in his welcome, although they were all gathered around the dining-table rather as a welcoming committee. It was as if Sam recognized in the film company his kind of people—his whites, as it were. Angela fully expected him to apologize for his foreign wife and her wog family. She took a seat at the table next to Giulietta, who was sorting out seashells with her brothers, though the latter were paying little attention. They seemed fascinated by this new persona of their brother-in-law, his hitherto unnoticed swagger. 'You're going to need the co-operation of the natives,' he was saying. 'Accommodation, board, for instance. Employment of extras. I'll give you a hand if you like. Worked on a couple of movies back in the States.'

'We would be grateful,' Mr Worcester said politely.

'People round here,' Sam almost whispered, 'don't

123

take too kindly to foreigners. They don't even trust the Romans. But once you're in with them, they'll eat out of your hand.'

Angela wanted to spit.

'I could be your liaison officer,' Sam was saying.

'We wouldn't want to take you away from your work,' Mr Worcester said. He didn't particularly like Sam, but he knew that the services of such a man in such a village would be invaluable. 'It would be a full-time job for you,' he said. 'Interpreter, liaison officer and general dog's-body for the eight weeks we shall be here. I would offer you a good salary of course, if you could give up your own work for that period.'

Sam moved over to where Mr Worcester was standing. 'Come,' he said, 'I'll show you to your room,' and they went off together and negotiations were presumably completed on the way. Giulietta got up from the table, and picked up Angela's case. Tom Welland had to argue it from her, for she was reluctant to let it go, and then, leading the way, Angela and Tom followed her. Hal settled down with the brothers and wordlessly they sorted the shells.

In the next few weeks, the village was transformed. Workmen arrived from the surrounding hamlets—masons, plasterers, cabinet-makers, carpenters. Tents were erected on the edge of the beach where it melted into a maize field behind. Further down by the caves, they were building a villa façade, and sundry interiors. Within a month a full-blown English garden had sprouted along the villa drive, with plastic lawns and imported rhododendrons. The summer retreat of Caroline and Julian Strong, the central characters in Tom's story. Tom hovered round the builders most of the day, marvelling at his inventions. 'That's just how I envisaged it back in Hampstead while I was writing,' he would exclaim each time a new piece of decor was installed. Wallis, the set-designer, acknowledged the compliment. He had had little to go on from Tom's script directions. He had tried discussing the sets with Tom, but it was clear that the writer had no notion of what he wanted. So he had gone ahead on his own, with Hal's occasional advice, and he knew that it was the fruits of his imagination that had evoked Tom's whole-hearted approval, and that that was the correct order of play. Meanwhile Mr Worcester and Angela, with the tiresome but necessary interference of Sam, had organized amongst the villagers accommodation for the whole company. David, with whom Mr Worcester was in spasmodic touch through the rather unreliable postal services of the village, had spent the last two weeks in Rome negotiating finance and crewing arrangements, and he was due to arrive in the village with the rest of the company on the following day. Things had gone well in the pre-production in the village, and the shooting-date was met with two days to spare. That night Mr Worcester decided to throw a party on the beach for the villagers and workmen in token of their swift and helpful co-operation.

Before preparing for the party, Angela called into the village post office to collect the day's mail and messages. Among the cables was one for David, and Angela, thinking that it had to do with the production and possibly needed her attention, opened it. 'Million thanks for birthday present,' she read. 'Love love love Carol.' Business-like, she put it back in the envelope and added it to the pile. She walked quickly out of the post office, fighting back her resentment. The woman after all must have a birthday, and she was entitled to receive a present from a man with whom she lived, even if that man happened to be your husband. She managed to accept the fact of it, but what needled her was its quality. What kind of present had he given her to merit such an effusive acknowledgment? She would never be able to find out, short of asking him, and that she would never do. She would say nothing about it, and let him see that someone had opened the telegram, Mr Worcester perhaps, and let him sweat in the uncertainty of it. Yet it nagged at her, this concrete reminder of her unhappiness. For weeks now, in the pressures of the work, she'd managed to put it aside. She had been happy in the friendships she had made amongst the people of the village. There had been no hostility in her heart, that weary companion of her misery. Now she felt it creeping upon her, demanding a target, anything, anybody, on which to vent its spleen. It was no accident when later on, as she walked into the grand party-marquee erected on the beach, she was greeted at once by Tom Welland, as if he was waiting there for his arrest.

He was slightly drunk, and urged her to catch up with him. She took the wine offered her out of the small residue of her politeness. She did not need alcohol. She needed no agent to numb her sensibilities, no excuse for what might appear to be irrational behaviour. What she was going to do with Tom Welland, she was going to do cold. She had liked him too little to care about deceiving him, and why should she fool herself, since she liked herself even less.

He put his arm around her waist and motioned her into the dance. The village band were seated at the end of the marquee, mainly a brass affair, with the addition of the master plasterer from the next village who doubled as fiddler. The music was of the 'forties vintage, of the quick-quick-slow variety. Partners were positively partners. Some women danced with women, some men with men, but they were each a pair together, depending on the other's rhythm for their mutual enjoyment. The drink was the wine of the locality and very potent, and the villagers, as well as the English contingent, were merrily advanced. Even Mr Worcester had discarded his jacket, showing his braces shamelessly. He was dancing with Giulietta's mother, on his polite insistence, and she giggled with the embarrassment of it all, looking back continuously at her card-playing husband, as if to apologize to him for the situation she had been placed in. Tom piloted Angela round the floor.

'Are you happy with everything?' she said.

'It's all exactly as I envisaged,' he said. 'I think the sets are marvellous.'

'Have you altered the script very much? I haven't read it since the first draft.'

'Well, the ending's different of course. I fought against it for quite a while, but I think David was probably right. He hated that suicide ending.'

'Apart from Hal and David,' she said, trying to give him some outlet for his own honesty, 'd'you really think in your own heart that Caroline would have survived?'

'Oh yes, definitely,' he said. 'I wouldn't be talked into any changes simply because they were commercial. There's such a thing as integrity.'

Yes, she'd heard that one. It was a word often shouted in David's office or on the set. It was bandied around by writers, technicians and actors as if they each had some exclusive monopoly on moral rectitude. 'Are you writing another novel?' she said.

'No, I think I'll give it a break a while. Just write for the films.' Angela doubted whether the world of literature would suffer a great loss, and doubted too whether the film industry would greatly benefit through Tom's change of vocation. She felt his sweating hand sticking to her waist through her dress and she tried to wriggle out of its pressure. But he, mistaking the gesture as one of excitement, held her closer.

'Are you and David divorced?' he said.

'Would that make any difference?' she said. Then added, 'Oh I'm sorry, I forgot about your integrity.'

'I'm not given to poaching,' he said, 'except of course in my novels.'

'Well, let's pretend this is one of your novels, shall we?'

'You're giving me a licence, you know.' He smiled at her.

'I hand them out all the time,' she said, with utter honesty.

'What a pity,' he said. 'I hoped I was something special.'

'Well, in a way you are. I don't think I've ever given one to a writer before.'

"Dear Angela, I think we must devise a new system of book-keeping. We will drop the name column, since all are anonymous, and out of an academic curiosity we will keep the column referring to the Nature of the Account. Then we will add Profession. For, after all, very few people do what they are, and a note on how they earn their bread will reduce them even more to anonymity. We shall call the book *X*, and bind it beautifully to offset the

rottenness within, and this, together with my endless suicide scribbles in your direction, will be the sum total of
the bibliography of one Angela Morrow, who inconve-
nienced everybody by surviving. And here I go again,
Angela. Nature of the Account? Gratis. Profession?
Scribbler. Remarks? Stand by.''

The band took a break, and Tom guided her over to one
of the supper-tables. The women of the village had
cooked for the party, and Mr Worcester had been lavish
with their expenses. Hal Butler came over to the table to
join them. He had a Roman girl in tow, one of the production assistants from the Italian end. She was very
beautiful and Angela looked at her with envy, not of her
beauty, but of her plain lack of need to write letters to
herself. They found a table and Mr Worcester joined
them. He was alone. Giulietta's mother was happily
dishing out the pasta, a generous portion of which Mr
Worcester now balanced towards the table. Angela noticed that the men of the village were not eating. They felt
themselves the hosts and concerned themselves with
serving those outside their own community. But they
were drinking continuously and Angela watched the
passage of one of them as he staggered down the marquee, a plate of pasta in each hand. She knew instinctively that he wouldn't make the table he was aiming to
serve, and she watched him, coolly waiting for him to
fall. She could almost gauge at what point in his journey
he would surrender, and when he reached it, he did indeed pause, gaze about him glassily, pivot slightly on his
left foot, and then, with the grace of an aging flamingo,
he folded to the floor, the pasta slipping from his hands as
he fell, draping itself like sticky streamers around his best
serge suit. There was a silence after his fall, broken only

by the stifled giggles of the children. The villagers wanted to laugh, because he looked very funny lying there draped in spaghetti, but they felt they ought to show some shame that one of their number had so misbehaved. It was Mr Worcester who gave them their cue. He threw his head back and let out a large, English club guffaw, and went towards the man to help him to his feet. Now the others joined in his laughter and the incident seemed to give a licence to everybody to drop all pretences. Now the band started to play again. Men began to dance on their own and to sing. The marquee suddenly became very crowded and riotous, and it felt as if a breaking-point must be reached. Tom took Angela's arm. He was very drunk. 'Let's walk along the beach,' he said.

They threaded their way through one of the flap openings. The moon was covered with cloud, and the beach was lit only dimly by the few lights that shone down from the piazza. They walked along the shore line. The air was hot and damp, and Angela felt her hair swell into a fuzz. At the far end of the beach there was a cave. Sometimes on a Sunday the villagers could be seen trudging along the sands in their beating black, making their way to the cave to pray. For there was a Madonna inside, hewn out of the rock, decorated with two pearls on her cheeks for tears. The villagers would light candles to her, and on a Holy Day the cave would be flooded with light. Now it was dark inside. Tom took out his lighter, and lit a few stubs of candles at the foot of the statue.

"Dear Angela, There must be a better place to pursue the art of survival, yet there is something strangely fitting about it too. The Virgin is hewn out of the rock in tears, a stone celebration of affliction. There is no clutch after life. There is but an acceptance of a boring martyrdom.

She is a confirmation of the vale of tears, she is anti-life, so it is fitting that we come here without love, without desire even. With her pearly tears, she is a voyeuse on our debasement.''

'It's beautiful,' Tom was saying. 'I've simply got to work this location into the script. Instead of going to a hotel, Caroline could come right here with her lover.'

'Would you like a rehearsal?' Angela said, business-like.

They lay down on the sand, and she could almost hear Angela say, 'Action.'

He kissed her and she responded with simulated passion. She was rather good at that, and it fooled almost everybody except herself.

'Now I don't want you to go falling in love with me,' he said. 'It would only hurt us both.'

'Is that in the script?' she said.

'I believe that real love,' he went on, getting into his stride, 'is a combination of the spiritual and the physical. Such love between two people can only grow. There's no such thing as love at first sight. At least, I don't think so.'

''Dear Angela, This is a terrible script, and I do believe we both do it justice. 'Spiritual love and physical.' Jesus, I've swallowed better platitudes than that one and if I have to swallow any more, I'll shit a better script than this.''

On the smooth sand below the Madonna, he took her drunkenly but adequately, and they lay there side by side, though light-years from each other away. From her viewpoint now, she could see the Madonna upside down and found her less offensive. No symbolism from that angle, only a jagged interruption of the rock-face, climbing-steps for children in the folds of the dress, and a tidy heel-holder under the chin. She closed her eyes, but was yet aware of a sudden flash of light, as if a passing holiday-maker, his Pentax ever at the ready, had spotted yet another piece of touristiana. She sat up quickly, as did Tom, and they felt a sudden darkness enclose them, as if a chinkless door had been closed on the cave. Tom groped for her hand, and as he touched it, a great roar of thunder shuddered through the rock, and they heard the blustering rain outside. They got up and went to the mouth of the cave. Across the beach, lit in spasms of lightning, they could see the marquee billowing with loaded gusty cheeks, and the guy ropes vainly trying to hold down the flaps, like a frightened girl overwrapping her skirts. Shadowy figures in groups of twos and threes were leaving the tent, weaving through the flaps, some holding bottles and plates of food. Outside, they straightened into formation, and then with loud laughter they ran into the water, splashing each other around, bottles held high, while the lightning forked across the pockmarked sea which rolled and fretted with the itch of the rain. Then, as more and more figures were leaving the tent, as from a burning house, the rising wind met the fuse, and the whole canvas structure left its moorings, billowing high above the central pole in unashamed exposure. The band folded their instruments away and joined the others in the sea. Tom and Angela watched them, and then, as if the party had simply moved to another site, joined them in the water.

'I can't swim,' was the last Angela heard from Tom, and she went forward into the waves, calling back to him through the wind that he could lie in the shallows and be cleansed. She saw a passing guest hand him a bottle, and he sat in the water, tipping the bottle into his mouth, throwing his head back to receive it, and falling gently backwards, the bottle his periscope. Angela swam out, away from the others, then lay on her back. She needed to cleanse herself as she hoped Tom was doing, both of themselves and of each other, of the lie of their lying together, of the debasement of her own ways of survival. And as she watched the sky clear, and the sea-skin become smooth, she resolved that never again would she give herself and others such little worth.

It was twilight suddenly, as it had been when the party began, and it seemed a signal to all of them to leave the water and tidy up what was left on dry land. She swam back to where she could stand, and watched the unsteady pairs straggling to the shore. Tom was still lying there, but he'd dropped the bottle at his side. Some figures paused to look at him, and then moved on, leaving the ripples to lap away his hangover. But one of them, the young baker's apprentice from the village, with his girl on his arm, stayed to look at him more closely. They bent down, lower and lower, their heads touching like petals closing in the dark. Then the girl let out a shrill cry that echoed over the sands and brought the rest of the party back to the water's edge. By the time Angela reached the shore, a crowd had gathered. She saw Mr Worcester thread his way out of the silent gathering, and move slowly towards the dry sand, and there she saw him kneel. She could hear faint crying now, the wailing of men and women. She moved away from the crowd. She did not want to be seen with Tom's body lest she still betrayed some mark of their coupling, but she watched it as it was lumbered high above the crowd, and carried unsteadily towards the tent. Hal Butler stood on the wet sand, bewildered, watching Mr Worcester, whom he could not bring himself to join. Angela went towards them both, and Mr Worcester rose as she approached. Then the three embraced each other in trembling shock.

'How did it happen?' Hal whispered.

'He vomited,' Mr Worcester said, 'and it choked him. He drowned in a paltry six inches of water.'

They started back towards the tent. Angela would have wished Tom a better death, at least five fathoms to conquer him. She shuddered. She wished that she had been able to love him a little, so that his death would have had some defiance. But she had unleashed an evil eye in the cave, and it had come after him, following him to the shallows, where six inches of water was more than enough for it to flower. And then she sobbed aloud, for her heart shrieked that she had killed him.

The men carrying the body had stopped short at the tent, while another went inside and picked up a folded white tablecloth. Then the cortège turned and, steadier now, wound its way back along the shore. The villagers had taken over. It was their death now, and their sorrow, and it was to their Madonna that they were taking Tom for comfort and absolution. Angela shivered. She did not want to go into that cave again, to the site of his trial and sentence, and to the beginnings of the death that she had wished on him. Yet she followed Mr Worcester and Hal as they joined the end of the line of mourners.

As the head of the procession approached the mouth of the cave, the chanting swelled slowly over the line, tuneless at first, a repetitive and insistent protest. Then slowly a melody fingered its way through the chant, and the rhythm of protest waned to give way to a mournful, harmonious acceptance. The bearers stopped at the entrance to the cave, waiting for the mourners to enter and assemble as a congregation. One of their number carried candles, and he distributed them, lighting some himself to illumine the shrine. Angela followed Mr Worcester into the cave, and she saw something glinting on the sand. Tom's lighter. She stood still, hoping that everyone would ignore it and let it lie there as a legacy. For it belonged to no one except perhaps to that shrinking Virgin who, by its light, had viewed their sin and sent Tom to his deserts. But Mr Worcester picked it up, turned it over in his hand, and passed it sadly to Angela as a terrible souvenir. She clenched it in her hand as she joined the others, who formed rows each side of the cave. Now the Madonna was fully lit, and Angela had to turn away, though her pearly stare pierced her back like the eye of Cain.

The bearers brought the body through the aisle where the assembly had parted, and laid it, covered now with the white cloth, at the foot of the statue. How long ago was it that he had lain there, with her alongside, shrouded both of them, each in their separate impenetrable fantasies. Now his were shed, as he lay in his own white sad truth under the Virgin's recognizing eye.

On each side of the aisle, the mourners knelt and prayed. Then they moved in single file towards the body, crossing themselves and praying all the while, until they followed one the other out of the cave into the luke light of the sudden dawn. Now only Mr Worcester, Hal and Angela were left staring at Tom and each other in total disbelief. Outside, along the sands, the canvas flapped shapelessly around the centre pole. Inside, the tables were still strangely neat, the plates in their piles, and the pasta congealed in the bowls. On another table a big loose-tapped barrel dripped its red wine on to the sand.

The women began to clear away, while the men started to wrap the tent. There was a great fever of activity, of lively clatter, anything to drown the death and the silence that shrieked from the cave along the sand. Angela went to help the women, and Mr Worcester and Hal joined those who were loosening the guy ropes. Nobody spoke. The men hammered the pegs in their desperate fury, and the women clattered the dishes out of their sad anger. Occasionally Angela looked back at the cave, and she knew from the shadows on the rocks outside that the candles were still burning.

"Dear Angela, Never again. Never, never, never again."

Chapter Nine

Tom Welland's body was flown back to England the following day. Mr. Worcester, with Sam Weiner's help, had handled the arrangements, and all was completed before the rest of the company arrived. Angela had driven down to the village station with Mr Worcester, slowly following the hearse along the narrow roads that wound through the mountains, inland from the sea. They waited on the station platform with nothing to do but disbelieve. At the end of the station a cluster of village women were waiting. They were dressed in their best, off to Rome for the day, and embarrassed by the long box that would accompany them. The Naples-Milan express whistled through the station and the two railway porters stood discreetly in front of the box and the women held their skirts about them. Now they moved forward a little, for the next train was theirs, the local one to Rome, with fourteen pick-ups on the way. When it came, shunting down the line, they gathered their packages, anxious to board the train, and distance themselves from their fellow-traveller. But as soon as they boarded, they rushed for the windows, where they could view the proceedings like any other detached spectator.

The porters carried the coffin into the last carriage, and Sam got in after it. As they placed it on the wooden seat, with the dull thud of wood on wood, Angela understood for the first time that Tom Welland was dead. She had woken early in the morning, convinced that she'd had a bad dream, and she'd run quickly to the window that overlooked the beach. She was in time to see a party of barefoot fisher-men trundling the box up the cliff steps that led to the village post-office. Still she could not believe it, and even in the car to the station, she was convinced of her continuous sleep-walking. Now the thud of the wood had woken her, and she knew that no one would ever see Tom Welland again. She fingered the lighter that was in her pocket, and wondered what she should do with it. To whom did it belong, this inheritance? Did he have a wife? Children? What was known about the man, and by whom? Who knew of his hobbies, if he had any; what he thought, if anything, of Mozart, the Rolling Stones, space travel, Zap comics? Did Mr Worcester know, or Hal, either of whom had possibly come as close to Tom as she had? But theirs had been a closeness of people in a rush-hour tube, of body cleaving body, unknown to each other, yet closer to one another than a woman and her lover in bed. Their coupling had been a conjunction adrift between two irrelevancies, and nothing was known from it. Only a lighter, a piece of lost property, remained.

Suddenly the blinds were drawn down on the last carriage and the porters left quickly. She waited with Mr Worcester until the train left the station; then sadly they returned to the village.

The rest of the company were due to arrive in the afternoon. David would be coming too. She had given him very little thought since reading Carol's telegram, and now its contents appeared to her very trivial. She looked forward to David's coming. He would put his arm round her and comfort her perhaps, though he would wonder why she grieved so acutely for a comparative stranger. Word of Tom's death spread quickly on their arrival. To most of them it meant little, beyond the sadness of a young person who dies. Most of them had never met him, but the event served to cast an irritation, at least, on their arrival. Besides, they themselves had had a tiring journey, having had to hang about in Rome for three hours—as if that were a penance—because the collecting car-drivers had been misled on the plane's arrival time. And when the stars saw the nature of the accommodation provided for them, their temper was not improved. To cap it all, Mark Baines, the leading man, had brought along with him his secretary, or so he chose to call him, and his person had neither been budgeted for nor accommodated.

'There's no room,' Mr Worcester said coldly. 'We have taken over every single spare room in the village. Your friend will have to stay in the hotel about five miles from here.'

There was Tom's room of course, and Mr Worcester was not unmindful of it, but the man was not yet buried and there was something faintly immoral in assigning his bed while it was still warm. Yet Mr Worcester knew it was in the nature of the film business, or any other business for that matter, that by the end of the day, at most, some rationale would have been found to commandeer Tom's bed, and by the morning this same rationale would have confirmed that not to have taken it over would have been a sacrilege.

David was lodged in the village baker's house in a large room with a double bed. Mr Worcester had been personally responsible for that allocation. He had hoped no doubt that, what with the sun, the beauty of the place and the excitement of the work, Angela and David might grow together again, but he had seen her promenade with Tom Welland on the night of the beach party, and he grieved for her as well. It was altogether a bad beginning for a picture, and though Mr Worcester, unlike most of the company, was not a superstitious person, he knew from experience that once a production was on the turn, it could only get sourer.

That evening they all ate together in Sam's café on the beach and everybody kept away from the cave. David sat next to Angela, and she tried obliquely to find out from him what he knew about Tom, but he knew less than she did. He was deeply distressed at the news, and swore that out of respect for Tom's memory not a single line of the present script would be altered and he passed this strict instruction on to Hal, though he knew that over the shooting-period more rationales would be found for convenient changes.

After dinner they walked along the beach together, saying little, and touching not at all. Then, as it grew dark, he told her that he was tired, that he needed to sleep and to be alone. She had expected nothing else from him and she didn't understand why it hurt her that he was going without her to his bed even though over the last few hundred nights he had done exactly that. She ascribed his depression to Tom's death, but even in doing so, she feared that she was falling into the trap of all of them, of using and exploiting the event to explain away everything.

As she undressed to get into bed, she felt the lighter again in her pocket. She knew she should have given it to Sam, who had packed Tom's effects, but she felt she had some right over it. Not that she needed any reminder of their pairing, but it was part of her penance that she should feel its weight about her. She put it in the pocket of the jeans she would wear the following day. It had become part of her wardrobe.

"Dear Angela, I am someone else from what I was. Have you changed too? Perhaps we have freed ourselves a little, but I shudder at the cost. But if David reaches out towards me, will you bear the lighter, please, when the time comes?"

David was woken by the smell of baking bread. It was still quite early, but he was no longer tired. He got up and put on his swimsuit underneath his trousers, and threw on his shirt as he left the house. The sun was already high and it was warm. He climbed over the railings on the piazza and, ignoring the steps, slithered down the rock to the beach. He heard a baby cry in the village and the clang of opening shutters. He picked his way carefully through the water, as if he were trying to avoid the site of Tom's drowning. Tom's death had filled him with a strange fear, and a deep self-discontent. He had experienced too, on hearing the news, an urgent pull towards Angela, yet at the same time an inability to touch her. Tom's death had sobered him into an astonished recognition of what was real, and in that reality he saw his own weakness, his own guilt, his own cruelty. For some reason that morning he had prayed and given vague thanks, but as he felt himself lured by resolutions, he had dressed hurriedly and scrambled down to the beach because he knew, with more certainty than he had ever known, how desperately uncommitting he was. He barely could admit to himself what concrete matter disturbed him, apart from Tom's death and his own chaotic way of living. At the airport, before he'd left London, Carol had turned him inside with her news, and it nagged at him, so he dived gently into the sea, hoping to drown it. He swam out, thinking of nothing except his stroke, and counting them to turn his mind away from other thoughts. At a hundred, he turned back towards the shore, floating, occasionally standing to test his depth. Then he walked to the shore and lay exhausted on the sand, feeling the water-drops on his skin as the sun blotted them. Then he got up, dressed and walked towards the cave.

Angela was watching him. The opening shutters had woken her, and she too, untired yet fretting, had decided on the sea. But as she drew the blind across the window, she saw a figure swimming towards the shore, and she knew, even from the fleshy blob of him, that it was David. So she watched him guiltily as he lay on the sand, and then as he rose and dressed and walked towards the cave. She wanted to call out to him to stop, that he was trespassing, that he went into that cave at his peril. For she felt herself still inside it with Tom, and she wondered whether she'd left any evidence behind, a sigh, a tear, an echo of their coupling, that would for ever cancel out the gentleness towards her that she knew was creeping upon him. She saw him enter the cave and she timed his stay. Three minutes. That was long enough to see everything. Five minutes. That was long enough even to pray. Ten minutes. What search was he carrying out inside? After fifteen minutes she dressed hurriedly, feeling the lighter rub against her thigh. Then, barefoot, she ran across the beach.

When she reached the cave, she held back. She hadn't meant to go in there again. Besides, since she knew David was inside, it might be tactless to disturb him. So she called his name, and it echoed around the rocks, reverberating back from the cave. Then suddenly he broke out of the darkness, blinking on the sudden sunlight. She went towards him and he held out his hands. They walked back along the shore and up the rock-steps to the café on the piazza. There they ate breakfast together, and talked with the non-talk of strangers or of people who know each other too well.

At nine o'clock the company assembled on the main lot on the beach edge. David sat in their midst and welcomed them all. This was the first time that Angela had seen David surrounded with the paraphernalia of his trade. He was very different from the man she knew in restaurants, or in car interiors, in fearful encounters and stormy partings. He revealed a self-confidence that she rarely saw in him, but the gentleness was familiar. He was obviously well liked by those with whom he had worked before—he had kept the same basic staff for years. He respected the skill of each man in his department and never interfered with a problem that he wasn't technically equipped to investigate. He trusted everybody. That was part of his innocence too, but rarely did his trust misfire. He praised the designer for his sets, and acknowledged the efficiency and dedication of Mr Worcester. He spoke about the need to respect the people of the village and to intrude as little as possible in their privacy. He asked for a measure of decorum in company behaviour since they were all in a way guests of the village. And finally he spoke of Tom. He told them what little he knew about him, and it was clear that he wished he'd known him better. His death, he said, heartbreaking as it was, placed them all under an added obligation. Tom would be remembered, if at all, by his work, and it was incumbent on all of them to do that work justice, to treat it honestly as he would have wanted. It was the only memorial they could give him. When he had finished, Hal took over, and the production was under way.

Over the course of the next two weeks, Angela saw little of David. She spent much of her time on the set with Mr Worcester while David ran the general administration, headquartered in the hotel some five miles away. They met only in the evenings, when most of the company would gather in Sam's café on the beach for dinner. In the first few days, David was occupied in fending off the queue of reporters who had come from all over Europe to gather the spices of Tom's death. But beyond the pure simple fact of it, nothing was known and it was up to the reporters to make what they wished of it. Over the first week, the press-cuttings that David received were so diverse in their reportage that there was little indication that they referred to the same event. Most went to town on the *dolce vita* aspect of the affair. 'Creative writer'—what was the opposite of that one?—'dies in beach orgy' was a Swedish version; while another hinted darkly, but too light for libel, that the event was the outcome of a conflict between the director of the film and the writer, who had refused script changes. But amongst all the coverage there was one small paragraph from a Roman paper that was deeply disturbing. It described the accident in straightforward terms, and added: 'The writer was last seen in the company of Angela Morrow, the estranged wife of the film producer . . . They were seen together hand in hand entering a cave at the far end of the beach. Mrs Morrow was not available for comment. She is reported to be in a state of shock.' The matter of the report troubled David enough, but he was more disturbed because he could not guess at the source of the information. Mr Worcester had instructed everybody not to talk to the press and to leave the whole business in the hands of the press officer. Harry Block, who had been David's press man since he had started in pictures, was much too discreet and loyal to offer such information even if it were true. It was unlikely either that any of the villagers had talked. They were suspicious of strangers and would have preferred the story to have been kept within their confines, since they felt themselves very superior to those villagers along the coast who had lent themselves to tourist seductions and were giving the Church a bad name. David asked Harry to try and trace the informer, though he knew that no reporter would willingly divulge his source. It nagged at him right through the day. Now he understood why Angela had been so keen to discover what he knew about Tom. He wondered how long the affair had been going on, or whether there was an affair at all. But for what other reason would two people enter a cave hand in hand, in the middle of a party? By what right had he to ask? Only very occasionally did he acknowledge that there were certain rights he had forgone, but in his mind Angela was still his wife. But he would not ask her. In fact he would hide the cutting from her. Neither would he probe amongst the others of the company who were at the party. He feared to acknowledge what he might discover. Yet he needed to know who had passed the information, and he toyed with the idea of driving into Rome himself to find out; but he realized that if he made an issue of a tiny paragraph in a little-read paper, it would balloon into monstrous proportions and filter through the national press beyond anyone's control. No. He would sit tight. Sooner or later he would ferret it out.

That night he met Angela at Sam's café. She was sitting with Hal and Mark Baines. Mark had put his pullover on the seat next to him, keeping it for Alex. Alex's 'secretary' role had been dropped with little ceremony after the first few days, when it quickly became clear what his role was. He had moved into Hal's quarters shortly after his arrival, and Hal had moved in with the village priest, whom he had got to know and like after Tom's death. For the first few nights Hal had kept to his original lodgings, staring across at Tom's empty bed. Then Mark had moved in and slept respectfully on a mattress on the floor. It was only a question of time before he would climb into Tom's bed, and that same night Alex took over the mattress. Together they played the role of hosts and did their best to make Hal feel at home, but it was an untenable situation. Hal had left the following morning.

Alex would spend most of his days sunning himself on the beach. He kept away from the set and the company, and joined Mark only in the evenings. Now he came into the café with his week's bronze, his shirt carefully unbuttoned, boasting the depth of his tan. His hair, fair at all times, was now bleached by the sun, though his eyebrows and lashes retained their original dark brown. He knew, and the knowledge was writ on his face as he walked in the café, that he would never look handsomer. He squeezed Mark's shoulder and sat down beside him. He nodded shyly at Angela. He would not speak unless he was spoken to. He knew his place. He was there for Mark and Mark alone and only Mark could, if he wished, include him in the conversation. When David reached the table, he got up and offered him his seat, but David dragged a chair from the next table and placed it next to Angela. 'Some tan you're acquiring,' he said.

'So would we all,' Mark said, 'if we spent our days like Alex.'

Then Mr Worcester joined them, and Giulietta came over to set the table. Since the film had started, some of the village women had been recruited to help with the running of the café, and what had been a small holiday bistro had now become almost a works canteen. The strain was showing on Giulietta's face. She smiled wanly most of the time, and when she spoke, which was seldom, she insisted on Italian. She saw little of Sam these days. He spent most of his time on the set, or shuttling back and forth to Rome on company business. She was obviously not happy with the situation, as she watched Sam become more and more part of the company. Now he swaggered into the café with Alison the continuity girl, and sat down at one of the tables as if he too were a client. She tried to catch his eye to smile at him, and Mr Worcester, seeing her distress, called Sam over to their table and he drew a chair beside him for Alison. Sam was now placed at the end of the table next to David, and at last Giulietta was able to catch his eye. She went over to him and laid a knife and fork at his place. He caught her arm. He leaned back in his chair and smiled at her, and it was quite clear from the nature of the smile that he had issued it as separately as a garment in order to offset the hurt he was about to give her. 'You know,' he said, for the benefit of the others in a language she found difficult to follow, 'I'm getting terribly homesick.'

Nobody spoke at the table, though each of them knew that Giulietta's marriage was about to founder.

'I'd like to see America again,' he said, as if he had not already said enough. 'Or England. Maybe it's just the language I miss. And conversation,' he added.

But mercifully Giulietta had by then left the table and was setting places at the other end of the café.

'How d'you think Giulietta would take to America?' Mr Worcester asked. 'Or to England, for that matter.'

'It wouldn't work,' Sam said, 'unless I took her whole family with us.'

'Have your folk ever met her?' Alison asked.

'God no. They'd have apoplexy. Though my mother's very like Giulietta. A compulsive feeder. I'm going to miss you all,' he said, 'when you go.'

'We've got a few weeks yet,' Hal said. He didn't like Sam too much, but he felt sorry for him. His marriage had been a mistake. Giulietta was much too good for him, much too serious a person and far more honest. He would have been better off amongst his own dilettante kind.

Giulietta returned with the pasta. She put a plate in front of each of them.

'None for me,' Sam shouted. 'It's coming out of my ears.'

'Marvellous stuff,' Mr Worcester said, mixing it with the sauce.

'You haven't had it every day for the last two years,' Sam said.

'She's a great cook, your wife,' Mr Worcester went on, ignoring Sam's objection.

'She's lots more too,' David said quickly.

'I don't need you to remind me,' Sam said coldly. Then he called over to his wife, holding out his plate, 'I've changed my mind, Giulietta.' She served him, knowing that his change of mind was for the others' benefit. Sam started eating, feeling their eyes on him. He wanted desperately to change the subject. 'What gives with Daphne?' he said.

Daphne Wells, the star of the film, was sitting alone at a small table near the door. She was eating her pasta with little appetite, staring vacantly ahead. After each mouthful she would take some wine, with the bored certainty that no matter how much she drank, she would remain for ever sober.

'There's nothing the matter with her,' Hal said. 'She just likes being on her own.'

'It's more than that,' Mark said. 'She's very touchy. I think she's got husband problems.'

'She's doing a pretty good job anyway,' Hal said. 'She was great today. You've got to give it to her. That bathroom scene. And it's not an easy one. The dialogue was very stilted. Had to change quite a bit.'

Angela looked up suddenly, and David put down his fork. He wanted to shout at Hal, just on the principle of any change, but he knew there was no point in hanging on to unspeakable words in a script simply out of respect for a dead writer. After all, Shakespeare was dead, and his texts were mauled enough in film versions. Tom Welland and William Shakespeare. What's happening to me, David thought. I'm getting as mediocre as the rest of them.

'I hope you're not changing too much, Hal,' was all he could say.

'Well, you see the rushes,' Hal said. 'I don't think Tom would have objected.'

Tom's name had rarely been spoken aloud since he died. David looked quickly at Angela and he noticed how she gripped her fork.

'I'm sure Tom would have approved,' Mark was saying.

That was twice in less than half a minute. Now the licence had been given, and within a few days his name would be bandied around without ceremony, and with it his script. All sanctity had melted from the event. There was an audible sigh of relief round the table. A taboo had been broken, and Tom's name could already be heard from the other tables, not even in a whisper, but with loud and raucous assertion, as if it had been a toy denied them as a punishment, and now, retrieved, they were making up for lost time.

'Was there much about it in the press?' Sam asked.

'No,' David said. 'A few papers reported it. Just the bare facts.' He knew suddenly that Sam had been the informer. 'What else was there to say?' he asked.

'Well, they could have made quite a story out of it, I suppose,' Sam said. 'Sort of thing journalists like to go to town on.'

'Yes,' David agreed, 'but they've got to have a story to go on.'

'They usually make them up.' Sam laughed.

'They might,' David said, 'or they could be fed one.' He put a spoonful of pasta in his mouth and watched Sam out of the corner of his eye.

'I'm surprised at the Roman papers,' Sam insisted. 'It's the kind of story they'd make an apple-pie of.'

The rest of the table, with the exception of Angela, were still kicking Tom's name around, and the subject of press coverage was not only between Sam and David. David leaned towards him, and placed his elbow almost in Sam's chest. 'How much did they pay you?' he hissed. He knew he was taking no risk in identifying the informer. It could have been none of the villagers. They had too much pride. And amongst the company there was a like pride, twisted perhaps with professional loyalty. Sam was a rank outsider to both parties, and he had a great need to feed his own sense of self-importance. Sam dropped his fork, then quickly picked it up, as for Take Two, and then put it down quietly.

'How much did they pay me for what?' he said, deliberately keeping his voice down.

'Don't worry,' David said. 'The others won't be told, and if you want to stay on the pay-roll, you'd better answer me.' David didn't want to fire him. He would have to give too many explanations which might end in compromising not only himself but Angela too. He wanted to keep the matter strictly between the two of them. 'You know exactly what I'm talking about,' he went on. 'Your little tit-bit to the *Roman Courier*.'

'Oh, that,' Sam tried to toss off a laugh. 'They didn't print that, did they?'

'They paid for it, so they printed it. How much?'

'Nothing,' Sam admitted. 'The reporter's a friend of mine.'

'That's all I wanted to know,' David said. He turned his back on him. He found his fist clenched in anger. He didn't know what to do. The discovery of the source had in no way lessened his fury, and he knew that if he looked at Sam again, he would kill him.

Over by the door, Daphne Wells was leaving her table. David got up too, as he felt he had to do something. 'Just going to have a word with Daphne,' he explained. He followed her outside the café, taking her arm. 'Is everything all right?' he said.

'Why not?' she turned to him.

He smelt the wine on her breath and in her hair and all about her, and then he noticed that she was carrying a bottle. He recalled all the bottle-carrying stars of his former productions, and the women were the worst. They were never filmable till after lunch, when their eye-bags would settle. He hadn't known that Daphne was one of them, and it disturbed him a little. 'What are you trying to drown?' he said, touching the bottle and trying to laugh. Then he thought of Tom and his live hand in Angela's and he hoped that Sam would have gone when he got back to the table.

'Nothing,' Daphne was saying. 'I just like the wine in these parts.'

'Are you happy with your rooms?' he said, making conversation. 'You've got the best in the village.'

'Yes, I know,' she said softly. 'They're very comfortable.'

He had hoped she would complain, to give him something to do, something to put right at that very moment so that he could unclench his fist and postpone his anger.

'Good night,' she was saying. 'I'll see you tomorrow.' She kissed his cheek and made for the steps up the cliff.

David turned back to the café. Sam had gone. He must have left by the side door which eventually gave out on to the cliff rock. David went outside again and looked towards the steps. He saw Sam jump from the rock to Daphne's side. He took the bottle from her, and then he took her arm. Daphne stopped to kiss him. David went back into the café, and saw Giulietta standing at the side door watching, covering her face with her hands.

Chapter Ten

The following Sunday, most of the company spent the day on the beach. They lay in the sun separately, dotted amongst the day-trippers from Rome. Angela sat near the water's edge. From time to time, people joined her, but mostly she was alone. She wondered why David did not join her. Since he had arrived, he had not exactly avoided her, but he had not once come forward in a positive meeting. She could see him sitting outside Sam's café. He was drinking what looked like a large orange juice. He was alone, his towel drooped across his knees, and he looked towards the water. He could see her of course, as he could see the others between him and the sea, and he could stare at her, she knew, without her being aware of it.

Which indeed was what he was doing, with the sea as a cover. He did not intend to join her of his own accord, but he would go if she called. That would give him the freedom to attack her, which he would forgo if he went to her voluntarily. Since reading the item in the *Roman Courier*, he had itched to confront her with it, and he knew that until it was done, one way or the other, he could not rest.

Angela watched him until he'd finished his drink. Then she raised her hand, and rubbed her forehead, a gesture that could have been mistaken for a wave. He didn't move. He wasn't too sure. Let her make herself perfectly clear, he thought. She rubbed her forehead again.

"Dear Angela, Why can't we just come together, he and I, naked of the past, unthinking of the future, and face each other only in the honesty of the now. Here is the dialogue and it won't win any prizes for drama and the words are hard to say. But I'll write it for you and try not to listen. 'He: Forgive me. I love you. I want to come back. She: I forgive you. I love you. Please come home.'

"I don't suppose there are two actors in the world who could put that across. Nor any director who would handle it, much less an audience that could stomach it. But it is a dialogue that needs no guidance or witness. It must surely be being said off-stage all the time and all over the place. I would say it, Angela, but I need him as a feed. All right, stop nagging. I'll make the first move."

She waved to him positively, calling with her hand. He got up, then sat down again, toying with his glass. It was clearly on a second thought that he rose and came towards her, and she did not know how to handle his hesitation. She got up as a more welcoming gesture, and when he reached her, she sat down on the sand again, smoothing an area for him beside her.

'Let's walk,' he said.

She got up, but he did not wait. He was already a few yards in front of her. She knew he was making for the cave.

'You been in the sea?' she shouted after him. 'Don't you want to swim?'

'Later,' he said. 'The sea's always there.'

So is the cave, she thought.

'Come on,' he shouted back at her.

'What's the hurry?'

He slowed down and waited for her. 'Seen Sam?' he said.

'No, but I'm not particularly looking for him.'

'Seen Daphne?'

'I'm not looking for her either.'

'Neither of them are on the beach.'

'Jomo Kenyatta isn't on the beach either. Neither is the Queen Mother. It doesn't follow that they're together.' She noticed how he kicked the sand as he walked, as if it had offended him. She knew he had something to say to her. Everything in his manner pointed to a pent-up showdown. She was not totally ignorant of what it was either, as he propelled her, the palm of his hand on her back, towards the cave. At the entrance she stopped. 'Let's not go in there,' she said. 'It's dark and cold and full of God.'

'It didn't stop you before,' he said.

Now it was dribbling out, like the pus from a weeping sore, and he was prepared to let it dribble, hint by hint, innuendo by innuendo. 'Or perhaps you needed the dark,' he said.

She grabbed his arm. 'What are you talking about?'

'Do I have to elaborate?'

'No,' she said, dropping her hand, and half smiling, seeing how ridiculous it all was. 'No, I know what you mean, and what you're trying not to say. But what happened in that cave was something between Tom and me.

It is something that I have to live with. It has nothing whatsoever to do with you.'

'Really?' he said, losing his cool. 'Not even when it's splashed around the papers that the wife of the film producer was the last person to be seen, hand in hand, I may add, in the company of the deceased, I quote, entering a cave together?' Now it was out and he had nothing more left to throw at her, and he felt suddenly defenseless.

She looked at him and said nothing for a long time, so that he could feel his exposure. Then she laughed. 'I'm sorry if I have disturbed your reputation,' she said. She had deliberately misunderstood him, but she was not prepared to defend herself with Tom. That was her own affair, and needed defending only to herself. And then he hit her, hard across the face, because she refused to hear what he was really telling her, which had nothing to do with reputation, or even poor Tom, but that she was his wife and that he wanted, he couldn't say when exactly, to come back to her. Her face smarted with the pain. 'Why?' she said. 'Just why?' But he was walking away and he knew that he had achieved nothing.

"Dear Angela, My face hurts, and I don't know whether I'm crying because the pain smarts my eyes, or because I'm sad, or outraged, or simply bored. Fuck him."

She turned in the opposite direction.

"Dear Angela, What do I do now, now that the old outlet for revenge is stopped up? Since Tom, that way is barred, even in an emergency. What other roads to survival? Find me some good works and I'll do them. Or a pack of cards to patience me away from self-destruction. Or some real real problem, whatever that means, to turn my mind away from this boring, monotonous, unchangeable, repetitive thing, yes, thing, I say, between him and me. Why is there still the pain? Am I making a cult of it? Haven't I said all this to you before, or did I say it to myself when you were eavesdropping? Recede, Angela. Put yourself at cable distance. I have a sudden loathing for fluency of words, for attributes of all kinds, for metaphor, for idiom. I no longer want to dress up my tongue; I will make do now with the basics.

"Help Stop If Message Already Received Please Ignore Stop Advise Address Nearest Leucotomist Stop Must Get Mind Off Mind Regards Angela."

She reached the end of the sands and then the rocks took over. She did not want to turn back, so she climbed, not knowing what was beyond. The rocks were smooth—the tide rarely came in this far—and climbing was easy. She climbed at an angle, and unless she looked behind her, she could not see the sea. In front was a long stretch of almost flat rock with the hint of a drop at the end. Her feet burned on the stone, and she sat down a while, holding them up in the air to cool. Then she ran forward on her toes until she found a small rock-pool, where she could dip her feet. Still she could not see what lay at the end of the rock-table and she was anxious to reach it, for the silence on that stretch was frightening. She could not even hear the beach sounds from the other side nor was there any aural hint of what was beyond. She got up, and climbed to the edge of the rock, and saw the sea again. She was very high over the water, and below her she saw a long slit across the stone, hardly wide enough to slip a foot between. She lay on her stomach and looked through. Far below was a stretch of sand shaped like a cone between the rocks. Some people were in the bay of water, and a small boat was swaying near the rocks on the far side. She wondered whether there was another road to the beach, for the route she had come upon seemed much too bothersome. But she was determined to find her way down to that stretch of sand, though it meant clambering down an almost sheer rock-face. It is only when people are at ease with themselves that they can avoid putting themselves in peril. But in Angela, peril, in the sense of physical danger, was unknowable. In her unhappiness she felt immune to the natural accident. So she clung to the rock and slithered down, feeling with her feet for holds. Had she seen herself from the bottom of the cliff, she would have hidden her face in her hands, as the others on the beach were doing, not daring to shout in case she looked back at them and lost her balance. Slowly they joined together, not taking their eyes off her and walked in a silent line to the base of the cliff.

She did not fear that she would not find a foothold. There was always one waiting. So that when, about half-way down, she stretched her leg and found nothing, swinging it across the rock for a hold, she looked down for the first time and saw the drop beneath her. She tightened her handgrips, and the one foot that was settled, and she laid her head on the rock and was afraid. She was cold suddenly and she stiffened, afraid to tremble lest she should lessen her already precarious hold. She felt the sweat on her forehead and in her armpits, and she knew it had nothing to do with the sweltering sun.

"Dear Angela," she whispered, "I don't want to die. Not this way, not any way really, except in my bed of old age and sadness maybe. I don't want to die, Angela. I want to live: I want to love. I'll forgo that even, just for the living. Find me a foothold, Angela. Oh, why can't there be a bloody Madonna on this rock with folds of a

dress, or a lap or an arm to secure you. What a coward I
am, Angela. You and I have been courting death for so
long. But, by God, we were never serious. We flirted
with death, you and I. We prick-teased with our talk of
ovens. Don't leave me now, Angela. For God's sake,
find me a hold.''

She lowered the arm opposite her loose leg, and her
body lay crouched like a crab on the rock. Those below
turned away their faces. They knew it was the only move
she could make, the only chance she had, but her one
fixed foot could slip in the meantime and that would be
the end.

She swung her foot gingerly over the rock, feeling for a
jagged edge with her toes. Then she heard, 'To your
right, Angela.'

She recognized Mark's voice, and his use of her name
encouraged her. But whose right? Did he mean camera
right, or hers? She tried hers. No hold. Then she moved
her leg in the opposite direction. 'That's right,' she heard
him say.

'A little more over.' That was Alex's voice. She suddenly felt safe in their hands. She stretched her leg as far
as it would go, but still no hold.

'Another foot,' Mark shouted. But another inch was
impossible. She dangled it loose again.

'Move your right hand further to your right,' Mark
said.

But there was a shortage of handgrips too. She looked
across and saw one, but could not gauge whether it was
within her reach. There was no testing it out. She could
only risk heaving herself in its direction.

''Angela?''

Her left foot now cramped at the heel and she knew she

would have to reach a new handhold if she were to relieve the pressure on her leg. She counted up to ten, and at ten she gave herself to twenty. She knew that the longer she left it, the surer fear would paralyse her altogether. But supposing she missed? Supposing when she heaved across and struck out her hand, there was no ace underneath for all her patience, and the game would be dead.

'You can do it,' she heard from below, and the voice seemed distant and short of confidence. She stiffened her body once more.

"Dear Angela," she shouted, "this is no way of living."

She heaved herself across, and caught her hand on a peg of rock. She heard a cheer from below, and now she let her body tremble a little. She let down her left foot. A hold was waiting below, and another for her right. She seemed now to be running and she heard them shouting below. Then arms were around her, carrying her down to the beach, wrapping her in towels, and laying her gently on the sand. One of them brought out a flask of brandy and she sipped from it. Then the trembling turned to laughter and the laughter to tears, rinsing the shock out of her body. Mark and Alex sat by her until she was still, smoothing her forehead until she fell asleep. While she slept, they lay on each side of her, talking in whispers.

Her sleep was light, for she stirred and turned often. Then after a while she sat up, her eyes still closed, and said, 'How do I get back?'

Mark woke her up, and reassured her. 'You don't think we came that way, do you?' he said.

'Is there another?'

'Of course. Alex found it by chance. It's partly swimming. When you're ready, we'll go back.'

He put his arm round her, and so did Alex. Then she got up to test her legs. 'I don't want you to tell anyone about it,' she said.

'Don't worry,' Mark said.

'What about the others?' She nodded to the handful of bathers around them.

'They're from the next village,' Alex said. 'They come here by boat.'

Angela nodded to them. They gesticulated with the occasional Italian expletive, hands on heart, mouths opening in horror, aping her tangled leg movements on the rock. She responded with gestures of thanks, and then the three of them walked hand in hand to the peak of the sand-cone. At the top of the triangle, the rock opened into a low and narrow tunnel. They moved in single file on their knees. The tunnel stretched for about twenty yards. It was dark inside, but Angela followed the whites of Mark's rubber soles. Suddenly she heard a splash, and she saw Mark's hands stretched towards her. He was in the water at the end of the tunnel and she could see the beginnings of their beach and Sam's café only a hundred yards ahead. They waited for Alex to emerge from the tunnel, then they swam together towards the shore.

There was some commotion outside Sam's café. A small crowd clustered about the entrance and loud voices could be heard. As they neared the café, the crowd dispersed and they could see Mr Worcester urging them away. In the space left, they could see Sam's father-in-law struggling with two men from the village who were trying to restrain him from attacking Sam. Sam stood on his own, shrugging helplessly at the by-standers. His father-in-law was screaming at him and shaking his fist, the only part of his body that his restrainers had let free.

At last, the men managed to get him back into the café. Sam walked away. 'He's mad,' he explained to no one in particular. 'He doesn't know what he's talking about.'

But nobody wanted to know. So he latched on to Angela who was just approaching with Mark and Alex.

'What was that all about?' Mark said.

'Something he concocted about me and Daphne. He was yelling about his daughter's honour. Jesus, what a bunch of primitives.' Sam tried to make a joke of it, but it was clear, even to him, that the others didn't find it funny. In fact, they'd left him, standing alone, embarrassed by his own tapering laughter. And then his father-in-law appeared at the café door again, shaking his fist and yelling at him across the sands, so Sam ran into the sea and swam far out, away from the humiliation of it all. The older man watched him, and, still shaking his fist as if to make his intentions clear to everybody, he sat down heavily at one of the tables. It was obvious from his settled angry air that he had every intention of waiting.

As the sun went down over the beach, people gathered their towels and bags to return to the village or the railway station. The old man sat there doggedly, his eyes on the solitary floating figure in the sea. From the café on the piazza overlooking the beach, Angela watched the two of them as the light faded, and both held their stand. But Sam couldn't stay in the sea for ever and, short of crossing the horizon, there was no other exit. So the old man waited, as he could afford to.

In the interval, a crowd had grown on the piazza, and Sam must have seen them and known that the longer he tarried, the greater the spectacle, so he turned and started making for the shore. The old man didn't move. He watched and waited.

When Sam reached the shore, he hesitated. There were about a hundred yards between him and the old man. He could have turned swiftly and clambered up the cliff rock, but he feared the anger of a hostile crowd even more than that of his father-in-law. So he hovered, hesitant, like a bull entering the arena, while the crowd on the piazza fell audibly silent, waiting for the old man's move.

Eventually, he got up and stood in front of the table. Sam took a few steps forward, then stood still. The old man moved too, as pawn to pawn, a formal opening gambit. Sam took a few more steps, but the old man made no further move. He had made his gesture. Now Sam could come to him, and take his punishment. And as Sam approached, it was clear to those in the crowd that there would be no battle. Sam had publicly stained the old man's reputation, and it was Sam's duty to give him an opportunity to restore it. And the crowd stood their ground to bear witness, as the old man would have wished.

So Sam stepped to within a few yards of where his father-in-law stood. Still the old man didn't move. It was important that Sam was seen to approach him, to offer himself for retribution. Sam understood, and placed himself directly in front of him. Then the old man put his hand on Sam's shoulder. From the piazza it looked like a gentle gesture of greeting, but in close shot it was an iron grip. Then, with the other hand, the old man laid about Sam's face and ears, unburdening himself of his anger, punching out his shame. And Sam stood with his hands at his sides, and accepted it. Then the old man paused, and he picked up a towel from the table and folded it round Sam's shoulders. He took off his own jacket, and draped

163

it around the towel. Sam's ears were ringing, and he wiped the blood from his face. He was shivering too with cold, pain and a measure of relief. He was glad to feel the old man's arm around him. Together they walked to their house at the end of the beach, and on the piazza the crowd dispersed.

Daphne Wells had been sitting alone at the café table. She had not joined the crowd at the cliff edge. She had thought it best to keep out of sight. From the look on the crowd's faces, during the beach encounter, she could see that someone on the sands was taking a beating, and it was clear from their sick witness-pleasure that it was Sam. She was surprised when David joined her at her table.

'Nobody won,' he said, sitting down. 'But it wasn't a battle. The old man had a point to make. That's all.'

Daphne said nothing. She sipped her drink.

'Daphne,' David said, leaning forward. 'Sam's got a wife. I don't want any trouble.'

'I'm a wife too,' she said stiffly. 'Or at least I was. Nobody told the slut that my husband went off with that he had a wife.' She sipped her drink again. Then she too leaned forward, smiling. 'Did anyone ever tell Carol?'

'What's that got to do with you?'

'As much as you have to do with Sam,' she said. 'In any case, it takes two to ignore a wife, so don't you come moralizing to me.'

She got up and left the table. David turned in his chair and looked about him. Angela was sitting with Mark and Alex. He should not have felt threatened, he knew. Then why, even of them, should jealousy gnaw at him?

Chapter Eleven

On the set the following morning, Daphne was not filmable. She had arrived for the eight o'clock call, punctually like the good trooper she was, depending on some miracle from the make-up department. Her eyes bulged out of the bags beneath them, bloodshot with tears, lack of sleep, drink or a combination of all three. Mr. Worcester took one look at her and calculated the overtime. Sam looked at her too. Swollen and bruised himself, any facial reaction for him was painful, so he contented himself by muttering, 'Jesus, she looks worse than I do.' Though he felt sorry for her, he decided there and then to end their relationship. It just wasn't worth the physical battering.

Hal conferred quickly with David, and decided to change the shooting-schedule. They would do the exteriors in the mountains behind the village. The sequence involved only Mark and his film girlfriend, Wendy. At this point in the story their affair was in its beginnings, and it was on this walk through the mountains that it would be consummated. Daphne was ordered to sleep the day away, and the rest of the company prepared for the drive out of the village.

'You can take the day off too,' Mr Worcester said to Sam. 'As long as you spend it in bed,' he added, immediately regretting the offer. He suspected he would spend it in bed with Daphne.

'No,' said Sam, relieving him. 'I'll feel better if I'm working.'

'Why don't you bring Giulietta along?' Mr Worcester suggested. 'We won't be eating in the café today.'

'That's a marvellous idea.' Sam was suddenly very grateful. 'I'll go and get her.'

'Can Alex come too?' Mark said. 'You know he's never in the way.'

'If you like,' Mr Worcester said. 'He can look after Giulietta.'

And so they all piled into the cars and drove out of the village. Angela travelled in the camera car. The choice of vehicle was haphazard. It just happened to be there and have a spare seat. As she climbed into the back, she found herself squeezed next to David. Quickly she stood up, and transferred Tom's lighter to the pocket on the other side. Then she sat down again, pressed against him, and she found their proximity embarrassing. She was relieved that the noise of the engine was so loud that conversation was impossible. She had not spoken to him since he had hit her on the beach and she felt he owed her an apology.

"Dear Angela, Will I ever learn? Not everybody acts according to accepted patterns of behaviour. Why must I then be so conventional in my judgment of him? When he hit me on the beach, he was saying he was sorry, as he has said he was sorry with every rotten gesture he has made over the last two years. With every scream at me, with every blow, with every hurt, he is saying, 'I am guilty. Forgive me.' Possible, Angela? Or am I being generous? Or intelligent? Or merely my very own masochistic self. Yes, my lord, I did kill my wife. But I was only trying to say that I was sorry, and I'm sure that she would have understood. And the bloody trouble is, Angela, I do understand. That's what it all means, this rash of platitudes that assails me. To have and to hold, for better or worse, in sickness and in health, till you know who. I have looked at other people's marriages and I have wondered. I have wondered why men step on their women, and why women lie there in the first place. I have wondered at women's appetite for shit and men's compulsive feeding. When I have seen it in others, I have been filled with contempt, but it is me lying on that floor, Angela, and I know that it is I or you who put us there, and what standards we apply to others we must in all honesty apply to ourselves. But rather than self-contempt, we will fashion a rationale for all prone ladies everywhere. So listen, sisters, and spread the good word amongst those prejudiced vertical women standing up for their silly rights. Join the Daughters of the Doormat, and let us link our supine hands. For Masochism is Beautiful.''

The car bounced along the unmade road, churning up sand and dust.

'You worried about Daphne?' Angela said, when the car reached the main road, and the engines were quiet again.

'Not really,' he said. 'As long as she's all right tomorrow.'

'Is she always like this?'

'She's never easy. But she's a professional, and somehow or other she always pulls through.'

'What's her problem?'

'I think the Sam business last night upset her.'

'There must be more to it than Sam. Sam's just a holiday affair. She can't be taking it all that seriously.'

'She has marriage problems, I think,' David said, then immediately regretted it. But Angela was generous. She said nothing and stared out of the window.

The car was climbing again, weaving through the mountain roads, surprising the blind bends, losing and catching sight in turn of the cars ahead. The silence intensified as they climbed. All of them in the car were driving. Most of the road was without a wall on the far side, and far down you could see the sea and their beach and the corrugated iron roof of Sam's café. It would be quiet there today, and the villagers in their respite would know what change had been wrought in them, and they might well be hankering for the days before the occupation.

'I shall miss that village,' Angela said.

The engines rumbled again over a stretch of half-made road. And taking advantage perhaps of the noise, David whispered, 'Shall we have dinner tonight? Just the two of us?'

There was a faint possibility that she hadn't heard. But such a request and at such a time would have been audible for Angela through an earthquake. She looked at him. 'We can drive south to the next village,' he was saying. 'There's a little place just off the road. Get away from all this for a while. We haven't really been together since I arrived.' He was almost pleading with her.

She leaned her head against his shoulder and he ruffled her hair.

'We're stupid, aren't we. Both of us,' he said.

She didn't want to pursue it. It could have led as easily to war as to love. Perhaps he himself would elaborate later on.

"Dear Angela, I am learning. I accept. I question nothing. You will berate me for making do with the crumbs from his table. So what if that is true? Is pride a better diet? I have tried that one, and it leads to starvation. Is dignity more nourishing? To hell with that too. I shall take the crumbs, Angela, together with the consequences. And I shan't come running to you."

The car pulled up in a lay-by behind the others. Hal crossed over into the fields to check the camera set-up, and off-loading began. Angela joined Mr Worcester. Sam was dispatched to the inn further down the road to check on lunch arrangements. The actors concerned in the sequence were in the make-up van. David was talking to Hal. Suddenly everybody was very busy, and Mr Worcester looked round and was content. After the bad start he was prepared to believe that they would have a good day. Only Alex and Giulietta stood on the sidelines, conscientiously keeping out of everybody's way. It took an hour for Hal to arrange the set-up and start to rehearse. He was going to shoot the last section of the sequence first, when Mark and Wendy, after a silent walk through the woods, come upon a clearing, where they claim fatigue, sit down to rest, and inevitably make love. Hal had chosen a known beauty spot. They had cleared it of picnic traces, stuffed pine cones into old footprints, so that it looked as if it were discovered for the first time. The ground was crackling and autumnal, but a distinct summer sun shone through the trees of the sparse forest behind and lit the clearing with yellow shafts of light. It was a lighting cameraman's delight. A single small tree, a pine sapling, trembled in the middle of the clearing, like a stray from a litter, and the love-making was to be shot through the filigree of its branches. Hal was coming into his own. If David hadn't drawn the line, he would have ordered Vaseline on the lenses.

There was a verge behind the cameras, and those not directly concerned with the production took their places on the grass to watch. Giulietta was sitting with Sam, who had returned from the inn, and Angela found herself with Alex.

'Have you seen Mark working before?' she asked.

'No,' he said. 'We've only been together for the last six months, and most of that time he's been working in television. It's a bit difficult to be a spectator in the studio.'

'Well, you ought to see him in a new light,' she said. She sensed that Alex was nervous. He was shifting himself on the grass, backing away, as it were, as if he regretted he had come. Angela looked in the clearing. Mark had his arm round Wendy and was easing her to the ground. Although it was only a rehearsal for camera positions, Mark was putting his heart into the job, whereas Wendy was almost stiff in his embrace, concerned only with landing on the right spot. Alex obviously dreaded the real thing.

Hal watched the movements in front of the actors, then he checked them in the camera. 'Fine,' he said. 'Let's go from your entrance, Wendy. Mark, you're about four seconds behind her, but keep behind the trees till then. Stop when you're about four yards from the tree. About here,' he said, showing him. 'Then you put your hand on her shoulder. O.K.? Then walk together, up to Wendy's line "I don't know," and then down both of you by the tree. Let's have a run-through.' He stood back while Mark and Wendy disappeared behind the clearing. Then he called, 'Action.'

Wendy entered the clearing like a startled gazelle. It was her big scene, the scene on the basis of which she might or might not get other work, and she was going to play it as her very own cameo, with sublime indifference to what went fore or aft. When Mark touched her shoulder, she responded as to a thunderbolt, and she sank to the ground like an asp-sucked Cleopatra. Mark was clearly embarrassed by all her shenanigans, as indeed were all of the spectators. Hal called a stop, and went up to them so that his comments and directions would not be heard by the others. 'Try it again,' he said, walking back.

This time Wendy underplayed. She stepped into the clearing, and without a pause, went mechanically to the tree as if she was sulking. There she waited for Mark's hand on her shoulder, and obediently folded her knees under her. It was now incumbent on Mark to arouse some semblance of passion in her, which he did with what seemed effortless enthusiasm.

Alex got up. 'Let's go,' he said to Angela.

She went with him immediately because she feared he might make a scene and he was clearly disturbed. They ran down the verge and heard Hal's voice, 'Let's do it again.' Then she took Alex's arm and they walked back towards the cars.

'What's the matter?' she said.

'Mark's been married once. He could do it again.'

Yes, that was logical enough, and there was not much she could say to reassure him.

'But he's not made that way,' Alex was saying. 'I

171

know him. I understand him. He won't accept what he is.'

'Which of us does?' said Angela, and her logic was equally irrefutable. 'In any case,' she added, trying to comfort him a little, 'Wendy's not his cup of tea at all.'

'That's not the point. She's a woman. She represents a breakthrough. She's some kind of proof for him. But he knows it doesn't work. He's had proof of that too.'

What could she say to him? All his surmises were very secondary to his prime feeling of loss, as her criticisms of Carol were secondary and irrelevant to the basic fact of rejection. The quality or otherwise of one's rival was independent of the pain that gnawed with a stubborn constancy, whether or not the rival was admissible. 'Jealousy won't hold him,' she said. 'Not if you show it, like now. Petulance and sulks are a bore, and they'll drive him away.' She knew that surely from her own experience, and between them, as two people who loved and who were threatened, there was no difference. 'Let's go back,' she said. 'After all, you wanted to see him work, and that's how you must look at it. For exactly what it is. Acting.'

He went back with her reluctantly. At the edge of the verge, and far from the others, almost out of earshot, they sat down. They were still rehearsing, and Wendy was in Mark's arms. She'd loosened up considerably, and she was responding with appetite. Alex looked green. It didn't matter that they were out of hearing. What the actors were saying couldn't have made matters worse.

'It's only acting,' she whispered to Alex.

His response startled her. He moved close and put his arm round her shoulder, fondling her hair. He no doubt hoped to catch Mark's eyes.

'You see,' she said, smiling. 'You can do it too, and you don't mean it any more than he does.'

'That's not true,' he said doubtfully. 'I wouldn't use you in that way.'

Still she let him fondle her, while the rehearsal proceeded. Hal stopped them often. He was clearly not satisfied. Then he called for a break. He felt perhaps he was pushing them too hard. Besides, he needed a cold drink himself and a little time to think of a new approach. The company broke up and made for the refreshment car. Mark leapt up the verge to join Alex, but Alex turned away, gripping Angela's waist, leading her from the crowd. 'Let's go for a walk,' he said.

Angela took his hand away, slowed him down, and forced him to wait for Mark. He clearly wanted a quarrel for the sheer pleasure of making it up. She waited for Mark, then muttered some excuse and left them. When she reached the refreshment car, she looked back and saw them still standing on top of the verge. Alex was kicking the grass about him, sulking. Mark was gesticulating helplessly. Then he ruffled Alex's hair and roared with laughter.

'Want a drink?' Angela shouted to them. They waved and came running down the verge. Hal was talking to Wendy, and as Angela passed them with the drinks, she overheard Wendy pleading, 'Yes, but he's not exactly a man to make love to.'

'Has it ever occurred to you,' Hal said, as kindly as he was able, 'that half the best actors around are homosexual, so you'd better get used to that fact if you want to keep in work. In any case,' he added, 'Mark probably has the same feelings about you.'

"Dear Angela, Documentary films are far cleaner."

The three of them sat together by the road. 'Mark and I

are having dinner together tonight,' Alex said. 'Want to come with?' They were both for some reason grateful to her, and they wanted her to share their joy of each other.

'Thanks,' she said, 'but I've already got a date.' This very proudly.

'Uh-huh,' Mark said. 'Dare I guess?'

'You can have a try.'

'Hal?' Mark tried.

She shook her head.

'Mr Worcester?' was Alex's offering. Then they ran out of possibilities.

'That's a pretty poor reflection on me,' Angela laughed. 'Can you think of no other eligibles?'

So they went through all the male members of the company, even including Sam. Everybody, that is, except David.

''Dear Angela, Why is something that is so desperately obvious to me so absolutely unthinkable to anybody else? Or are they deliberately withholding the name to spare me the hurt of their possible blunder?''

'My husband,' she said, straight as she was able.

'Really?' There was a glow in Mark's eye, hopefully envisaging future possibilities.

'No,' she said, quenching it. 'We're just having dinner.'

'Well, you never know,' Alex said, surer now, his hand on Mark's shoulder. 'Dinner for two. Candlelight.'

'It's not that easy,' she said.

Hal called them back to work and Angela was glad that she could get off the subject. Although she trusted Mark and Alex, probably more than anyone else in the company, and knew of their goodwill, she didn't want to discuss her marriage or lack of it with anybody. Except perhaps with Angela, and sometimes she saw even her as an intruder. As for this evening, she wanted to play it by ear with no anticipation and no rehearsal.

Mark and Wendy were rehearsed till lunch-time, and Hal hoped to get the scene in the can by early afternoon. The light would have changed too radically to shoot the mountain-walk sequence. He was none too happy with the way the day had been spent.

It took another hour of rehearsal after lunch before Wendy was just about passable. Four takes in all and each take worse than the last. At tea-time, Hal decided to call it a day. He had to face the fact that Wendy had given him of her best and that her best was not nearly good enough. Her poor performance had affected Mark too, and nobody, except perhaps Wendy, was pleased with the day's work. It put David in a bad mood too. Mr. Worcester held out a possible hope of a reshoot before they left for the final shooting in Rome. Perhaps over the next couple of weeks Wendy might improve. But no one had much confidence in that possibility. All in all, they returned to the village dejected, and in each car, except that which carried Wendy, they held accusing post-mortems.

The piazza café was deserted when they arrived. It was too early for the evening aperitif and most of the villagers were still working. Angela offered to check on Daphne's health and countenance, but Mr Worcester suggested they left it till dinner. The company dispersed to their various beds, baths, self-recriminations and resolutions. Only Wendy looked happy. But by about seven o'clock, as the piazza filled and the sun warmed with its setting, the company was resilient again. The bad day's work was resolved to be forgotten, even by Hal who was drinking it away at the bar. Mr Worcester, who had gone to visit

Daphne, was now seen walking with her, arm in arm, along the road that led to the square. From the distance she looked radiant, and one could hear her laughter. 'My God,' Hal said. 'Some transformation. What happened?'

'She had a wire from her husband,' Penny, the publicity assistant, said. 'I took it up to her this morning. He's in Rome on business and he's coming down tonight to see her.'

'Her face must have been on ice all day,' Hal said. He walked out to meet them and ushered them to the table where David sat with Angela. She did indeed look beautiful. She had little make-up, but her cheeks were glowing with a child's excitement. The deflated bags under her eyes had left the skin milky, and a clear blue vein underneath proclaimed a certain frailty. Mr Worcester brought over drinks for all of them and they drank to Daphne and her recovery. No one spoke about her husband though it was obvious that everybody knew, and soon it seemed unnatural not to refer to it. 'You're busy tonight, we hear,' David said, bringing it into the open.

'We'll have dinner together, I suppose?' she said, trying to make light of it. She obviously didn't want to talk about it, and yet she had to tell somebody what she feared, what she could hardly believe possible yet which filled her with dread. Angela noticed her reticence and intuitively felt the need to break it down.

'Have you thought where you're eating?' she said, to keep the conversation going.

'Oh, I don't know,' Daphne almost shouted at the table. Her happiness was on the verge of hysteria. Then quietly she said, 'How can I be sure he's coming on his own?'

'Oh, he wouldn't,' Angela said, and she felt David

nudge her under the table. It was a mistake to dismiss it as a total impossibility. He knew Daphne's husband, and that was just the sort of gesture he was capable of.

'You can't,' David said to her gently but with authority. 'But if he's not alone, you can refuse to see him. Or you can make the best of it.'

Hal sighed. He began to reschedule for the following day.

'Look,' David went on. 'Angela and I are going down to the Medici tonight. If the going gets tough, come and eat with us. It's easier when there are more around.'

'D'you think he'll bring her?' Daphne said, now understanding that it wasn't such a remote possibility.

'I don't know,' David said. 'Everything's possible.'

'No, no, no,' Mr Worcester interfered, dabbing Daphne's eyes as he saw the tears welling. 'You look beautiful. Don't spoil it, and we're all on your side. Now drink up. We're ready for another round.'

'What time is he coming?' Angela asked.

'He didn't say. Just this evening.'

'D'you want us to wait around?'

'No,' she said. 'There'll be plenty of people here to catch me if I fall.'

'You'll be all right,' David said, getting up and squeezing her arm. 'You have to be. We're making a picture. Remember? Anyway, we all missed you today.' He took Angela's arm and led her to the car. Mr Worcester looked after them benevolently. 'Don't forget,' David called back. 'We're at the Medici.'

They settled in the car and drove off. 'Poor devil,' Angela said. 'She's terrified. You don't think he'll bring his girl with him, do you?'

'Anything's possible with Peter,' David said. 'I like

177

your dress,' he went on, anxious to change the subject. 'Is it new?'

She laughed. 'You bought it for me three years ago. For our wedding anniversary.'

He changed gear. History. They said nothing as they climbed the hill out of the village, and the following mile of unmade track silenced them further. 'You've altered it,' David said, when they turned into the main road. 'The neck was different.'

'Yes. I cut it low. This evening, in fact. Thought I'd seduce you.' She laughed.

'I don't need that kind of bait. Not with you.' He put one arm around her. 'I had to ask Daphne,' he said. 'You understood, didn't you?'

'Of course. But I hope for her sake, as well as ours, it won't be necessary.'

They were travelling easy. With his arm round her shoulder she felt whole, fretless, and totally in the present. She took his hand and lowered it to her lips, and he leaned sideways, kissing her head.

There was no traffic on the road, and David was driving more or less in the middle. Since they'd left the village, they hadn't met another car, so they were surprised when, in the distance, they heard the heralding roar of a sports car. Its driver, too, was driving in the middle of the road, and as they approached each other, they gently curved to their own sides. The car passed with a wave from its driver. At his side, or rather welded to his side, was a girl, and from what Angela could see of her face, half hidden in the man's shirt, it was very young and beautiful.

'Good God,' David said.

'What's the matter?'

'That's Daphne's husband.'

'The shit,' Angela said. 'Well, I reckon we can expect company. Poor Daphne.'

'She'll either hit the roof,' David said, 'or she'll play the star. Either way, those two will get their money's worth.'

'Why must people hurt each other so?' Angela said, almost to herself.

'Not everybody. Some try to make amends.'

She moved closer to him and they drove the rest of the way in silence. The lights of the Medici could be seen from the road. Its buildings straggled across the top of the hill, and as they turned off the main road they could hear its music. Angela was excited. 'I feel like dancing,' she said.

'Do you? Anything you feel like, you shall do. We're going to enjoy ourselves.'

She wished he wouldn't make such a decision about it, as if one had to make up one's mind to happiness.

'Whether the others come or not,' he added, and that rider eased her a little.

They parked the car at the top of the hill, on the outskirts of the gardens. He took her arm and they walked along the paths skirting the lily-pond and flower-beds. Most of the diners were sitting outside on the long patio. Inside they could see the dancers. The music was old fashioned, and called for close dancing and dependence on your partner for steering. The band had the sort of repertoire which unfailingly included somebody or other's 'our tune'. Yes, it augured well, all of it: the flowers, the wine, the music and even a token crescent moon that later on would assert its yellow against a darker sky.

They found a table in a small niche at the end of the

balcony which kept them unseen though open themselves to a view of the hills.

'What will you drink?' David said. 'Campari?'

She nodded, smiling. 'I'm in your hands. You order everything for me. You know what I like.'

He was gratified. Nothing had changed. 'Let's dance,' he said. 'If I haven't forgotten how.' He led her through the balcony on to the floor. Only a few couples were dancing, and all of them very close. It would have seemed almost disrespectful on that floor to keep a distant partner. He held her close, gently but somehow desperately, as if he would lose her. Angela trembled. She was suddenly unfamiliar with the sensations under her skin. She had known them long ago, and their association was totally virginal. They were feelings that could be induced at will by recollecting, step by step, a loving encounter. She remembered how, as a schoolgirl, her friend's brother, Richard, down from University, had taken her out. They had walked over Hampstead Heath, and had taken two hours to touch hands, and then only by apologetic accident. And then sensations had pricked her skin, and at night she had lain in bed retracing their steps over the grass, to the point of the touch, and the joy on her skin was almost unbearable.

David held her closer as the music crescendo'ed into finale. When the band stopped, they held together for a while, and then he led her back to their table. She hoped he would say nothing, and indeed he hoped the same of her. The waiter arrived with their drinks, and to take their order. 'We have time,' David said. 'Shall we have our drinks first?'

The waiter bowed himself away. Yes, they had time, Angela thought, and for them it was only just beginning.

A waltz wafted to their table. They looked at each other, shook their heads and laughed. They had met over a waltz, when he had practically crippled her. No training on earth could have touched him with triple time. She had nursed her foot as he helped her off the floor. 'Don't write me off altogether,' he had said. 'There are certain things I *can* do.'

Well, he'd proved that all right, and she didn't want to think about it. Neither did he, and he lifted her glass to her mouth, toasting her. 'Stay with me tonight?' he whispered. Then he realized what he had said. He thought of Carol and what she had told him at the airport, and a sick lump leapt into his throat. He swallowed and said it again, knowing that he had no right to ask. 'Will you?'

Suddenly Angela broke into her, setting off an alarm of fear. She nodded without smiling. He was telling her, and there was absolutely no doubt in her mind, that he was coming home.

He leaned back and called the waiter over. They studied the menu together, but she let David choose for her. When the waiter left, David looked out over the balcony, and from the expression on his face Angela could see that their evening had been broken. She leaned across. Daphne, starring in the centre, her husband and the girl on either side. They were walking towards the balcony. Only Daphne was smiling, as much as her stiff upper lip would allow. David waved, standing up and motioning them to the table. 'I'm sorry,' he shrugged to Angela, 'but what can we do?'

The waiter brought them more chairs, while Daphne introduced her partners. 'My husband,' she said pointedly. 'Peter, this is Mr and Mrs Morrow.' She had chosen her lines with care. 'And this,' with freezing cordiality, 'is Carol.'

"Dear Angela, What else? Are they all called Carol, this race of parasites that batten off married backs? I would like to lay her fair and beautiful head on this table, and pound it with these forks; take the cheeks between my thumbs and fingers and manually maim. I would ravage her to the brink of dying, and pray that her demise be slow and infinitely painful."

'How do you do?' Angela said, keeping her hands firmly behind her back.

They all sat down and wondered what to say to each other. It was Daphne who kept the ball rolling. She was an intelligent woman, but capable of small-talk when it was in order. 'Is this your discovery, David?' she said. 'And have you been keeping it to yourself? Is the food good here?'

David answered each question in turn, spinning it out, knowing that Daphne was too hurt to keep this kind of chit-chat going for too long. He waited for the waltz to peter out and then he asked her to dance. It would get her away for a little while at least. He looked to Angela for her understanding. She nodded and smiled, and turned her smile as it froze into Peter and Carol. Then she turned it slowly on Peter. 'Do you go to Rome often?' Small-talk for small people.

'I do business there. Typewriters.'

'And you're the shorthand side of it, I suppose,' Angela withered at Carol. Carol giggled. She could see a joke when one was offered. Back to Peter. 'Are you staying long?'

'I've got to be in Rome tomorrow.'

'You'll have to drive back tonight then.'

'No. We'll probably stay in the village and leave early in the morning.'

You filthy rotten bloody swine, she thought, and she put his head on the table too and mashed them both to pulp.

'Have you been in the business long?' Peter was saying.

She didn't want to talk to him any more, but because she had to say something, she was going to make it short. 'Yes,' she said.

He heard the finality of it, and turned to Carol, taking her hand. 'Carol's in films,' he said. 'The other side of the cameras of course.'

But Angela didn't react. She opened her bag, took out a single cigarette, lit it quickly herself, and picked up her drink. Had she had a book with her, she would have started reading.

So they sat, the three of them, without talking, until Peter got the message.

'Well,' he said, 'will you excuse us. We're going to dance.'

'Of course,' she said, glad to be rid of them.

So she was left alone at the table with a drink to occupy her—and, "Dear Angela, I have the violence and it frightens me. Not that I shall turn in on myself—you and I have ways of skirting that—but that I shall vent it on someone else. Yet I am killing all the time, am I not, in my cosy intellectual way. Stuart and the rest, to say nothing of poor Tom. Yet I sit here, inches near these two monsters, symbols of my pain—the pain, God knows, of a million other women. I sit here, with four sharp knives within reach, my heart butcher-breaking, and I have to solder my hands to my side. How else can I use my anger? If it were only breath that one could exhale with water at the ready to quench the fire. If it were only a sudden scream that, once discharged, would break the barrier of pain. But it is not so easily discardable. It lodges at no constant site, it keeps no natural season; it has no process or degrees of growth. It arrives and remains in its prime. What is Daphne doing, Angela? What role is she playing, and where has she hoarded her anger? I could never play such a part. Is there some extra strength or virtue in her that we lack, or is this *her* survival-kit? I dread the remainder of this evening, and I'd like to go home right now. It was all so miraculous until they came, but somehow their company is doom-laden. Yet there is something almost farcical about it all. Such extremes of insensitivity are, from a certain viewpoint, laughable. But my God, Angela, they're us. Daphne's us, Peter's David, and she's her. Then why can't I find that viewpoint and fall about laughing.''

David and Daphne came back to the table. She had wanted to leave the floor as soon as she had seen Peter and Carol dancing. She still looked radiant, though the high colour on her cheeks might have indicated the beginnings of a small fire. She sat down and took a cigarette. 'I made it, you see,' she said to Angela.

'I think you're doing wonderfully.' She didn't want to say more than that in case Daphne would be broken by her dignity. But she had to infer that she and David were on her side.

'What are we going to eat?' David said. They studied the menu that the waiter had left on the table. Daphne, like Angela, left her dishes to David, and David was happy to order for the three of them. Peter and Carol came back shortly afterwards, and their ordering was apart, as if they had separate tables. Angela noted Carol's taste with contempt. A prawn cocktail, steak and chips, which sounded more passable as *allumettes,* and a Coca-Cola. Daphne sniffed, but whether from disdain or an attempt to hold back tears was hard to say. Angela smiled at her, just slightly, knowing well how a lump in the throat can so easily explode to kindness or praise. Each of them hoped the food would come soon. It had become an evening that had to be swallowed rather than enjoyed.

Carol's cocktail was the first to arrive. The others had ordered asparagus, which took longer to prepare, but Carol started on her dish immediately, sulking for her Coca-Cola, so that by the time the asparagus arrived Carol had finished. She lit a cigarette and puffed over the *hollandaise.*

'How's the film going?' Peter directed at David. He wanted conversation. The idea of not thoroughly enjoying the evening had not occurred to him. He could see no reason why they shouldn't all be very happy.

'We're on schedule,' David said. 'It seems to be going pretty well.'

'And how's my wife doing?'

Angela shuddered at the word. It was all so familiar.

'She's wonderful,' David said, putting his hand on hers. 'As she is always.'

"Dear Angela, D'you notice how moved David is by Daphne's situation, how considerate and understanding he's being towards her? Does he see for one moment that Daphne is me, and that that man whom he so patently loathes across the table is his own reflection? Do guilty men grow image-insulators, current-taping their vision and understanding? Or am I being clever again. Stay around, Angela. I had hoped I wouldn't need you, and I am hoping still.''

They continued talking about the film, with Peter making most of the running. He seemed genuinely interested in Daphne's work, and spoke of her as if she weren't there. David included her all the time, but she was content to sit smiling, probably because she daren't risk opening her mouth for fear of explosion. Carol fretted for her steak and chips and another coke. So it was Peter and David who held such fort as there was. Angela kept to the side-lines. Everyone was relieved when the second course arrived. David and Daphne had ordered pheasant. Angela was trying the local lamb dish that looked more Provençal than Italian, while Peter's looked the same as Carol's only bigger. They started together, and when the conversation ceased, Angela realized that Daphne hadn't uttered a word since she had returned to the table. She was looking fixedly at her food, and the colour on her cheekbones was threatening. Suddenly she wanted the evening to end, and she started to eat quickly as she could see David was doing. Both of them sensed the danger in the situation, in their artificial togetherness, in their cold politeness to each other.

'I don't suppose you've got all that time,' David said, as if to excuse his own hurried eating. 'It's a long drive back to Rome.'

'Take your time,' Peter said, and Angela's heart lurched. 'We're not going back tonight. We'll find some bed in the village and leave early in the morning.'

Daphne put down her fork, and Angela could see that her hand was clenched. David was not quite sure that he had heard correctly. 'Did you say that you were staying in the village?' he said.

Daphne didn't need to hear it twice. She raised her two hands and held them in front of her. She looked as if she were gently studying her palms. Then her fingers were seen to bend and stiffen like the rigid pincer of a crab. Only Angela noticed what was happening, because she felt and could predict every movement with her own hands, so she understood when Daphne turned her hands steadily as if on a pivot and with them framed Carol's face. Carol looked up from her chips, startled. David watched and waited. Peter went on eating unawares, and it was not until Carol shifted sharply in her chair that he noticed that anything untoward was happening. Daphne had clamped Carol's face and placed her two thumbs like a gag over her mouth. At this stage, Angela's hands ceased predicting. In seconds, Daphne had torn down Carol's cheeks, drawing blood. It was the kind of action that had to be done quickly before thought could temper it. For one second she let go the thumbhold on Carol's mouth, but only to punch viciously at her gums. The blood spurted along with remnants of steak and chips that poor Carol had relished only a few seconds before. She opened her mouth to cry out, but Daphne's thumb was quick on the draw, and left just enough opening to reveal an ugly jagged gap where a tooth had been. Carol's dress was smeared with blood and food, and what looked like a pearl button on the bodice dropped to the table as the tooth. Daphne picked up the steak knife and Angela sprang to her feet. David and Peter sat as if transfixed, watching, glued to their seats. Angela tried to get the knife out of Daphne's hand while shielding Carol's face. But now Daphne's fight was with Angela too, and she managed to knock Angela backwards and Angela had to release her hold. Now Daphne had time. Thought could have caught up with her long ago, but she held the knife close to Carol's face, and for a few seconds waited. It was this pause that she gave herself before cutting into Carol's cheek that robbed her of the long-held role of victim. Angela hated her then and she pushed her back with all her strength, so that the knife fell from her hand and she reeled back on to her chair.

Angela held Carol close, dabbing the blood with a serviette. Because of the isolated position of their table, none of the other diners had seen what had happened. It had been a quick and silent retribution. Carol was crying, and Angela comforted her, holding her fair head to her breast, and rocking her gently.

"Dear Angela, What am I doing?"

At last, Peter and David reacted. And both towards Carol. 'We must get her to hospital,' David said. 'She needs stitches. I'll take you. I know the way. We'll go in my car.'

Angela wrapped her coat around Carol, smoothed her hair and handed her to Peter. David had already gone to fetch the car.

'I'll carry you, my darling,' Peter said, lifting her in his arms. She was sobbing quietly. 'It's all right, sweetheart,' Peter was saying. 'No damage done. You're still beautiful.' He said it with little conviction. Carol would never be beautiful again.

As he carried her down the slope, Daphne spoke for the first time. Her voice was low and controlled. She picked the tooth out of the mess on the table and held it towards him. 'Here,' she said with disdain, 'you might need this. You never know. They perform miracles nowadays.'

When they had gone, Daphne was able to cry, and Angela didn't know whether or not to comfort her. Her sympathy for Daphne had waned considerably, but now that she was alone and with so much damage done, she was so clearly the loser that Angela could not help but be sorry for her. 'How do you feel now?' she asked, and her concern was equal only to her curiosity.

'Sorry,' Daphne said. 'Just sorry. Thank you for stopping me. I would have killed her.' She shivered. 'She's in a bad shape, isn't she?'

'Nothing that cosmetic surgery can't cope with,' Angela said. 'She'll survive.' Then, after a pause, 'But will you?'

'I've thought of doing what I've just done every day for the past year. Though it was killing I was after. But now, I don't feel any better for it.'

'Did you ever think of doing the same to Peter?' Angela asked. The question was purely academic.

'No,' she said. 'Isn't that strange? I blame her totally, though I know that's stupid. But I suppose it's because I still love him.'

The waiter came to their table and exploded at the state of the cloth. Angela apologized. It had been an accident, she told him, and she helped him clear the debris. Then she ordered coffee and a brandy for them both.

It was an hour before David returned. They were keeping Carol in the hospital and Peter would stay with her until she slept. He'd come to take them back to the village, and then he would return to take Peter to his car. He settled the bill while they waited in the car for him. Then he drove them away without a word.

"How is she?" Daphne dared to ask.

'D'you care?' David said coldly.

'Of course she cares,' Angela shouted at him. 'Can't you see she's sorry?'

189

'She'll live,' David said, 'though her face is likely to be a mess for some time. God, what an evening.'

The drive to the village was silent. At the back of the car Daphne was crying, and as her sobs became louder David said, 'Look, Daphne, I know you're feeling pretty bloody, or you ought to be, but I want you on the set tomorrow morning at eight o'clock, and I want you filmable. So stop blubbering.' He did not attempt to disguise his anger. Daphne gave one last wail and was silent. By the time they reached the village she was composed again.

It was only eleven o'clock and the piazza café was full. 'Go straight to bed,' David ordered. 'Both of you. There's no need for anyone else to know what's happened. Peter will probably drive straight back to Rome, so no one need ever know. Eight o'clock tomorrow,' he said, opening the door for them. And harshly to Angela, 'I'll see you in the morning.' He made a quick U-turn and was gone.

'I'll walk with you to your place,' Angela said. 'Let's go round the back and avoid the square.'

Daphne was crying again, as if it were permitted now that David had gone. 'Will you be all right?' Angela said when they reached the door.

'Yes. I'll take a couple of sleeping pills.'

Angela was loath to leave her. Her distress was so plain, beyond apology to anyone, even to herself.

'I never thought I would feel like this,' Daphne said as she opened the door. It was the one road she had possibly banked on with all her despairing lack of logic, and it had led only to a dark pit.

'See you in the morning,' Angela said.

Daphne closed the door. Angela heard her going up the stone steps inside, pausing from time to time. She listened until she heard another door click, and then she ran, by-passing the square, down to the beach, and to her own lodgings.

She lay in bed not able to sleep. She had not wholly abandoned the hope that David would come to her.

"Dear Angela, I have a feeling we learned a lesson tonight. If nothing else results from this evening, it is clear that Daphne has lost Peter for good. She knows it too. What has happened to her anger now that it is vented? She has it still, impotent now, and so more violent. I hope that she is sleeping.'

She lay listening to the noises from the piazza. She heard a few faint 'Good nights', then the pulling down of shutters. The café had closed. She strained her ears. She was listening for a car. She wouldn't sleep until David came back. It was only a few minutes drive from the hospital. By now he must have dropped off Peter at his car. That left twenty minutes to drive back to the village, and all that time had already elapsed. So she listened and was glad when all other sounds ceased, and nothing could muffle his return.

"Dear Angela, Why am I waiting in order to be disappointed yet again? In order to hear his car arrive, and the echo of his footsteps as they by-pass the beach road. But I am entitled to hope. More entitled now than Daphne. Oh Angela, I hope that she is sleeping."

She heard the car screech on the gravelled car park. And she waited. The door slammed. She could not help but run to the window. She saw him cross the piazza with not even a side-glance at the beach road. So she went back to bed.

"Good night, Angela. There is some consolation in knowing that there are certain things that I have *not* done."

* * *

She woke very suddenly, and looked at her watch. Three o'clock. Why had she woken? There had been no noise, no dream to struggle out of. It was the thought of Daphne that had woken her, the thought with which she'd gone to sleep, and it had knocked on her mind for answer. She noticed that she was trembling. She dressed quickly and ran along the sand. There was only the light of the moon that picked out the road on the cliff, and that was dim, filtered through heavy cloud. Through some sense of urgency that came from outside her own thoughts, she started to run. She tripped over the first step of the cliff and grazed her calf. She cried out with the stiff stabbing pain, which was quickly gone. At the top of the cliff, she climbed over the piazza wall. It was quicker than going to the end of the steps and round the square. There was no light on in the village and she had to grope for the café steps. There was a short-cut through the side-entrance and she prayed that the gate was open. But the fixed chain glinted at her approach. Without thinking she jumped over it, and realized only when she landed what she had done. Her heart beat with terror of what she knew she would find. Down four more wide steps, and the length of an alley to Daphne's front door. It was open. She had never been to her room before, but she knew it was the best in the house, and therefore the one on the balcony. The door at the top of the steps was shut, and she prayed that Daphne hadn't locked it. She knocked, and for the first time since she had woken she considered the possibility that her imaginings were of her own, and had nothing to do with Daphne's sleeping soundly in her bed. And what reason could she give for coming if Daphne woke up? She knocked again, nevertheless, louder this time, but there was no answer. Gently she tried the door. It was locked. But a woman was entitled to lock her bedroom door in the house of strange people. But when she knocked again, very loud this time, the only response was from the owner of the house, whom she recognized as the barman of the piazza café. He spoke no English and she tried to tell him with what little Italian she had, together with contortions of her body, that something might have happened to Daphne, and she had to get inside to see. He understood at once, and motioned her to follow him outside. There was a ladder on the patio that he leaned on to the balcony, and Angela scrambled to the top, hoping that he would not follow her. She climbed over the wrought-iron balustrade and saw that the french windows were mercifully open. She could see Daphne lying face down on the bed, and it was clear that she was more than sleeping. She rushed to the bed and tried to wake her. Daphne was breathing very deeply and with a slight snore.

She tried to turn her on her back to look more closely at her body, as if it might give some clue. And as she pushed the body over, three empty pill bottles fell to the floor. On the bedside table was a note.

"Dear Angela, What am I doing? A woman's dying and I'm standing here reading her letters."

'Peter darling,' it said. 'No time to write. I am in a terrible hurry. I leave you all my love. Daphne.'

Angela stuffed the note in her pocket, unlocked the door and ran from the house. David's lodgings were on the other side of the square. Her knees ached with the unfamiliar speed, and as she came within shouting distance of David's house, she called his name. By the time she'd reached the stone steps leading to his door, he was leaning out of his window. One or two other faces appeared, but she ignored them. 'Come quick,' she called. 'Daphne's taken an overdose.'

'Get Mr Worcester,' he shouted. 'I'll go right over.'

She leapt over the fence to the cliff, and scrambled down on her belly.

"Dear Angela, What a night."

She knocked at Mr Worcester's door as gently as the urgency would allow. He answered immediately and she went in and told him. Up the cliff once more and straight to Daphne's house. David was already there and they met him carrying her down the stairs. 'I'll take her to the hospital,' he said. 'I think she'll be all right. I'll need your help, Mr Worcester.'

Together they carried her limp and heavy body to the car. Angela opened the door. 'Shall I come with you?'

'You go back to bed, Angela,' Mr Worcester said. 'You've had enough for one evening.'

She went round to the driver's seat. 'Go to bed, darling,' David said. 'Someone's got to be fit for tomorrow.'

She watched them down the gravel path and out of sight. If she walked down to the square, she could wait and see the car on the mountain road. Within minutes it had climbed to the flat and she watched it as it disappeared down the slope, and she waited till its noise had faded.

In her room, she lay on her bed and let her body throb. She was tired, with a physical exhaustion she hadn't felt for a long time. She undressed slowly, lying down, and as she kicked her jeans to the floor, Tom's lighter fell with a thud.

"Dear Angela, Tom almost got his way with the script tonight. She tried to give Tom his due. She faced her own fragility, and she tried to die. What will Peter say? Has she, with this action, gained on the swings what she lost earlier on the roundabouts? Is everyone back to square one? But Carol still has the advantage. Apart from everything else, she has the scars, and will always have them. Daphne can only utter a verbal reminder. Why do I feel safe tonight, as if it was only my neighbour's house that caught fire? Tonight we are really surviving, Angela.''

She pulled the covers over her. A child cried out in the village and she heard the distant hooter of a ship. Tomorrow the story would spread around the company, and they would try to keep it from the village and the papers. Superstition would breed and morale would be low. It was as if Tom's death had doomed the picture from the start.

''Good night, Angela. I hope Daphne isn't sleeping.''

When they arrived at the little hospital, carrying their bundle between them, they met Peter who was just leaving. He stared at them, open-mouthed, and followed. He watched as they pumped her stomach of pheno and pheasant, and he had waited with David and Mr Worcester until six o'clock when she had been allowed into a legitimate sleep. Then the nurses wheeled her into the women's ward. Her bed was practically opposite Carol's, and David was glad that he didn't have to be there in the morning when they woke to each other. He and Mr Worcester drove back to the village, while Peter stayed a while in the ward looking from one bed to the other. For a moment he thought of asking the nurse to put them in separate rooms—but how could his scant Italian begin to order the chaos that he had engendered? He knew the words for both 'wife' and 'mistress', but what entangled gestures could bridge the gap between them both and show the span was perilous? He couldn't explain it to anybody. He hardly understood it himself. So he left, and at the door of the ward he shrugged and, to no one in particular, said, 'Women!'

Chapter Twelve

David and Mr Worcester returned to the village in the early hours and spent what was left of the night in rescheduling. At seven they went for a swim, and afterwards David had gone to Angela's bedroom to wake her. When she saw him standing over the bed, she knew he was no part of a dream. She had gone to sleep half expecting him and it was right and proper for him to be there. Her first thought was of Tom's lighter and whether he had seen it and gratefully scored her infidelity. Then she realized that she was naked and had kicked the covers off during sleep. She wondered how long he'd been standing there watching her, shocked perhaps by the extra two years of vein and mother-of-pearl and at the change that had been wrought when he wasn't looking. Quickly she covered herself, embarrassed, wanting to explain to him how it had all happened, that it wasn't her fault, that time, neither his nor hers, but the neutral passing of years had overtaken her. She felt him gently shake her shoulder. She wished she had been more prepared, and when she turned and looked at him squarely, and saw that he was dressed and that it was morning, she was relieved.

'Get up,' he said. 'Mr Worcester's getting us breakfast.'

She sat up in bed, covering herself with a sheet, and smiled at him.

'O.K.,' she said, 'I'll dress if you leave the room.'

He understood. He seemed almost relieved to have been asked. 'Five minutes,' he said.

Then she realized that she had not thought of Daphne, though since watching her limp body into the car the night before she had thought of little else and she was appalled how David's presence could abolish all concern. 'How's Daphne?' she said.

'Living. She hadn't taken much. It was probably only a gesture.'

'Did she have to die,' Angela asked coldly, 'before Peter could understand her hurt? I'll be five minutes,' she said, not wanting to pursue the subject.

'They're letting her out this evening,' he said. 'You'd do me a favour if you picked her up. I've had enough of that hospital.'

'All right,' she said, knowing that the hospital had nothing to do with it, 'I'll go tonight after the shooting.'

He left the room, stepping over Tom's lighter, with such deliberation that he had obviously seen it and chosen to ignore it.

As soon as he'd gone her body wanted him.

"Dear Angela, Have we been apart too long, he and I? Too long for him as a lover, and history precludes the stranger. Then how shall we come together? In what roles save those of mutual penitents. And if ever we do come together, shall I, God help me, be nattering away to you all the time?''

The cooking smells from the kitchen made her suddenly hungry. Mr Worcester was grilling fish that Giulietta's father, only a few hours ago, had taken from the sea. David was cutting bread, and there was a rich smell of coffee. Angela set the table, and felt suddenly at home, married again, with Mr Worcester as their guest. She set each place with care, and then took over from Mr Worcester and ruled the stove with an animal, and almost angry, domestic instinct. She served them both and they both noticed how she glowed.

'Angela'll pick up Daphne tonight,' David said.

'That's a good idea. It'll be less embarrassing for her,' Mr Worcester said. 'She's had a rough ride. Let's hope she'll be able to work tomorrow.'

'Do we have to tell them what happened?' Angela said. 'Can't we cook up some story that she had to go to Rome for the day? We could tell Hal, but only Hal. It wouldn't be much fun for her to come back on the set knowing that everybody knew. And they would have to know everything, the Carol story too.'

'We could try,' David said. 'It's certainly worth a try. Though sooner or later the story would break. Nurses from the hospital, the waiter from the restaurant and Pino from the bar. He helped me carry her down the stairs.'

'Yes,' said Mr Worcester, 'but in the beginning they'll probably only talk about it amongst themselves. Sam will get to know, of course, and he's their link with the company. Perhaps we'd better let Sam in on the story and tell him to keep quiet.'

'That's a risk,' David said.

'It's worth taking,' Angela tried to persuade him. 'Think of the embarrassment for her otherwise.'

'Well you tell Sam?' Mr Worcester asked David.

'All right,' he said, 'I'll see to Sam and you tell Hal. As soon as they get on the set. Now let's enjoy our breakfast and try to forget about it for a while.'

But it was difficult to think or to talk about anything else, so they ate in silence, commenting occasionally on the goodness of the fish or the coffee. It seemed natural to both David and Mr Worcester to look upon Angela as their host, as the one who would serve them, and this she did gladly.

'Can I have some more coffee?' David asked, and as she handed him a fresh cup he smiled and said, 'Just like old times, isn't it?'

His smile saved the remark from any nuances her fear might have scratched it for, so she was able to answer, 'Yes, and they were good times too.'

Mr Worcester looked from one to the other like a benign matchmaker, hoping for some follow-up from David. But the water was deep now, and both of them perferred to wade to the safety of silence.

''Angela Morrow Enjoyed Your Absence Stop But Sense Your Imminent Return So Be It.''

They arrived on the set shortly before eight. Sam was already there, his diligence noticeable. David took him aside while Mr Worcester waited for Hal. Angela watched Sam's face as David told him Daphne's story. It registered very little, possibly because any facial reaction still pained him. Once he opened his mouth in astonishment. Angela thought she saw him smile, but it could have been a grimace of pain. Again he opened his mouth and again, and Angela could not recollect so many points

199

of climax in the story. Yet David would not embellish it. It was clear that on the whole the events of last night had disgusted him, and frightened him a little, possibly because he had felt threatened, and he would not embroider them in the telling. She saw Sam nod his head emphatically. He was obviously offering his whole-hearted co-operation.

Hal was not taking it as well as Sam, and with more reason. He had staked a good deal on this picture, waiving his usual fee for a percentage of the gross, for David Morrow's pictures were known to make money. This constant rescheduling meant less time for reshoots if they were necessary, and the way things were going, they could have done with a second take on practically everything. 'I'll never use her again,' Hal was saying. 'She's too unreliable.'

Mr Worcester saw no point in discussing it. Hal's lack of compassion brooked no argument and he set straightway to reorganize the shooting. As the company arrived on the set, they were told that Daphne had had to go to Rome with her husband for private reasons, and though they nodded their heads, none believed it and there was much speculation as to her absence. David kept his eye on Sam and walked about him if his conversations seemed too long or too lively. He began to doubt the wisdom of lying to them. Sooner or later it would be out. He could only hope that it would be later, when it was less newsworthy. Angela was dispatched to the Press Office for the day in case anything leaked out, for she, knowing the truth, would make a more convincing liar.

It was a hanging-about day for her. The office wasn't busy, and every time the phone rang, she rushed to answer it, reporting for duty. But the whole day passed without alarm. The story was no doubt circulating in the village, spread and exaggerated by all those who'd called in at the bar on the piazza. By evening, the company would probably be in the picture, but by then Daphne would be back and, with luck, able to laugh it off.

At six o'clock, she picked up David's car and drove to the hospital. She drove slowly, wishing to delay her meeting with Daphne.

"Dear Angela, Is there something humiliating about a failed suicide? Would her point have been made more acutely had she succeeded? Is there not in her mismanagement the same contempt that attaches itself to all failures? And is she made a fool of by the failure or the attempt itself? I wish I could rid myself of this tedious tendency to analyse everything, which precludes all spontaneity, and is in itself a defence. I should go to Daphne and play my greeting by ear, for that would be the right one and the one that she would need. Take these thoughts away, Angela, and lie low with them, and let them rot in putrid analysis."

In spite of her leisurely driving, she reached the hospital well before the appointed time, and she decided to go straight in and have it over and done with. She was surprised to find the hospital so small. There was no one about. She walked along the corridor, passing the empty office and intake room until she came to two doors, one clearly marked 'Women', and the other 'Men'. She peeped into the Women's door, thinking that it was a lavatory, and was surprised to find herself in a large ward, crowded with women and children. Then she realized that there were only two wards in the hospital, and she thought of Carol just before she caught sight of her. Or what she thought must be Carol, for the face was practically obscured by bandages, but she was somehow recognizable by the woman who was sitting on her bed. Daphne.

Angela stood for a while and watched them, though neither of them could see her. Daphne was holding Carol's hand and seemed to be doing most of the talking. Occasionally she put her ear to a little hole on Carol's face where her mouth was and then she would throw back her head and laugh. For some reason Angela knew they were talking about Peter, either loving him or mocking, but probably the latter for they looked allied enough to have a common enemy. Angela felt like an intruder.

She walked slowly towards the bed. Carol saw her first out of the slit in the bandages. She waved and nudged Daphne. Daphne stood up, holding out her arms in a 'come and join the party' gesture. When she reached the bed, Daphne hugged her. 'My saviour,' she laughed. 'Come and say hullo to Carol. It's all rather one-sided, I'm afraid, but there are enormous advantages. You can sit here all day and insult her and there's nothing she can do about it.'

A rather back-handed joke, Angela thought, but she smiled, willing to reinforce Daphne's defences. It seemed inappropriate to ask either of them how they were. So, taking Daphne's hand, she said, 'I've come to pick you up. I've brought you some clothes. Hope they're the right ones.'

'Thanks, Angela,' Daphne said, taking the suitcase. 'Anything's better than going back to the village in a nightie. I'll have enough problems going back there at all.'

'Nobody knows,' Angela said. 'We said you had to go to Rome for the day.'

'I hope they believed it.' Daphne's smile was unbelieving. 'I'll go and dress. See you in five minutes.'

Angela found herself alone with Carol and not knowing what to say. She sat on the bed and Carol touched her and motioned her to come towards her mouth. Angela put her ear to the hole.

'We're best friends now,' she heard faintly. It was a school-girl's voice, of whispered conversations heard in locker-rooms buzzing with rumour of prefects and the latest crush. 'We've sworn a lifelong friendship,' Carol added.

'In blood?' Angela recalled her locker-days. She heard a faint giggle through the slit. She wanted to hold her in her arms and kiss her for her innocence. 'Is Peter coming today?' she said.

'I don't want to see him again,' Carol whispered. 'Daphne said she'd arrange to get me back to England. Daphne'll tell you everything,' she sieved through the hole. Then she took Angela's hand and nodded emphatically. Speech was obviously difficult for her, but she wanted to assure Angela that the decision had been made and that it was the right one for everybody.

"Dear Angela, I don't understand anything any more. Did somebody win after all, or did only Peter lose? When they woke up, each one this morning, both throbbing with recollection, and looked across the ward and saw each other, from whom came the first gesture? Did Daphne cross the line and offer the kind of friendship that was only possible after punishment? And are they now to be lifelong buddies, Carol, Daphne's pet Black or Jew? I would sooner store the maiming in my mind, enacting it in fantasy, than contract myself to such a partnership of victims. Perhaps neither of them really *like* men, in the same way that Peter doesn't like women. And David too, perhaps. That men and women are a social front for each of them, stalking areas, an entrée to social acceptance. Save me from that, Angela.''

Daphne was dressed and was coming towards them. 'I hate leaving you,' she said to Carol, 'but I'll be back before we leave for Rome. I'll get Mr Worcester to make all the arrangements. Don't worry about anything. Just get well.' She kissed her through the hole, and Angela shivered. Then she whispered something in Carol's ear and Angela was glad not to hear it. Angela took Carol's hand and said goodbye. They would see each other again, she was sure, though she knew that back in London, it was unlikely. She didn't want to get involved in their relationship. In her mind it was sick.

''Dear Angela, Sicker than mine with David? How sick is sick?''

In the car Daphne said nothing for a while. Then she put her hand on Angela's arm. 'Thanks for everything,' she said.

Angela took the farewell note out of her pocket. 'Here,' she said. 'No one saw it. I thought you'd like it back.'

She took it and read it over. 'Jesus,' she said, 'what a bloody fool I was.' She started to cry. 'I wish I could go back home.'

'Getting straight back to work will help,' Angela said. 'And the company knows nothing. Except Hal. And he understands.'

'You saved my life, didn't you,' she said again.

'Well, don't do it again,' Angela laughed it off. 'I may not be around.'

As they turned into the village road, Daphne asked Angela to drop her off behind the square so that she could go straight to her lodgings. She wanted to make an early night and she would be ready for work in the morning. 'You're right,' she said. 'Work is the only salvation, but somehow when that sort of remark comes from a woman, it hides behind a mountain of despair.'

Angela smiled at her. They had a lot in common. She dropped her off and parked the car on the piazza. It was dinner-time and the company were down in Sam's café. Mr Worcester got up when she came in. 'David's gone to bed,' he said. 'He was dog-tired, as you can imagine. He asked me to tell you to go and say good night to him after you've eaten.' Mr Worcester tried to suppress a smile, and in doing so had to raise his eyebrow, thus giving a totally different impression from the one of hope and happiness that he wished to convey.

"Dear Angela . . . Dear Angela, Why don't you answer me?" She was trembling.

'Come, sit at my table,' Mr Worcester was saying.

Angela noticed how the others eyed her curiously and she wondered whether they all knew of her assignation. 'Do they know?' she whispered to Mr Worcester.

'I'm afraid so. It was all round the village and they heard it at the bar. The whole story. Carol too. That filtered back from the hospital.' Angela laughed with her own relief. They sat down and she noticed how quiet it was. They were obviously waiting for her to say something.

'She's fine,' she told them in general. 'She'll be on the set in the morning.'

They went back to their food and chatter, and when Angela's pasta was put before her, she had no appetite.

"Dear Angela, How far away are you? How often

205

have I begged you to recede and you have clung anchored to my side, my greedy correspondent. And now when I need you, you are far away. Angela Morrow Possibly London Stop Advise Suitable Technique Imminent David Encounter Stop Return Immediately.''

She fiddled with her food.

'Have some wine,' Mr Worcester said, pouring it into her glass. He felt her nervousness and hoped that alcohol might give her a little courage. 'Don't eat if you don't want to.'

She pushed her plate aside and drank the wine greedily. Then she regretted it, not wanting it on her breath as a sign to David that she had needed artificial aids. She would go to her room first, she thought, and prepare her body like a bride. Or she would go straightway to him, as she was, unrinsed of all her survival encounters, for they were stains on her that he had spilled and must now accommodate.

'You'd better go,' she heard Mr Worcester saying. 'He said not to leave it too late.'

Leave what too late, she thought. And if I don't go tonight, is it then too late, for ever too late? Is he still dictating the terms?

''Dear Angela, You have come back laden with my resentment, and now I want you to go, and let me go to him alone, with no hope and no expectation, but only with the desire that creeps upon me which you will corrode if you stick around.''

She got up from the table.

'Shall I walk you a little way?' Mr Worcester said.

'No. I'll go on my own.' Then, pressing his hand, 'You understand.'

He nodded. He wanted to say something, but 'Good

luck', or 'Hope it works out', would have sounded tasteless. But that's what he meant. She would need all the
luck she could get. 'Take it easy,' he said, and that
seemed to cover everything.

She walked slowly up the cliff steps, breathing deeply
with her mouth open to exhale the smell of wine. Then
she began to whistle and kick a pebble aimlessly along
the road, shrugging her shoulders, a performance of nonchalance that she tried in her heart to feel. But the more
she whistled and the more she shrugged, the more their
history encrusted her heart, and she knew that it was no
good going to him so burdened. So she stood still and
said aloud, 'I am meeting him for the first time,' and she
heard Angela laughing. Suddenly she was angry. "Go
away," she shouted. "It is you who morse-codes the re-
minders like an eternal hammering on the back of my
brain. It is you who encumbers me with our past. I'm not
carrying that baggage any more. Leave me in peace, I
beg you."

Her hand was in her pocket fingering Tom's lighter.
She took it out. It was the easiest of the impedimenta to
discard, but she had to make a start somewhere. With
it would go the Stuarts, the Pierres, the Jameses, the
Jacks—the cabin luggage of her survival. The freight she
would deal with later. She would need David's help to
offload that. She walked to the top of the cliff, and without looking at it again, she hurled the lighter into the sea.
She did not stay to see it hit the water. She turned
quickly, and strangely lightened, ran towards David's
house. The door was open and she ran up the stairs. His
room was on the top floor but she didn't stop running.
The lightness in her heart dictated her speed, and when
she reached his door, she panted his name and entered.

He was in bed, reading. She noticed that his pyjama-top lay on the chair beside him. She hadn't remembered his chest so hairy, but the sight of the small mole under the left nipple eased her into familiarity.

He put out his arms towards her. 'Come,' he said.

She did not move. She put her hands up to her shirt and started to unbutton. She remembered reading something, probably while sitting under a hair-dryer—a genuine seat of learning, that, when the mind is stuffed with useless trivia that will do no more than get you by in a dicey drawing-room—she remembered a magazine article which had laid down the rules of undressing on such an occasion. And, if she remembered rightly, the siren worthy of her name took off her shoes first. The article had been laid out like a recipe, with a list of ingredients first, which, if she rightly recalled, did not include trousers, to say nothing of the folds on the flesh or any of the scars of neglect. She remembered the admonishment, in a footnote, to conceal one's worst feature till last, for by that time, the article assured its readers, if all the instructions had been followed, the partner's appetite would be so acute that his critical faculties would be blunted. So what was her worst feature? Worse in comparison to what? Neglect singles out no feature in its particular; its effect is overall.

She turned her back to him, because she was suddenly shy, embarrassed by the long days and nights in which he had managed not to touch her. Mercifully he turned off the light of the bedside lamp, and the room was lit only by the half-moon and the lights that still burned on the piazza. She undressed slowly, and then she turned to face him. He had opened the bedclothes, half concealing his nakedness.

'Come on, you old bag,' he said, and suddenly she was able to relax because he had articulated what she feared she might be for him, and he had made a joke of it.

He held her in his arms. 'No sobbing,' he said, as he felt a hot tear on his shoulder. 'It'll be all right. Have you ever thought of those thousands of men who went to wars, and the thousands less who after years came back, and held their women again? It is possible,' he whispered. She listened, and knew it to be only half-apt, and knew it too to have been rehearsed, but she loved him for the attempt of it, for his anticipation and concern. She drew him towards her. He's had his war, she thought, and whether this was truce or armistice did not concern her. Those fears that had fed her hopes, and in their turn had fed on each other, she had shed them all with Angela outside. She was in the here-and-now, and all the 'if onlys', and 'might have beens' had been stifled.

He put his hand to her face, outlining her features, familiarizing himself once more with the contours of his past. He did likewise with her body, and there was no hesitation in his movements, no startled halt, no faltering at change, just a gentle and gradual acclimatization, the conquering and gentle coward, who after years of foreign occupation now returned to occupy his own.

She slipped beneath him and held him very close, and fingering his back, recognized the old landmarks, which she had never sought to find elsewhere. She heard the silence within her, and in that silence he took her. The gap that over the years vocabulary had widened and imperilled, now, without words, was closed.

Chapter Thirteen

Mr Worcester breakfasted alone and chuckled to himself. He had gone to Angela's room to wake her, his heart beating with hope that she wasn't there, and when she didn't answer his call, he opened the door on to her neat, unused bed, and he saw that it was good.

He ate heartily. Things were not going too badly. They were almost up to schedule, Daphne would be back on the set, and David and Angela were together. There were enough reasons for a third cup of coffee. He was dawdling really. He didn't want to be too early on the set. He wanted David and Angela to be already there, and Daphne installed in her dressing-room. He wanted to avoid the initial greetings. He was not good at breaking ice, and in his desire to say the right thing his enthusiasm was often misunderstood. He wondered sometimes whether others pitied him for his curiosity and concern for others, which compensated, they might have thought, for his celibate life. And he knew he could not entertain such a thought if he did not sometimes pity himself. This was one of those moments and another reason for the coffee. But it was quickly over, for he was able to rationalize his present position and find nothing pitiable about it.

His widowed mother had died only two years ago, and for her last fifteen years he had lived with and looked after her. At her funeral, he had met his cousin Ellen, who had been living in Australia for some years, and now, widowed herself, had returned home. He loved Ellen, but she knew nothing of his feelings. Though they saw each other frequently, he had been too shy to voice them, and each time he went away he was terrified that in her ignorance of his feelings, and his absence, she might contract with somebody else. It was a situation he could have dealt with admirably had it been another's problem, but in his own case his timidity precluded any solution. Often he thought of writing to her and declaring his love, but he could not face the encounter afterwards, and her possible kind but firm refusal. He thought of Angela, and how she risked everything all the time, and how she loved and put her love at risk together with her pride and self-respect. Even Daphne availed herself of failure, and he wondered what was lacking in him that he continually played safe. It was up to him to break the pattern, he knew, and, with the thought of Angela and Daphne, he finished his coffee and decided to write to Ellen. He would write today while he yet had two weeks before his return. Daphne had failed, and Angela had probably succeeded. He too had a fifty-fifty chance. He would go up to the post office on his way to the set, and he would buy an air-letter form.

It was still early, and as he crossed the beach, he saw no activity around the set area. He climbed the steps to the piazza, and when he reached the bar he found Angela and David having breakfast. They shouted across to him

211

and he was glad that they had made the first move. He gesticulated that he would join them later.

He bought an air-letter form, then decided on two in case he needed a change of style, and when he got back to the bar, they were gone. He was relieved. He looked down over the cliff and saw them walking hand in hand along the shore. Yes, he would write the letter to Ellen. He would compose it in his mind during the day.

Most of the company were on the set. Daphne had not yet arrived, but it was still early. Hal put on a look-out to advise him of her coming. He was very edgy. At last, a shout came that she was coming down the cliff, running even, and that put heart into him. The company dispersed in groups, none of them knowing how to handle Daphne's arrival, and when she came on the set, glowing, she looked like the victor. There were murmurs of casual greeting all around. Only Sam had the courage to approach her. In front of them all, he put his arm around her, and said, loudly enough for all to hear, 'I'm glad you're back, Daphne. We missed you.'

She responded immediately. She had dreaded the silent greeting, the nods from those who knew it all and didn't know what to say. She would gladly have talked about it, and told them the whole story herself, drawing attention to the silliness of it all, and thus anticipating their censure. But Sam's greeting had obviated the need for that, and now they came towards her as she made for her dressing-room. Hal followed her. Mr Worcester hoped that he'd let Daphne do the talking.

The day went well. There was almost an end-of-shooting festivity about it, and indeed they managed to make up for all their lost time. David and Angela spent the day side by side, and Mr Worcester, composing his letter, glowed to see them. By evening, his mind was seething with his declaration. He went home before supper to commit it to the thin blue paper. He left it till after supper to take it to the letter-box and he was glad that he had missed the post. That would give both of them a day's grace. He calculated the day she would receive the letter and generously gave her a week to mull it over. He had given her an address in Rome. With luck or otherwise, he might have a reply before they left for England.

Now the regrets assailed him, and his fears, and he had constantly to think of Daphne and Angela to justify what he had done.

The last week of the filming went smoothly. There was even time for Hal's reshoots. Wendy didn't improve, and each take was worse than the last. Angela's bed remained empty, neat and made. Each day Mr Worcester ticked off the progress of Ellen's consideration, and as the day for a reply approached, he let others go through his post. There was little work for him to do on the set during this period, so he spent his time arranging for Carol's return and medical care. Angela was now beyond his reach and he had to care for somebody. Once or twice he took Daphne to the next village for dinner, or Sam and Giulietta were his guests. At times he was filled with hope that Ellen would accept him, and he felt entitled to have a last fling at playing Miss Lonelyhearts.

They left for Rome at the end of the week, and the villagers had mixed feelings at their departure. Pino at the piazza bar would feel it most, and though he frowned upon their foreign antics, the odd attempted suicide was more than worth the lire that showered into his till. The women of the village had put aside the lodging moneys, so that even in a poor sea-year, no one would go hungry.

Some, like Giulietta, wept to see them go, and Sam, whose work was finished, remained to comfort her, and no doubt would fret ever after for a return ticket home. After a while or so, the village would forget them, except for Sam and Giulietta, in whose domestic realm they had left a pocket of disturbance.

In Rome, the accommodation was hotel. David booked a double suite for himself and Angela. Rarely now did he think of Carol, for he dared not. Her airport farewell was now a sour residue. In time he could turn it into a nightmare, from whose lie he must surely wake. He had come to regard the present time as their honeymoon, and he did not attempt to hide it, and it was this public declaration of their love that pleased Angela most of all. Her fears had evaporated, and with them her hopes, in the knowledge that both were sterile. She was living and loving in Rome, as Mrs David Morrow, and it was Angela at home, dusting the mantelpiece, who was still suffocating in history. And good riddance to her, Angela thought, and the only hope that she entertained was that they would never meet again.

They had been in Rome for three days when the letter arrived for Mr Worcester. He had woken in the morning with a strong suspicion that today was his Waterloo, and he had sent Angela to check on the post. While she was gone, he delved for reasons why Ellen hadn't written. She had been deeply affronted by his letter and would ignore it. Or she needed more time to consider it. Or she preferred to wait for his return so that they could talk about it. By the time Angela came back to the office, he had resigned himself to a letterless day.

She brought in a pile, putting it on his desk.

'Would you sort it out for me, dear? I've got to finish this accounting.'

He had nothing to do really, but he couldn't bear to discover the absence or the presence of it himself. In any case, he knew that if Angela said there was no personal post, he would check the pile himself. He scribbled nonsenses on his pad, a busy frown on his face, and his heart thumping.

'Nothing much,' he heard her say. 'Mostly from the London office, which you'll have to deal with. And there's one marked "Personal" for you.'

She threw it singly on his desk, and for a moment Mr Worcester disliked her. It fell face downwards, and it took a little time for him to turn it up. And when he did so, he could surmise only from the postmark that it was from her, for he realized for the first time that he didn't know her handwriting. He put the letter in his pocket. There must come a time during the day when he would have courage enough to open it, and later on perhaps to read it, and later, to . . . His fingers itched, but he would wait for privacy, and that was not likely to come till the lunch-hour. He would have to busy himself during the morning and try to ignore the bulge in his pocket. He was not due on the location till the afternoon. They were shooting the penultimate sequence of the film on the Spanish Steps, and he was due to meet the Inspector of Police there shortly after lunch. But there was little for him to do till then. He might as well play the tourist in Rome and try to take his mind off the words that possibly dictated his whole future.

He took a bus to the Vatican, and walked across St. Peter's Square, tapping his pocket now and again, even feeling inside sometimes, teasing himself unplayfully.

Once he actually took the envelope out and examined the handwriting, as if that might give him a clue to the yea or nay inside. Quickly he put it back, almost as if he was tempted to open someone else's letter.

He bought a packet of peanuts and sat on one of the benches along with the tourists, feeding the pigeons. He was trying to find a peace of mind that no upsetting news could disturb, and which good tidings could only underline. But he was restless sitting there, unbelonging, and he gave the peanuts to a little boy and walked quickly out of the square.

Rome, as always, was full of tourists, and there was something safe in following their numbers and letting their official guides guide you too into their potted histories learned by rote, into their tired jokes and outstretched palms. He remembered how once, on location in Delhi, he had taken the day off to visit the Taj Mahal. He and many hundreds of others, and most of different tongues. He had attached himself to an English guide, but tiring of him and his patronizing delivery, he had opted for an Indian, who promised to be more reliable. But the latter's guiding was radically different from the Englishman's and his information might well have referred to an entirely different building. On the beach at the back of the Taj, a holy man was ranting, promising those tourists who gazed over the ramparts that only he could tell them the truth, the whole truth and nothing but the truth about the building. The guides on the terraces ignored him, pontificating with great self-confidence, in French, German, Spanish and Italian, and, to judge by a small group of black listeners, Swahili. He had wandered around on his own. You couldn't really trust anybody.

He found himself in the Sistine Chapel. The guide had

given his flock exactly ten minutes inside, during which time they could check on the information he had previously fed them. They walked round, craning their necks at the ceiling, ticking off the items in their guidebooks. After the appointed time, they were ushered out, having 'done' the Chapel.

Mr Worcester remained, and savoured the silence of their departure. But he was not alone for long. Yet another group of drawing-room name-droppers were let loose from their guide, and the Chapel buzzed with their wonder and their scribblings. Mr Worcester lay flat on a bench amongst them, contemplating the ceiling, his eye fixed on the finger of God. Around him, people stumbled, coughed, argued and preached. It was like a market-place, and he decided that amongst this anonymous meaningless noise lay the exact privacy that he sought. He sat up on the bench and opened his letter.

'Dear Hayzell,' he read.

He turned the letter over. Was that good or bad? That mode of address was confined only to his closest family. From anyone else, it could have been insulting. It augured both good and bad. He read on.

'Please don't think me familiar to address you in such a way, but if I am to be your wife, I cannot for ever call you Mr Worcester.'

He jumped up from his seat, and grabbed the arm of the tourist nearest to him. Then he realized what he had done, so he loosened his hold on the man's arm and sat down sheepishly. 'It's just that I'm getting married,' he said.

The tourist, a distant Finn, had not understood him, and took him for one of those religious maniacs that the

217

guidebooks insisted hung around the Chapel from time to time. Mr Worcester resumed his reading.

'I was so happy with your letter,' he read. 'I have had vague suspicions of your affection towards me, but I was too fearful to give you encouragement to speak. Your letter has made me very happy, and I look forward with joy to your homecoming. I am as impatient as a child to see you again. Till then, Your deeply loving Ellen.'

He read it over again, unbelieving, resenting that he had kept such momentous news sealed in his pocket for so long. He had denied himself at least two hours of happiness, but he had a lifetime of love to look forward to. He lay down and looked at the ceiling again, while the party of Finns trickled out, and the few minutes' grace before the next onslaught, when he was alone with his unbounding joy, he was to treasure all his life.

He lunched opposite the Spanish Steps, and tried to contain his giggling. He took a whole litre of wine, which he could subsequently blame if a fit overtook him during the afternoon's filming. He decided he would tell nobody. He was still too overwhelmed by the news to believe that it was true, and he kept checking on the contents of the letter till he knew it by heart. Over his dessert, he recited it to himself. He overtipped outrageously, and it seemed right and proper that the first people he noticed as he left the café were Angela and David, walking arm in arm up the Spanish Steps like lovers.

During the afternoon filming it occurred to him to phone Ellen, and he could hardly wait till the shooting was over. He placed a call from the privacy of his room, whispering his love to her. He was astonished at the intensity of his own feelings that had been stored and unused for so many years. He swore his undying love to her, wondering whether he could repeat it to her face. Now he began to count the days to his return, and he was glad that there was enough to occupy him.

They finished shooting late on the Thursday night, and their plane was due to leave the following afternoon. In the morning Carol arrived from the hospital. A car had been sent for her and she was taken straight to Daphne's room. The morning was spent in packing and shopping, and the company did not reassemble until half an hour before the flight departure. Daphne was the last to arrive, with Carol. The company were curious and tried not to be seen looking at her. David and Angela went towards them, thus sanctioning the others' approach, and they crowded around, viewing Daphne's handiwork.

Carol's face looked like a toy-railway terminus. The stitches had been removed the day before and they crisscrossed the vertical lines of the scars. 'It'll fade,' she kept reassuring everybody. 'It'll take about a month and then nobody will ever know.' She smiled, and the gap of her missing tooth, together with the grooves on her face, gave her the look of a child-clown. Daphne was very protective. Alex and Mark did not question their companionship. To the others in the company, Daphne's patronage of Carol was all very quaint and they laid small bets on how long it would last. But Angela knew that that relationship was reliably permanent, for there was guilt on both sides and an avenue for both for atonement.

Mr Worcester watched them all as they left to board the plane. Daphne, her arm around Carol, Angela and David, Mark with his Alex, and he himself with his throbbing letter. The flight was like a package deal for honeymooners.

When they reached London, David insisted on taking Angela home. They took a taxi from the terminal, and he held her hand in his all the way to the flat. When they arrived, he told the taxi-driver to wait, and he helped her out of the cab, taking her case. It looked as if he might be taking her up to the flat, and suddenly she was frightened. She didn't want him to take her up, to drop her case and to leave her there. She preferred him to leave her outside as he had always done over the past two years, and that when the time came for him to take her up those stairs, there would be no turning back again. Now she wanted to celebrate that last temporary parting. She wanted to go upstairs alone, to face the mantelpiece alone, which must in her absence have gathered sufficient dust to be disturbed by the outline of their names that she would draft gently between the ornaments. She knew that this was the last time that he would leave her there. Soon, very soon, as he himself had said, perhaps tomorrow. Soon, he had said, as soon as he could extricate himself. A split second was all that that took, she knew. Either that or an eternity. She smiled her fears away. 'I can manage it,' she said, taking the case from him.

He turned back to the cab. 'I'll see you soon,' he said, and Carol's news thundered back at him, and echoed his terrible lie.

She went up the steps. How soon was soon, she thought. But everything that had happened pointed to his certain and quick return, and for the first time since David had left she did not feel alone. Over the past few weeks, Angela had slowly ebbed away, always a sign of her own content. She looked forward to going to bed, to lying on the high pillow that had served her over the long months and years as a muzzle for her pain. She would lie awake for a long time, savouring the joy of their coming together, holding it in her mind's eye to carry it through her sleep and greet her in the morning, her trust undimmed.

She opened the letter-box, and collected the pile of post that had accumulated during her absence. In the old days, and they were already history in her mind, in the lonely days, she would pick up her post and take it upstairs to her flat without looking at it. She would hide it from herself until she'd made her coffee, and then she would sit at the table with the pile face downwards, so that she could discover each one singly. In her days of utter and desperate loneliness, when even going to the lavatory was an event, every single happening had to be attended by some measure of ritual, so that any time unconnected with her loneliness could be spun out to its full. Now all that had changed, and on her way to the flat she looked over the post as an interim affair, because there were so many other things she had to do and think about. One large envelope from a Life Assurance Trust. She put down her case and opened the letter, and scanned the information that on payment of a certain subscription she could, in case of natural death or retirement, accrue a nest-egg. She smiled. Now she could really entertain the possibility of dying from natural causes, and the letter seemed a confirmation of that chance. She opened the door of her flat, and put the rest of the letters on the table. She carried her case into the bedroom and left it there. The unpacking could wait. Back in the living-room, she went straight to the mantelpiece and stared with total calm and triumph at the dust which had gathered. In the corners of the room were cobwebs, and the place had a musty smell. And all about it pleased her. Idly she went through the rest of the post.

There was a 'Welcome home' note from Stuart, written on House of Commons paper. She remembered that the by-election had taken place while she was away, and Stuart was concerned with informing her of his victory. A couple of At Home notices from friends for dates that had well passed. A bundle of coupons for free detergents, a note from the Gas Board which she presumed was a bill and left unopened. Then she picked up a blue envelope, its gum-edge crinkled. It looked as if it held scented notepaper. It was marked 'Personal', and underlined, and suddenly Angela was afraid. Of late, her life-style had been too monotonous for secrets, and this letter, heralding its personal warning, indicated that it held information that must not be known by others. She looked at the postmark but could not decipher it, and she knew, by some animal instinct, that she must not look at the mantelpiece again. She put the letter down and went to the kitchen to make coffee. She felt the pattern of ritual overtaking her, but she had enough faith in David's return not to slip back so wantonly into her old life-style of despair. She made her coffee, and then sitting at the table, she tore the letter open. She knew that the address would give her a clue, so she tried to avoid it, but it was embossed in black on the blue paper, and shrieked Fulham. A telephone number was beneath the address, two pieces of information she had for so long contrived to be ignorant of. Now they stared her in the face. She had no alternative now but to read the message.

Dear Mrs Morrow,

I hope you do not mind it very much if I write to you. David says that he hasn't seen or heard of you for over two years but that he has written to you many times regarding the matter of a divorce, but that his letters do not receive your attention. I know that you do not want to give him his freedom, but I am writing to tell you that we are expecting a baby in four months time, and I am writing to ask you to give him a divorce so that we can get married because of the baby and of course lots of other things. In anticipation of an early reply,

> I am, Yours faithfully,
> CAROL (BATES)

She dropped the letter on to the table, but she felt it still between her fingers, and there the pain started, creeping over her hand, cramping to her elbow, and then, by no discernible route, crash-landing into her stomach. She ran to the mantelpiece, shivering with her grief, and swept the ornaments to the floor. She felt her knees buckle, and she sagged with them, embracing her body closely as if to still the tremors that threatened to explode inside her. 'Sois sage, O ma douleur, et tiens-toi plus tranquille.'

"Dear Angela, Hold me close, hold me close into yourself, and together we shall contain our pain."

Chapter Fourteen

There was little sleep that night for either of them. Between them, decisions were made and rejected, hopes were offered and crushed. Tossing on her bed with her hatred and her fear, and the terrible love that would not leave her, she succumbed in early morning to the fatigue that had nothing to do with David's or Carol's story, but with the long journey behind her, and the accumulation of weeks of lost sleep. A very natural process, as hunger will eventually drive a man to food, whatever his sad preoccupation. In the morning, the contents of the letter, which in her sleep she had never totally relinquished, now came to wake her. She felt the skin on her face dry and burning, and she knew that she had cried herself to sleep.

"Oh my God, Angela, you are still so solidly with me. Do you remember, aeons ago, our yesterday's Italian journey. Were you a spectator at that *pièce de théâtre?* Did you know all along that it was but a play, another act of that weary drama, that long-running, record-breaking failure that we invested in? And now in a few months another member joins the cast. But the plot shall not thicken, Angela. We're pulling out of the play, you and I, once and for all.''

With enforced energy she got out of bed and went to the window. "It is enough, Angela," she said softly. She would not go to a work that day. All that was over. She would go to a lawyer and get started on a divorce. She would not tell Angela. She could not risk her mockery. She was as sure of her decision as ever in her life she would be, and she knew now that only its implementation could make it a certainty. But she had to do it right away, to set the wheels turning even though they might then spin so fast they were unstoppable. She had to find a lawyer, and if possible to see him today. But she had never had any law dealings. That was David's department, and she could hardly phone him, for his recommendation, though the thought did cross her mind. But she did have friends who had been divorced and she decided to ring them. It was only eight o'clock, much too early to phone, especially with such a request. Besides, at eight o'clock in the morning it would seem to others to be an impulsive gesture, not to be taken too seriously. Ten o'clock perhaps was the threshold of her earnest intent, but by that time Mr Worcester would have phoned from the office, wondering where she was. She would give it another hour.

It didn't really matter how seriously her friends would take her decision. She bathed and dressed, talking all the while to herself as if it were an ordinary un-David day. She picked up the ornaments from the floor, surprised and a little disappointed that all had refused to break, and she put them back haphazardly on the mantelpiece. She forced herself to eat breakfast, and at eight thirty started on her calls. By nine o'clock she had a list of four reputable lawyers, all specializing in divorce, and all recommended as expensive, notwithstanding their sympathy. She said their names aloud, as if that might determine her choice. Baines, Watson, Wade and Price. No bell rang. She switched the order, but still the same interchangeable quartet. She tried ascribing to each one an instrument. Watson, for some reason, claimed viola, not overburdened with solos but without whose participation the ensemble would not scan. She saw Wade with the cello, and favoured him, though she knew that out of the four the second fiddle, with his subservient indispensability, was best equipped to understand the nuances of marriage and divorce. The choice of a lawyer was almost as important as the choice of one's psychiatrist, and probably in the long run just as expensive. She phoned Baines and Price, and neither could see her for over a week. Wade was on holiday, which left Watson, and he was free and sounded almost anxious to meet her immediately. The fact that he was so easily available marked him down as possibly incompetent, but now she had no choice. She arranged to see him within the hour.

She decided to take her car. She rarely used it for work; it was mainly a pleasure vehicle. And though her present pursuit could hardly be called pleasurable, today was positively a non-working day, and so the use of the car was in order. She was glad to get out of the flat and away from the inevitable call from the office. The car, a yellow Mini, started without any trouble although she had not used it for weeks. She looked upon that as a good omen although she could not imagine what good could come out of what she was about to do.

As she drove out of the garage, she heard Angela laughing.

"Dear Angela. No. This is not just a gesture. It is not a lever to get him back. I'm going to go right through with it. It should be plain sailing. He won't defend it. What grounds could he have? Of course he'll try. It'll shatter him. He'll ignore the lawyer's letters. He'll pretend that nothing has happened. He'll refuse to see it, and hope that it will go quietly away. But I'm not going to weaken, Angela, despite your mockery. I dislike you a little this morning. Why can't you trust me? No, on second thoughts, it is better that you mistrust my intent. It's your doubts that put fight in me. Will we ever, both of us, be equally assured?"

The traffic built up as she neared the town centre. Mr Watson had offices in the City, and she had to use her road map to find her way. Not that she could read a map, but, unfamiliar with the district and reluctant to ask, it seemed the proper thing to do. It took her three red lights to find the right page, and then three more to find the appropriate square. And then the trouble started, for the print was small, and difficult to read when mobile. At last, with a cry of discovery, she found it. Maplehouse Street, E.C.I. She kept her finger on it, not trusting it to stay where it was, and at the next red light, she trapped it again.

"Dear Angela, Now that I've got it, what do I do with it?"

She found herself snarled up in the city traffic, in the middle lane, unable to get out and ask. She slid into the near-side lane, to much hooting and cursing from behind. A policeman stood on the kerb watching her. She intended stopping the car on the corner and to ask him directions, but he called her on, motioning her to pull up alongside him. She felt immediately guilty, and wondered what she had done to merit his waving her down. She decided as she stopped that she would remain seated in her car, and maintain her territorial security. Let him stand by the window and argue it out, whatever it was, through the half-open glass and the din of the traffic. But he was already opening her door. 'Will you step outside a minute?' he said.

'What's the matter?' She wriggled out of the half-open door.

But he was keeping it waiting for her to come round on to the pavement where he could tower above her on his own territory.

On the pavement she waited.

'Can I see your licence?' he said.

'I haven't got it on me. Look, officer, I'm late for an appointment. Why did you stop me?'

'Name?' he said. 'Address?' He wrote down all her so-called particulars, and instructed her to hand in her licence to her nearest police station within twenty-four hours.

'But why?' she practically shouted at him.

'Your car licence is out of date,' he said triumphantly, pointing to the disc on the windscreen.

'How observant of you,' she said coldly. 'I have renewed it. I've just forgotten to put the new disc on.'

'It's an offence,' he said, 'not to display a current licence.'

'So what are you going to do?' she said, leaning against the car.

'I shall have to report it.'

'Well, you do that,' she said, suddenly hating everybody, 'and maybe you know the way to Maplehouse Street.'

'You're in it,' he said, 'but you can't stop here.'

'I didn't,' she said. 'You stopped me.'

The traffic in the lane behind her had come to a stand-still. Drivers were hooting. She threw up her hands to them, pointing to the policeman, whom they were ready enough to blame. 'You've really caused a cock-up here,' she said to him. She hated him and all that he stood for, together with that part of the law which had necessitated her present journey. She got back into the car and drove away, weaving into the nearest alley around the corner. She was late. There was no time to find a parking-meter, so she drove the car on to the pavement in the lane, and ran away from it as if it wasn't hers. She knew that today was one in which everything would go wrong, and she began to have doubts about what she was going to do.

"Dear Angela, Let me take this decision so far that eventually it will overtake me. This is the only way I can make any kind of choice. Lead me to this man's office, and let us do what has to be done, though our heart is not in it, but where our heart is, is a cul-de-sac, a blind alley of stumbling-blocks."

Mr Watson's office was in a large building-complex. His rooms were on the third floor. A large piece of inde-finable sculpture dominated the carpeted foyer, and An-gela went towards it to read the bronze plaque on the pedestal, hoping that it might give her a clue as to its subject-matter. But it gave only the name of its benefac-tor. She turned inquiringly to the hall porter, who shrugged.

The lift was high-speed, and she'd reached his floor without any rehearsal.

She walked along the corridor, spotlit on its pictures. When she entered Mr Watson's offices, she was surprised at the contrast between his quarters and the common passages of the building. His office was pure nineteenth-century. There was a very high desk at the end of the room, and Angela had to stand on tiptoe to see the silver inkwells and paper-weights set out in meticulous order. In front of them sat Mr Watson in a high chair, a quill pen in his hand. His rimless glasses were fixed on the end of his nose, and the velvet lapels of his jacket were flecked with dandruff.

''Dear Angela, Do you suppose Mr Watson is aware of the new divorce laws?''

He motioned her to sit down, and she moved a chair into a position where she had a low-angle view of Mr Watson's head and shoulders. The position unnerved her. She couldn't possibly discuss any matters of intimacy from such an angle. 'Could you come down?' she said.

'I intend to, my dear, most certainly, just as soon as I have finished these documents. You won't mind waiting a few moments?'

She smiled at him. It would give her time to think what she would say. Well, it's like this, Mr Watson, I want a divorce, and I'm not using it as a lever or anything like that, and I don't want any maintenance. I just want to be free of him and put it all behind me.

''Dear Angela, How is he going to get down from that height, and why today am I writing to you so much? How can I stop my hands trembling without clenching my fists. I feel so old today, Angela.''

Mr Watson creaked as he descended. For a moment she lost sight of him as he came round the back of the desk, and then he reappeared, only a little taller than herself, his patent boots wrinkled with crow's-feet with all his climbing up and down. He took a chair opposite her, and sat down, placing his feet neatly together, and settling his long fingers in a steeple below his upper lip. 'Mrs Morrow?' he said, inclining his steeple a little. 'Forgive me for keeping you waiting, but I am now prepared to give you my total attention.'

That didn't please her. She would have preferred him to half listen, because she wasn't sure that she wanted to be taken too seriously, and as if reading her thoughts, he said, 'There is nothing irrevocable, madam, about this meeting. Let us regard it as purely exploratory. Perhaps you could tell me your wishes.'

She shifted in her chair. 'I want a divorce,' she said. Loud and clear.

She was astonished at her certainty.

'What grounds do you have?' he asked gently, positioning his steeple once again.

But all that was irrelevant. She'd said what she'd come to say and she wanted to get up and go, and leave her name and address and particulars with the clerk outside, and tell him to go ahead and to let her know when she was single again. 'D'you need grounds nowadays?' she said.

'I need at least the outline of your story.'

'Well, I've got every ground in the book,' she said. And then, as quickly as she was able, she spilled out the story, the bare bones of it, with no comment, no opinion, no tears. She hoped he'd heard it a hundred times before. She didn't want to be special, either with her story or with her misery. Countless women had been rejected in the same way, and countless women hadn't mended. Divorce perhaps was some kind of therapy.

'I'm sorry,' she heard him saying. He leaned forward

in his chair, his lips brushing the steeple. 'Has your husband been supporting you for the last two years?' he said. 'The question of maintenance must be discussed.'

'No,' she said, rather more proudly than she needed. 'I support myself, and I want no money from him. In any case,' she said, 'the easiest thing in the world to give is money. He would give me more than he could afford to assuage his guilt. I don't want to give him that possibility.'

'You may be making a mistake, Mrs Morrow,' Mr Watson said. 'You have been sorely wronged.'

And then she burst into tears. She was crying not for herself, but because she couldn't bear Mr Watson's innocence. She wanted to shake him into the reality of the woman who faced him with her stories of pig-faced Stuart, virgin James and mixing-bowl Jack, the sorry non-serial saga of her one-night stands.

'Of course,' he was saying, as if echoing her thoughts, 'you will have the opportunity of admitting to your own adultery if that is in order, in the event that your husband will not agree to a divorce by consent. Would you like a cup of tea?'

He didn't wait for her to answer, but he went to the far wall and pulled a cord. A clerk came in from the adjoining office, and Mr Watson ordered two cups of tea. 'It's a very trying time for you, my dear,' he said, moving towards her chair.

"Oh Angela, for God's sake don't let him touch me. I've taken people to bed for infinitely less kind words than this man has given me, and what else have I got with which to repay him?"

The clerk brought in two cups on a silver tray. He placed it on the table and poured from a silver pot. He was obviously well used to this procedure as if the same tray were set prior to any preliminary divorce discussions. They waited in silence until he'd gone.

'Mrs Morrow,' Mr Watson said, 'you are obviously not wholly decisive in your intentions. I could write to your husband and couch the letter in such terms that you will not be irrevocably committed to a pursuance of this action, and at the same time to advise your husband of its most pertinent possibility.'

"Dear Angela. Does he talk like that to his wife with his cracked shoes together and kissing his cathedral fingers? Where does he put his hands in bed? He's on your side, Angela. He doesn't take me seriously either."

'No,' she said. 'I am quite decided. I want to go ahead.'

'In that case, I must insist on urging you to make satisfactory financial arrangements. You are entitled to support. There may come a day when you will find yourself unable to earn a living. You are in a profession that is highly precarious and counts among its members a high incidence of unemployment. We must make provision for that.'

'My husband would do that in any case,' she said, 'without any legal binding. He would never see me in financial need.'

'That is a story I often hear, Mrs Morrow. But people change, especially guilty husbands. After a petition for a divorce is filed, they are quick to reverse the roles and assume the innocence of the abused party. Your husband is no different.'

'My husband *is* different,' she practically shouted at him. 'He would never behave in that way.'

'Mrs Morrow,' Mr Watson said, getting up from his

chair and walking away from her, 'I think you still love your husband.'

Oh you clever clever clever clever thing, she thought, but her hatred had nothing to do with poor Mr Watson. It was directed towards everybody who, with or without intelligence, could see through all the defences she had spent years constructing, and that finally had defended only the enemy and had exposed her more and more to her own frailty.

"Dear Angela, Nothing to say, but to know that you are alongside, exposed in the same way, but with your additional defence of mockery which in the end turns in on itself and destroys. Why am I writing to you so often today?"

Mr Watson had climbed back on to his perch, his quill at the ready.

'I shall draft a letter to your husband, Mrs Morrow,' he said, 'informing him of your intent. I shall advise him to consult his own solicitor so that we can negotiate together. I think that at this stage it would be advisable to free you from certain preliminaries. Of course,' he added, 'there is the possibility that your husband will ignore my letter. In that eventuality we will have to pursue other means, but we will hope that such steps need not be taken. Meanwhile, Mrs Morrow, I would be grateful if, over the next few days, you could write down on paper the facts that you have given me this morning. And I shall need a copy of your marriage certificate as well. These are mere formalities, but essential to the proceedings. I shall need also the birth certificate of your son. We have not at this meeting discussed the question of custody, but that procedure should be straightforward.'

'My husband will make no claim,' Angela said.

'You have a great deal of trust in your husband's generosity, Mrs Morrow, and if I may say so, he has, to date, given you little cause for your good faith. I am now about to speak out of turn, Mrs Morrow, which no doubt you will find a little strange. But what I am going to say is out of concern for you and your future. You must face facts. You must be unsentimental. Your husband is a weak man, a selfish man, a man who basically does not care about other people. A man incapable of love except for himself, endowed no doubt with a great deal of charm, who all his life will gravitate to women like yourself who are natural doormats. This pursuit of selfishness and vanity is often excused by innocence, a certain nobility of character, an unwillingness to hurt, but in the process of this reluctance, he has managed to injure not only his wife, but possibly the lady with whom he now cohabits, to say nothing of his son, and the child to come. He is not a good man, your husband, Mrs Morrow. You must learn to dislike him a little.'

Mr Watson had lowered his hand-steeple during his speech and he was salivating with anger. Angela looked at him with a mixture of hate and admiration. She opened her mouth to speak, but she didn't know what she wanted to say.

'If you are angry with me, Mrs Morrow,' Mr Watson went on, calm again, his fingers at his lips, 'you are of course at liberty to change your lawyer.'

She walked round to his side of the desk and looked up at him. 'Thank you very much.' She spoke quietly. 'I am happy to continue with your services,' she said, catching his mode of address. 'I shall go home and write the deposition that you require, and I shall forward the relevant documents.'

He smiled at her and stretched out his hand to take hers. 'You will mend, Mrs Morrow. You will mend when you will be able to forgive. But you cannot forgive until you recognize that you have been wronged. You may have contributed to it in your own unhappy way, but in this moment of time you are not guilty. Remember that, Mrs Morrow.'

She took his outstretched hand, and gripped it firmly. Then she walked towards the door. 'Are you married, Mr Watson?' she said, turning round.

'I'm divorced, Mrs Morrow, and I have yet to be forgiven.'

She did not take the lift in case there were people inside, and she needed to be alone with Angela, though she already heard her crowing with triumph and 'I told you so's'. She was right, of course, and so was Mr Watson, to whom she felt strangely grateful. She knew he was right, but to know it in the mind and face it in the gut were two entirely different propositions. In any case, to think badly of David, to condemn him out and out as a selfish person, only reflected on herself and the sickness of her choice.

''Dear Angela, O.K. So I made a mistake, and let's leave it at that, because quite frankly the whole bloody business is becoming a terrible bore.''

Outside the building, she stopped to get her bearings. She had no idea where she'd left the car. She had driven past this building shortly after the policeman had stopped her, and her sense of direction being totally inadequate, she had to turn her body in the direction the car would have taken and follow its course until she came to a recognizable landmark. After about fifty yards, with no familiarity in sight, she realized that she was walking against the traffic and that driving she would have taken the opposite direction. The mind's compass was askew with her unhappiness. It took a while to cross the road. She dodged the traffic, closely risking an oncoming lorry, but she had the confidence of one who knows that, with oven-avenues open, it was unlikely that she would die from natural causes. On the other side of the road, she started again, this time in the right direction, refraining from talking to Angela, and concentrating all her energies in finding the car. And then she came to the known alley on her left, and as she turned into it, she stopped. A policeman was standing by the car and taking notes. She walked towards him and recognized him as the same who had stopped her earlier. 'Oh no,' she said.

'Oh yes,' he echoed, writing copiously, his tongue licking his upper lip.

She leaned in front of the car. 'You get around, don't you?' she said.

'I do my duty.'

'I seem to be your sole duty this morning,' she said. 'Would you like to know my subsequent movements during the day, so that you can keep track?'

He ignored her, probably with little understanding of what she was saying. Then she noticed the white parking-ticket stuck to the windscreen.

'It seems I've already been fined,' she said. 'What more are you doing?'

'That ticket's just for parking,' he said. 'I'm reporting you for a faulty tyre.'

'Why don't you test the brakes while you're at it?' she said, opening the car door. 'The clutch slips too, and altogether the whole rotten thing is falling apart. The steering too. Have a look. Enjoy yourself.'

He looked at her as if she were mad, and licked his upper lip as he went on writing.

"Dear Angela, He's looking at me as if I'm mad, and he's right. I'm so full of hate, directed against everybody in this whole wide world. Everybody except the one person who in theory merits it. We cannot go on like this, Angela. We have driven each other to the brink of sanity, and we take it in turns to push the other over. Why is it not possible to cry it out of our body, to leave the site of our pain dry as the desert, dull perhaps, but preferable to the poisonous jungle we have so carefully cultivated, and which now overwhelms us?"

She got into the car.

'Change that tyre,' he said, 'and go easy.'

Instinctively he felt that she didn't mean what she had said, that she was simply unhappy. 'You've had an expensive morning,' he said.

Yes, she thought, and you don't know the half of it.

She drove slowly down the alley.

"Dear Angela, Have I ever felt worst than now? I should be feeling better, since at last I've taken a decision even though my heart is not in it, and it nags at me too that I should keep scribbling to you, pouring the loose letters of my sorry alphabet like molten lead into the cleft between us."

She decided to visit her old cutting-rooms. She would need a job eventually and now was as good a time as any to ask around. Besides, she didn't want to go back to the flat and face his phone call. She would be tempted to report what Mr Watson had said about him. But perhaps Carol had already told him she had written, and if that were so, he would be too cowardly to talk to her. She hoped that he wouldn't contact her again.

"Stop laughing, Angela."

When she went into the office, she met Robert. She had not seen him since before she'd left for Italy, and their last communication had been on the telephone, when she had told him to get himself another editor.

He welcomed her warmly as if nothing had happened and told her that his film had been chosen for the Irish festival. 'Congratulations,' she said, not in the least bit surprised. Robert often pulled off a prize-winner despite his shady manœuvrings. 'Who cut it in the end?' she asked.

'I did,' he said smugly, 'and I'll never use an editor again.'

'The time has probably come,' she said slowly, 'when you don't have any choice. How's that poor woman, by the way? The addict's mother.'

'How should I know? I finished shooting weeks ago. She's making out, I suppose.'

She looked into the cutting-room. She'd hoped to find Gavin, but according to reports, he'd given up the business and gone back to his painting. She went into the production office and inquired after work. There was a film coming up in two weeks' time, an industrial training job. Not the most exciting film on earth but good enough to remove her from the mantelpiece every day and to occupy the hours while the divorce arrangements were proceeding.

'Nothing sooner?' she asked.

'There's another recut needed on the art film. The sponsors want more commentary.'

The 'art film' had been hanging around the cutting room for over a year. When there was a lull in work, the current editor would have yet another go. Most of the

239

free-lancers had had a hand in it in the times when there was an unavoidable hold-up in their own films. The art film had become part of the fittings and fixtures of the company. It had become unspokenly necessary never to finish it to anyone's satisfaction, otherwise there would have been nothing to merit the editors' salaries in their off-weeks. Now it was Angela's turn, and her loyalty could be depended upon to find it uncuttable.

'I'll start on Monday,' she said.

So that gave her today and the weekend to swallow. She had the depositions to make to her lawyer, a cold pot-boiler of her marriage. She had to find the documents too, and hoped that they were not in David's possession. And she had to write to David.

"Dear Angela, I've got to. Of course I have. I can't have him getting a divorce letter out of the blue. I've got to prepare him in some way. I know what you're thinking. That the divorce letter will be a threat, and that he'll return. But how could he come back now? How *practically* could he come back with a baby on the way? The child is not a problem that can be solved. It is a hard fact, which with every year will grow harder. I hope to God, Angela, it isn't a girl. Don't let me wish it anything else but a whole being. My violence must not extend to the innocent."

At home, she got out pencil and paper. She would start on the deposition first. Cold, resolute, factual. Then she realized that for such a style she needed a typewriter, which normally, in a heartfelt document, would be an interference between her mind and the page. No, the deposition was merely mechanical. It didn't need a writer. It called for a typist. She slipped the paper into the machine, and centred it, and then in capital letters wrote,

TO WHOM IT MAY CONCERN. It was anonymous enough to be cyclostyled into thousands of copies and handed out on pavements just in case the passerby was one of the 'whoms' concerned. And then she typed, speaking it aloud, as it might have been read out in court. 'I, Angela Morrow, married David Morrow in London in June 1952. We have a son Jonathan, born November 6th, 1959. The marriage was happy . . .' This last she crossed out and replaced it with 'satisfactory'. No extremes for the court. Just satisfactory . . . 'until two and a half years ago when David Morrow formed a liaison with one Carol Bates.' *One* Carol Bates? Reduce that a little '. . . with *a* Carol Bates. In November 1970, he left me to co-habit with that woman'—all right, Angela— 'that *lady,* who now informs me that she is expecting their child in four months' time. In view of the above circumstances, I wish to petition for a divorce.'

She wondered if Mr Watson would approve of her style. She read it over. A mere hundred or so words was enough to encapsulate twenty years of history.

"Well, Angela, The Book of Genesis spends even less on the Creation of the World, so we mustn't be greedy."

She put the letter into an envelope and sealed it quickly. Now there remained the letter to David, and she wondered whether she should insult him with a typewriter. She decided to compromise. The letter would be cold all right, but it would be in her own handwriting so that he could not ascribe her indifference to machinery.

"Angela, are you there? Stand by."

She put the typewriter away and got out a piece of rough. She felt she would have to make a first draft. 'Dear David,' she wrote, and it came faster than she could put it down. 'I have received a letter from your present partner'—yes, Angela, *present,* for we must imply the impermanence—'who informs me of the impending arrival of your baby. She also writes that you haven't been able to contact me for over two years in order to talk to me about a divorce. Really, David! You could have had a divorce, or your "freedom", as your partner so naively calls it, at any time for the asking, but now in the circumstances I am asking it of you. I have instructed a Mr Watson to proceed with a divorce, and no doubt you will be hearing from him.'

"What now, Angela? Is there no more to say? Do I wish him well in a civilized manner, even at this late stage? Shall I make my voluntary exit on my B.A./Piano Diploma/Gold Medal Elocution dignity? Oh when will you let me be a fishwife again and applaud me while I tear her apart? But I can't now, can I? She's carrying. But I'll wait. Yes, Angela, I can wait. A hundred gestations wouldn't outlast my anger. Is there nothing more to write to him? After twenty years together, I write him half as much as I write to you—logical, I suppose, since you have occupied me almost twice as long. How shall I finish the letter? With something to appeal to his maudlin sentimentality? Do you remember when we, etc., etc.? Some aphorism? Some quotation from the classics to show him how clever I am, that terrible cleverness that lured him for so long, that diminished him with every syllable, and emasculated him with every breath? Some titbit from that forked tongue of mine to spear him into the ground? What can I say, Angela?"

She covered the letter with her hand so that Angela would not see. And then she signed it. With love.

She tidied her desk. She felt the need to put things in order, a will-making need almost. She sorted out what was left of the accumulated post. She noticed that she hadn't opened the letter from the Gas Board. She would pay that bill with all the others outstanding. But it was no bill. It was a letter informing her that after all their preliminary warnings, the fitters would arrive on the following Monday at eight o'clock in the morning to begin the conversion to natural gas.

"Dear Angela, They are coming to convert us to North Sea non-toxic gas, and I shall be like a distracted lemming vainly searching for a cliff-edge. Have we come back to where we started, Angela, after our great safari into survival? Ah well, 'tis better to have something or other than never to have whatever it is at all. We have yet two toxic days. Two strong days, as strong as the last turning of the Catherine-wheel before it splutters and dies. Let's get out of here, Angela. For the gas-oven exit changes nothing, and closes all avenues of change. It preserves only what has been. It encapsulates for ever an insult of the past, and freeze-frames it in stubborn rigidity. So let's get out of here. I don't feel safe, and I feel you're losing your stamina too. We must look after each other, Angela. Charity begins at home, but where does home begin?''

Chapter Fifteen

She could not stay in the flat. The letter to David itched to be posted, though it was far beyond collecting hours, but for the overnight post office at Trafalgar Square. She would drive down and post it there, giving herself no more time to reverse her decision. Moreover, she would treat the event as some ritual. She would put on a formal dress, and make up carefully; she would surround the posting with ceremony, and thus make it irrevocable.

She dressed with care. A long red velvet dress, caught up on one side to show the lacing of her boots. A heavy silver necklace, intricately filigreed, and over it all a black stole. A cross between mourning and celebration befitting the mission she was about to accomplish. It took her some time to adorn and scent herself, punctuated by long and tiresome conversations with Angela while the bath-water grew cold and the tears dried and make-up was remade, and it was almost midnight when she left the flat, catching sight of herself in the mirror in the hall and noting, with a certain fear, the still repose on her face.

There was little traffic about, and even Leicester Square seemed empty. She clutched the letter in her hand as she drove. It was unstamped. Whilst she had been in Italy, the postal rates had risen, and she did not know how much her questionable freedom would cost her. She reached the post office and parked on the studs by the zebra crossing. At that time of night there would be no parking problem. The post office was full. Large groups of Indians were gathered in unhassled chatter. As Italians will use Victoria Station as their salon, Indians will use post offices as their venue, though their business has nothing to do with postal communication. Of the others who were standing in line, she wondered what pressing urge had driven them here that an early morning collection could not satisfy.

She joined the line, and it was some time before she could buy the necessary stamp, and stand hesitant by the yawning hole in the wall beyond which all was final. She looked away and dropped the letter inside, and as she ran out of the building she was just in time to see the back end of her yellow Mini taking off towards the square. For a moment she thought it had gone off on its own, then she realized that she had left the keys inside with the flat and office keys on the same ring. She stood still, staring after it as it turned out of the square, and then she gave a little scream at the injustice of it, which turned into a laugh at the ridiculousness of it all. A passing policeman asked her if she needed help.

'My car's been stolen,' she said.

'Where did you leave it?'

'Just there,' she said, pointing, 'on the studs.'

'In that case,' he said, 'the police have probably taken it away. I'll check for you.' He talked into a receiver that hung on his chest in a code which she didn't understand but which must have been meaningful to him, for he informed her that her car was on its way to the King's Cross pound, where on payment of five pounds she could retrieve it.

'I only left it there for five minutes,' she said uselessly.

'Pity you didn't lock it,' he said, on her side. 'It would have taken them longer to get it away. You might have caught them in time. Then you'd only have the fine to pay.'

'What fine?'

'Leaving it on the studs. That'll run to five pounds too.'

'You mean I'll be charged with that as well?'

'Oh yes,' he laughed. 'We do a thorough job.'

And she laughed too. A pound for a taxi to the pound, five to retrieve the car, and five to pay the fine, plus three new pennies in stamps. Already her divorce had cost her over eleven pounds. It all figured.

She hailed a taxi. She was not in the least irritated by the nuisance of it all and her calmness surprised her. There was something right and proper in the way the misfortunes accumulated like a snowball hurtling to the end of a slope. Things were at least in motion, and when they ran themselves out they would dissolve, and something new, even something better, would begin. This hope perhaps explained the strange euphoria that, despite her situation, crept upon her. She wondered at it, this sense of well-being, mindful all the time of her loss, and the irretrievable step she had taken. There was something ominous about it too, a feeling that this night, some need, some drive, some compulsion would be consummated. It frightened her a little, yet it excited her too.

"Dear Angela, A woman can be alone by choice, and this is not a failure. What have I said? Have I struggled through survival for so long, through all the dreary encounters that have bored me and everyone else into the ground, have I writhed through all that simply to arrive at that conclusion, that truism, that almost platitude? When in the beginning, if I had had the sense to write to a woman's magazine, I would have got the same answer by return post? And laughed, maybe, and told them to stick it. Yet it is true, Angela. We have reached that conclusion via the sewers, but it is true. But, as they say, it's an ill wind, and, by God, in the course of our journey there was plenty of truth in that. Something is going to happen, Angela. I feel it. We are generating a great change."

At the station, she waited in line. The police had had a field night, and there were many waiting to pick up their offending vehicles. When her turn came, she had her money ready, and it was probably her nonchalance and total indifference to the power of the law that riled the sergeant who was dealing with her case. 'You'll be fined for this,' he said.

She smiled at him, saying nothing.

'It can cost you up to ten quid,' he said, irritated that she seemed to be taking the nuisance so calmly.

'Can I pick it up now?'

'You'll have to wait your turn. There are plenty before you, madam.'

She pitied his hostility, and saw a glimmer of her erstwhile self in his pent-up anger. She went over to the queue and waited, and it was half an hour before her turn came, and at no time did she get impatient. She moved forward slowly in the line until they opened the barrier for her.

She drove out of the pound, not quite knowing her whereabouts, and caring less, for she was in no hurry to get back to the empty flat. She followed the main roads and found herself heading towards Piccadilly. The neon was still burning though it was almost two o'clock. There were still numbers of people around and the traffic was suddenly heavy with home-going diners. She pulled up at the red lights in Coventry Street. Alongside her was a car, its front passenger-window open. The passenger's elbow crooked outside, and slightly brushed against hers. They looked at each other with smiling apology.

"Dear Angela, He is very attractive, and I have a taste for him devoid of any need to destroy. What great strides we are making, Angela."

'Shall we stop and have some coffee?' he said.

The lights turned green, and both cars travelled forward. After a short interval, the traffic lights held them parallel again.

'Follow us into Soho Square,' he said. 'There's a café open near there.'

When the lights turned, she let them go ahead, and found herself following them. She could discern three men in the car, but the back-seat passenger, either indifferent or uninformed, did not turn to look at her. She turned left into Wardour Street and followed them into the square.

"Dear Angela, I don't quite know what I am doing, but I feel this as a necessary encounter. Nothing that happens this evening can be accidental. My concern with destiny is probably a symptom of my despair, which we both know is the flip-side of this strange calm that engulfs me. Tomorrow, no doubt, I shall probably go to a fortune-teller."

She pulled up behind them in the empty square and waited for them to come to her. The driver and the front passenger alighted, but the man in the back was not seen to move. They came forward. She saw that they were both young, shortish, and their complexions swarthier than she had noticed in the glare of the Piccadilly lights. They came round to her side and opened the door.

'Isn't your friend coming?' she said, as she got out. She felt them looking at the full length of her with approval.

'He doesn't want coffee,' the driver said.

She noticed his accent, which recalled the accent of his companion. But it was difficult to place. Anywhere between Persia and Libya could have housed them, but it seemed suddenly irrelevant to know.

The passenger took her arm, and she did not withdraw it.

'My name is Wassan,' he said, 'and this is Eddie. And you?'

'Nancy,' with not a split-second hesitation.

''Dear Angela, Will you answer to that? Will you, as Nancy, mock me, raise my hopes, shatter them, cling to me, desert me, or consider yourself as this alibi totally superfluous and stand by until we are Angela again?''

They crossed the road to the café to find it closed. There was little surprise from either of the men.

'Come to our friend's place,' Eddie said. 'We can have coffee there.'

'Where is that?' she asked.

'Not far. You leave your car. We drive you, and drive you back.'

She noticed that her car was on a double yellow line, prohibitive at any time, day or night. She reckoned that during the course of the day, she had picked up at least five driving offences, too many to be taken seriously, so that an equalizer could only add to the ridicule. She would leave it there, brazen on the double line, uncaring. She had to give a chance for her luck to turn—she was due for a turning and there would be some kind of triumph to return later to the square, and find it still there and ticketless.

She walked with them to their car, and Wassan let her sit in the front, he himself settling in the back. She did not turn round to look at their companion until they had driven out of the square. When she did, she tried to hide her fear and her revulsion. She understood now why they had kept him hidden, for he was no inducement to company. A scar on his left cheek stretched from ear to lip, shunting along a purple track which sprouted occasionally with sharp grey stubble. But the scar was not his most disturbing feature. That was obviously man-made and understandable. It was the man's mouth that turned her stomach, with anger at first, and then with pity, for it was a brutal disfigurement to which the man, either with courage or with cowardice, had contributed nothing. In this birthmark deformity, the lower jaw had slipped sideways, and was for ever open and salivating. The inner lining of his lower lip was red-raw. He looked as if he wept with his mouth.

'Hello,' she said, stretching her hand to him across the back of the seat. 'I'm Nancy.'

He smiled at her, and the effect was hideous. 'My name is Andropoulis,' he said, 'but everyone calls me Bill.'

She turned away, not able to look at him, and then

caught sight of him in the driving-mirror, his smile fading.

'Where are we going?' she said, noting that they were driving through a district unfamiliar to her.

'Not far,' they kept saying, and after half an hour's drive the answer was still the same.

"Dear Angela, I try to think about this crazy thing that I am doing. I am exposing myself to a *tangible* peril, which will postpone the empty flat and the mantelpiece, and all its hidden dangers. I am so unhappy, I suppose, that I feel strangely innocent, strangely immune to any injury. It is the turning-point for us, Angela. Enough of this survival nonsense. Tomorrow we shall start to live.''

They turned into what announced itself as the Old Kent Road, meaningful to Angela only as the cheapest property on the Monopoly board, the one that was good to buy early and develop to its full capacity. She had no notion where it was in relation to her known haunts, and she began to doubt whether they would keep their word and take her back after it, whatever 'it' turned out to be, was over.

'You will take me back?' she asked.

'Of course. Naturally,' Eddie said.

They turned into a nondescript street, and pulled up at a nondescript house, an address that could never be found again. Bill was the first out of the car, and he came round to open the door for her. From this point on, he was obviously host, and she feared any obligation she might owe him. He took her arm up the steps, while the others followed.

Her calm was leaving her, and she knew that she must turn back, find some excuse—but what reason could she give them, having come this far, and then changed her mind? If she was going to turn back, she had to do it now, while still in the open air, and with the freedom to scream and be heard, and to run and to hide, and somehow or other to get back to that known and loved Mini on the double line. But Bill already had the key in the door and was ushering her inside.

The lights were burning in the large front room, which seemed to be lived in at floor level. There were no chairs, but the room was strewn with large cushions, and one elaborately covered mattress. Brass bowl-lamps stood in the corners of the fireplace and the room was trellis-lit. The smell was indefinable, not unpleasant, and somewhere between hash and incense.

They sat on the cushions, and Bill started to make coffee on a small burner. Eddie put on a slow and steamy record, and danced alone between the cushions. Wassan moved close to her, while stuffing and lighting an elaborate pipe. He got it going, and passed it to her, but she refused, smelling danger. She saw Wassan nod at Bill, and though it might have meant nothing but a passing on of the pipe, she feared conspiracy. Bill passed her the coffee, and she drank it greedily hoping that it would stir her into some kind of activity to save herself. The coffee tasted bitter. 'It's drugged,' she said coldly, terrified of the amount she had drunk. She put the cup down.

'No,' Bill laughed. 'It's a special herb that gives it a slightly bitter taste.'

''Dear Angela, If anything should happen to me here, who will ever know? There is no clue as to my whereabouts and only the unclaimed car will rouse suspicion of my disappearance. There is no one at home to expect me, no one to put out a search. What am I doing here? How and why have I put myself at such peril?''

It was Eddie's turn to smoke, and his dancing grew

lazier. He hung on to the pipe for the length of the record, till he gyrated to the floor, where he lay giddied into a stupor. As the record came to an end, he turned on his side, his back to them, and was heard to snore gently. Now they were three and she looked about for escape.

'I think I'd better get back,' she said to Wassan. 'Will you take me?'

She was surprised at the high pitch of her voice, and she hoped it did not betray her fear.

'We'll have to wait till he wakes up,' Wassan said. 'He's the only one who can drive.'

Suddenly it did not worry her. The effects of the coffee were taking over her fears. She felt a melting in the back of her knees and a mellow stirring in her thighs. She couldn't understand her erstwhile terror. It was a common ordinary everyday thing she was doing, sitting on the floor of a house, in God knows what forsaken part of London, at three o'clock in the morning, surrounded by strangers and drugged to the eye-balls.

Wassan got up to change the record. She was glad it was a dancing one, and the quickening pulses in her body responded to its rhythm. Wassan lifted her to her unsteady feet, and she clung to him as he danced her round the room, and out into the corridor into a small room at the end of the house.

It was dark inside, and she could discern only the outline of a small bed, with a table at the side. They could hear the music still, and he undressed her to its beat as her body fluttered in his gentle hold. He left the necklace. Its fastening was too intricate and too time-consuming for his eager appetite, and he carried her to the bed, laying her down, and fondling her as he took off his clothes. He would be easy to love, this man, she thought, whom she didn't know, whom she didn't want to destroy, whom she would probably never see again, in an unknown house on an unknown street. He would be the gentle shrine at the end of her survival pilgrimage, and after that she'd go no more a-roving. She would go home; she would begin to live again; she would begin to love herself a little more, so that never again would she stain anybody else with the dross of her own self-abasement.

He held her close and she gave herself to him freely and with peace. He talked all the while in his own language, knowing that she couldn't understand, but he too was with himself in their congress. He lay back beside her and they were silent for a while.

'I'd like a cigarette,' she said. 'A real one.'

'I have them in my jacket in the other room. I'll go to get them.' He rose sleepily from the bed.

'Come back soon,' she said.

He left the door slightly ajar, and the dim light of the corridor sieved through the crack.

''Dear Angela, I have decided. I shall make my peace. This is the end of our survival trek. This is the parting of the ways. Survival, as we have so destructively practised it, is a terrible pursuit, and the end is often sour. So let us part now before we are wholly curdled. I'm ready to live now, Angela, and that is an undeniable signal to your departure. For you are no part of my living. You were my bearer on our survival expedition, and now there is no biding baggage. I shall count the turns on the roundabout again, and I shall let the mantelpiece gather its natural dust. Oh yes, I know tomorrow perhaps, in the dull hopeless morning light, I shall call for you again, and you will come. For you will never leave me. It is I who must do the quitting. Farewell, Angela. We need never, but never, meet again.''

She lay waiting for her lover, her body mellowing with the aftertaste of satisfaction. She fingered the silver around her neck, and found it pleasantly cool. She heard his footsteps and she quivered for him again. Then he came into the room and bounded on to the bed on top of her.

She knew it was not he, and she screamed. She felt Bill's saliva dripping on to her chest, and she screamed louder and longer, her fear piercing the dark. Then he stopped her mouth with his own, or what passed for him as a mouth, dribbling his desire. She wrenched herself free and shrieked again.

''Morrow London Disregard Last Communiqué Stop Return Immediately.''

His greasy head landed a blow on her mouth whilst he busied himself with his nether animal fumblings.

''Angela,'' she whispered, ''I'm frightened. It's not fair. After all our resolutions, it's just not bloody fair. No more chances for us, Angela. We reneged all along the line. And what right have we, after all, we, who have been whoring together for so long, what right have we to choice? All of a sudden we want to be respectable. Do people actually die of dishonesty, Angela? Help me. Don't leave me, for God's sake.''

She felt his thumb on her throat, pressing the silver chain into her flesh, and a warm trickle over her breast that, in terror, she knew was her own blood. How long and how loud could one scream unheeded in a house in a capital city?

And he tired of the noise. He tightened his grip on her throat.

"Dearest Angela, It has come. It has come. If some, like us, survive by rejection, others, because of it, are entitled to do murder. He is entitled, Angela."

She felt her breathing stutter, and she could scream no more. Then with her penultimate breath, for even in her death-throes she knew that the last breath was yet another cliché, and was in any case required for the natural functions of quietus, so, with the last workable breath that he spared her, she whispered,

"Angela darling, I shan't be writing to you any more."

256